In Praise c

"In this sixth entry to the entertaining jack Beale series, ~~~~
and his friends in the wrong place at just the right narrative time. A fire on the
high seas, unexplained murders, and a mysterious "catch" in the form of a seduc-
tive and alluring shipwreck survivor keep readers guessing from start to end. Is
she really a threat to all who cross her, as Max believes, or simply a temptress, an
enigma, and a guardian angel in Jack's hour of need? Readers will be counting the
days until K.D. finishes the sequel." —Byron Petrakis, PhD

"K.D. Mason's sixth installment in these clever New England mysteries gripped
me more than ever as I dove into Jack's complicated and dangerous world. The
Atlantic Ocean plays a starring role in this life-and-death adventure for Jack and
his friends, who live, run, and work along its dynamic coastline. Humor sparkles
through the sinister and frightening events in *Unexpected Catch,* entangling Jack
in a net of ever-deeper intrigue. Fans will be pleased that Cat, the charming kitty,
continues to play a soothing role amongst the growing chaos. Thank you, K.D.,
for this exciting read!" —Vicki Miller, Durham, NH

"Once again, Jack Beale finds himself in the middle of a brewing mystery when a
deep-sea fishing trip ends up as a race to discover the details of an unintentional
catch. Danger follows Jack and his friends as they seek answers to questions about
highly unusual events that take place along the NH coast and Massachusetts' north
shore. As a local, I recognized many of the landmarks and could visualize the locations. As a runner, I related to Jack's need to run to clear his mind and develop
insight. As a reader, I liked the story's quick development and the realistic interac-
tion between the characters. This is another great addition to the Jack Beale series!"
—Curt L., Exeter, NH

"Jack Beale and his cast of characters are back to take you on a wild romp through the
seacoast of New Hampshire! Jack once again tests the limits of his tumultuous relation-
ship with Max after the strange and unexpected return of Sylvie, the femme fatale we
met in *Killer Run.* Unable to contain his instincts and curiosity, Jack is compelled to
answer Sylvie's pleas for his help, ultimately putting his life on the line. With *Unexpected Catch,* K.D. Mason continues a tale I can't walk away from!"
—Deb Wilkinson, Rye, NH

"Make yourself a Mai Tai, and head to your favorite recliner. K.D. Mason excels
at building suspense, tossing great clues, and winding the spring for the dramatic
finale. The author clearly enjoys his craft, and this is his best so far."
—Jim Bailey, WCRC

Other Titles by K.D. Mason

HARBOR ICE

CHANGING TIDES

DANGEROUS SHOALS

KILLER RUN

EVIL INTENTIONS

UNEXPECTED
CATCH

UNEXPECTED
CATCH

K.D. MASON

To Jeanie

K.D. Mason

Copyright © 2014, by K.D. Mason

The author may be reached through www.kdmason.com

Unexpected Catch is a work of fiction. All of the characters, places, organizations, and events portrayed in this novel are either products of the author's imagination or are used fictitiously, and any resemblance to any actual persons, living or dead, business establishments, events, or locales is entirely coincidental.

ISBN-13   978-1503097667
ISBN-10   1503097668

Cover and book design by Claire MacMaster, Barefoot Art Graphic Design
Copy Editor: Renée Nicholls | www.mywritingcoach.com
Back cover photographer: Richard G. Holt
Proofreading: Thomas Haggerty, Nancy Obert
E-Book Production: Marsha Filion, Bigwig Books | www.bigwigbooks.com

Printed in the U.S.A.

Dedicated to all those who work, fish, and play at Rye Harbor

* * *

THANK YOU'S

As with each of my books, I can't thank enough all the people who help and encourage me in this endeavor, and especially the following:

NHSPCA and Walter Franz
Special Agent Kory Cronin, CGIS
Byron Petrakis
Deb Wilkinson
Timmy Poole
Vicki Miller
Jim Bailey
Curtis Lindtvedt
Michael Sosik

PROLOGUE

SHE SHIVERED. "*WARM? MY ASS!*" she thought as she hung on to the cushion and assessed her situation. It was mid-afternoon and she was alone—twenty or so miles off the coast. Clearly, her options for survival had dwindled. Initially she had hoped that one of the other fishing boats they had seen earlier in the day would spot the smoke, come to investigate, and find her. As slim as those odds had been, especially when Richie's boat sank faster than she had expected, she had remained hopeful. What else could she have done? But now as she began to shiver, she faced the grim fact that time was not on her side.

Her mind began to drift as she thought back to how the day had begun. The heat wave that had smothered New England for the past two weeks seemed to be getting worse. Sleep had been impossible; the unrelenting heat and humidity saw to that. She had parked her car on a side street and, with a large coffee from an all-night convenience store in hand, she had walked back to the town dock in Newburyport to meet Richie. It had surprised her how many people were still out at three in the morning.

The town dock was next to a ribbon of a park, and in the distance she had heard the distinct sound of an idling diesel engine well before she had seen the boat. Every detail was so vivid in her mind. She remembered the two lovers, sitting on a bench in the shadows, kissing and groping each other, oblivious to the fact that they were sitting in the middle of a park. She remembered how the droplets of sweat had felt forming on her back, starting between her shoulder blades and then sliding in a slow tickle down her spine to be absorbed in the waistband of her shorts. She had stopped behind a tree and watched him, as he had waited for her.

She could almost taste and smell that convenience store coffee, uselessly hot against the back of her throat as she had stepped out from behind the tree and walked toward the boat where she had met him. "*Was his name even Richie?*" It was so cold. Her legs were going numb and the saltwater stung her eyes, causing her to blink. She heard a soft voice telling her to let go. That it was over. That she had failed, and now . . ."

"No!" she shouted—or at least she thought she shouted. She wasn't giving in that easily. Her legs began to kick. *They were kicking, weren't they?* The horizon was endless, until she saw the sun. "*The sun,*" she thought. She'd kick toward the sun. That was west. That was land and safety. He was going to pay. Richie had paid, and soon he would pay.

She didn't hear the boat approaching. In her mind she was still kicking toward the west, but that deep, bone-numbing cold was winning. Her eyes closed and she was running. Running through the woods. Then she fell. Her leg hurt and strong hands helped her up, but she couldn't stand. Voices. She heard voices. She opened her eyes and saw a familiar face staring down at her. Jack? It was impossible. She tried to speak, but couldn't. Comforted that he was there, holding her again, she closed her eyes and allowed the darkness to take her.

CHAPTER 1

"READY?"

It was five A.M.

"Yep," replied Jack.

He looked east toward the ocean in the general direction of Hampton Beach State Park. He could see that the inky blackness of the eastern sky had already changed to metallic gray as the night began its losing battle with the coming day.

Jack shrugged his pack onto his back and then walked around to slide a cooler filled with ice, beer, and sandwiches from the back of his truck onto the tailgate. With a grunt he hefted it off the truck and followed Dave down toward the dock. Dave, who was also wearing a backpack, carried their fishing gear and hurried ahead without offering to help with the much heavier cooler. Jack could clearly see that he was excited to be going out. They had been friends and running buddies for many years, and as much as Dave enjoyed running, Jack knew in his heart that Dave would rather be out on the ocean fishing over almost anything else.

As the sky brightened, boats that had made their appearance known only as dark shadows now became unique, each a different color, shape, and size. The men made no attempt to silence the clang of their boots on the aluminum ramp as they walked down to the floats where they would meet Dave's friend Bryan. "What's the name of his boat?" asked Jack.

"*Miss Cookie*."

"*Miss Cookie*?"

"Yeah, I know." Dave's tone made it clear that he had already told the story one too many times.

"Who would name a boat *Miss Cookie*?" Jack thought to himself.

He made a mental note to ask Bryan later.

The sky continued to brighten, and even though the sun had not yet risen, Jack could now see all of the boats in the harbor clearly, each with its own mirror image reflecting off the water's glassy surface. An engine coughed to life, and he turned his head toward the spot where the sound seemed to come from, but it wasn't until the boat began to move toward them that he finally saw it.

"That her?" Jack pointed toward the approaching boat.

"Yep."

From the side, the hull had the profile of a classic lobster boat, but above its sheer, all similarity ended. Instead of a short, mostly open deck house with the clear, large working deck area aft—as most lobster boats have—*Miss Cookie's* cabin was larger and enclosed, with windows all around. It looked more like the cabin on a classic motor yacht from another era than a fishing boat. This reduced the size of the aft deck area, but more than enough remained for their purposes, and Jack could see a number of rods already mounted along the stern rail. There was, on top of the deckhouse, what looked to be a low-profile, curved cowling that he presumed either provided some shelter for another steering station or perhaps an observation area. Aft, against the backside of the deckhouse, he could see a stout mast with a lifting boom that would be perfect for hauling large things into the boat.

The entire boat was painted a light gray, with dark blue accents along the sheer and around the cabin windows. The structure on the top of the deckhouse was painted the same dark blue as the accents.

As *Miss Cookie* glided toward the dock, Jack could see a man inside, guiding her in. As Jack stood there on the dock, something about the boat seemed familiar. Silently he watched, and then it hit him. The *Orca*. *Miss Cookie* reminded him of the *Orca*, Quint's boat in the movie *Jaws*. Jack found himself hoping that their day wouldn't be as eventful.

That's when the sun broke the horizon and *Miss Cookie* and all of the other boats glowed in the new day's early light. He squinted and watched as she was expertly laid up alongside the dock and brought to a stop, with a short burst of reverse from the engine followed by silence as the engine was shut down.

The man stepped out from inside the deckhouse and called a greeting to Dave. He was thin and wiry, with every day of a life well lived etched into his craggy face. Still, there was something about him that belied his weathered appearance. His bright eyes seemed to look out at the world with a mischievous glint, and his movements were quick and sure as he moved across the back deck.

"Mornin', Bryan," said Dave as he took one of the lines from his friend.

"Dave. Good to see ya'. Should be a nice day. Not much breeze so the ocean'll be pretty flat, good for fishing."

His voice had a strong Seabrook accent to it. "That explains a lot," thought Jack.

While Dave and Bryan tied up the boat, Jack looked it over more closely. The dark blue structure on the top was indeed a helm station. From a distance she had looked very yachty, but now, up close, Jack could see that she was well used. Four stacked plastic chairs and several coolers were in the back of the boat, along with two collapsed patio umbrellas, held closed with short ties. Looking forward, the door into the deckhouse was to the left side of the mast. On the right side was a ladder. In the moments it took Dave and Bryan to finish tying up the boat, the sun cleared the horizon and Jack could feel the temperature rise almost immediately.

Boat secure, Dave turned toward Jack and said, "This is my friend Bryan. Bryan, this is Jack. I've told you about him before."

Bryan reached out his hand. "Jack. Good to meet ya'."

"Mornin'." Jack returned the gesture.

Then Bryan turned back to Dave and added, "Glad you called me. Feels like it's gonna' be another scorcher."

Dave grunted in agreement. Then he looked out to sea and added,

"Seems that way. Least it'll be cooler out there."

Bryan shook his head. "Like I said, don't look like much breeze, so it may not be a cool as you'd think."

"Anything will be an improvement over what we've been dealing with the last few weeks."

"Well, we'll take what we get. C'mon aboard. Let's go fishin'."

CHAPTER 2

BRYAN DISAPPEARED INSIDE with their packs while Jack and Dave checked out the fishing gear on the back rail and un-stacked the chairs. As soon as Bryan reappeared, Dave helped him cast off from the dock and they were under way. The tide was full in and about to turn, so there was little current as Bryan steered *Miss Cookie* out of Hampton Harbor and pointed her east. A man and two boys at the campground waved as they silently fished off the breakwater.

Once clear of the harbor, Bryan pressed the throttle forward, and they could feel the bow rise up as *Miss Cookie* accelerated. As she reached cruising speed and leveled off, Jack was surprised that the ride was so comfortable.

Dave and Jack settled into the plastic chairs while Bryan drove the boat and watched as the distance grew between them and the land.

"You guys good?" Bryan's voice broke through the steady drone of the boat's engine.

Jack and Dave turned their heads back at the same time. "Yeah, this is great," said Jack.

Bryan came out of the cabin and Dave asked, "Who's driving?"

Bryan grinned, and Jack knew this must be a long-standing joke each time the autopilot was used.

"Otto," said Bryan. "You remember him."

When Dave had finished laughing, he asked, "What is it—about two to three hours 'till we get there?"

"'Bout that. I figure we'll head for the northern end of Jeffreys, out by the Fingers. I was out there a few days ago and we had some pretty good luck."

From his days spent sailing, Jack knew that Jeffreys Ledge was a long, winding, relatively shallow area that stretched from the coast of

Rockport, Massachusetts, to just southeast of Cape Elizabeth, Maine. It was a popular place for fishing.

"What're we fishing for?" asked Jack.

"Cod. Haddock. Pollock," Bryan said. "We'll have to see what's bitin'."

"Anyone thirsty?" Dave got out of his chair and moved toward one of the coolers they had placed by the stern.

"I'm good," said Jack.

"Not yet," replied Bryan. "Jack, coffee? I'm going to put a pot on."

"I could go for that."

Bryan turned, and headed back into the cabin. Dave pulled a beer from the cooler and settled back down in his chair while Jack stood and followed Bryan. Just as Jack reached the doorway, the boat lurched and he had to hold on to the doorframe. As he caught himself, he stopped, glancing around for whatever might have caused that lurch. The Isles of Shoals were in sight, but well off to the left. To the right of their position he saw a large sport-fisherman heading south at a high rate of speed. Looking astern, he noted that Otto was spot on as their wake ran straight and true. Looking right again, he concluded that it must have been from the wake left by that sport-fisherman that was now nearly out of sight.

Returning forward, he saw Bryan disappear through a narrow companionway door in the front of the deckhouse that was offset to the left of the helm. Jack stepped in and looked around. Four windows lined each side of the cabin, port and starboard. Two on each side were obviously fixed but the other two were on slides so that they could be opened. Thanks to this option, a refreshing breeze filled the cabin.

The front of the deckhouse overlapped the boat's forward cabin, making for a flat work surface in front of the four front windows, and each of those windows had a slight tilt outward at the top. "That's smart," thought Jack. Having the windows tilted like that really cut down on the glare off the water.

The door to the deckhouse had a window in it, and another was affixed next to it. Jack noted that he could easily scan all three hundred and sixty degrees around the boat, which would be a plus in lousy weather.

The inside was all mahogany. The varnish had seen better days, but its original dignity could still be felt. The ceiling was painted white between dark mahogany ribs, and hanging between the ribs were more rods, as well as several tubes with what Jack assumed to be charts sticking out the ends. A table jutted out to the center of the cabin from the left, with fixed benches on each side, one facing forward and the other aft. Not seeing any stove, head, or place to sleep, Jack guessed that those were through the companionway through which Bryan had just passed.

Jack moved forward to the companionway and looked in. He was right. Two steps down and to the left was the galley, where Bryan was busy lighting a small stove. Between the galley and the bulkhead that closed off the bow, which had its own small door, was what in a house would at best be a closet, but Jack was pretty sure that it was the head. On the right side of the cabin were two berths, one on top of the other, and he could see that their packs had been tossed on the upper. It was cozy, practical, and sufficient.

Bryan looked up. "Hey, Jack. Coffee's on. It'll just be a few minutes. How're we doing?"

Jack lifted his head out of the companionway and looked around. There was nothing in sight to be concerned about. The Isles of Shoals now were well off to port, and they were nearly past them. As he looked back, he confirmed that their wake was still straight and true. "Looks good."

"I'll be up in a minute. Could you keep watch?"

"Sure."

Next to the companionway was the helm, where Otto was hard at work. The wheel shared the same bulkhead as the companionway. A large, comfortable-looking chair on a modern pedestal—complete with footrest— had been placed in front of the wheel. Within easy reach was everything necessary for running the boat.

Jack climbed up into the helmsman's seat, which was as comfortable as it looked.

The throttle and engine gauges were located to the right. A VHF radio hung from the ceiling. Mounted on the console to the left was a twelve-inch multifunction display screen with a smaller fish finder next to it. Jack studied the multifunction display, noting that it had both full GPS and radar capabilities in addition to the autopilot controls. The GPS was active, and their position was marked on its screen with a small icon in the shape of a boat that was slowly moving across the screen. Their speed was a steady eight knots, and they were heading due east.

Even with the GPS, Bryan had left a paper chart out, and Jack picked it up. The Fingers, as the northern end of Jeffreys was called, were marked, and he could see that soon they'd have to change course to the north to get there. Glancing at the GPS again, he noted that the waypoint for making that turn hadn't yet come up on the screen.

That's when Bryan emerged with two cups of coffee. "You have a really nice boat here," said Jack.

"Thanks. Not the newest or fanciest, but she gets the job done and I'm convinced that she's just a lucky boat."

"How so?"

"Fishin's usually pretty good whenever we go out. She's sea kindly and there's been a few times over the years when she's really pulled my ass out of the fire," said Bryan.

Jack understood the first two statements, but wondered about the third.

CHAPTER 3

THE ENGINE DRONED ON and the ocean remained flat. As far from land as they were, as the sun rose in the sky they could feel its heat and only the breeze created by their forward motion provided any relief. Twisting around and looking back, Jack saw Dave reach for some sunblock and a hat.

"How long've you known Dave?" Jack asked. Bryan stood in the companionway, facing forward, cradling his cup between his hands while staring out toward the endless horizon.

"Long time. Better'n twenty-five years we've been fishing together. Met down South."

Jack looked over at him. That was news. For as long as Jack had known Dave, for as many miles as they had run together, he had never said anything about having lived down south.

"Thing is," Bryan continued, "he's the smart one and got out of it . . . and there. Took me a bit longer to wise up."

"Down South?"

Jack wasn't sure that Bryan even heard him. The captain continued to stare straight ahead, obviously lost in some distant memory. Then he spoke again, softly. "Feels like one of those hot, humid days down in the Gulf . . . nasty heat down there in the summer. Could be just like this, flat calm, then it'd change in a heartbeat. Thunderstorm, and you'd find yourself praying to survive, that you wouldn't get hit. Then as quickly as it came up, it'd be gone and you'd be bobbing on a flat sea, the heat and humidity worse than before."

Questions flooded his mind, but all Jack could spit out was, "Is that when you got *Miss Cookie*?"

"Hunh? Oh, yeah. Got her down there."

He continued before Jack could ask another question.

"Some guy who used to lobster down Maine. Got it in his head that more money was to be made down in Florida taking tourists out deep-sea fishing. Guess he was successful for a time, but . . . well, let's just say he found other, more lucrative ways to pay the bank."

"Drugs?"

Bryan shrugged and looked at Jack. "One day, she was found out drifting in the Gulf, no one on board. Official version was that he had been out fishing alone and probably hooked a big one and somehow ended up overboard. I got the boat at a salvage sale—kept the name. Seemed the right thing to do." He returned his gaze forward, tipped back his cup, and drained the last of his coffee. Jack knew that the conversation was over.

"How're we doin'?" Dave called in to them. He was standing in the doorway.

Bryan glanced back at the GPS screen and pressed a button on the autopilot. The boat made an easy turn to the north. Turning back to Dave he said, "Right on course. We'll be fishing within two hours."

CHAPTER 4

THAT LAST HOUR WENT BY QUICKLY. Jack grabbed a hat and sunblock from his backpack and joined Dave in the back of the boat while Bryan settled into the helmsman's chair.

"There's no one out here," said Jack as he surveyed the horizon.

Dave looked up from the rod he was prepping. After a quick scan of the horizon he said, "You're right. All the more fish for us."

"But isn't that a little strange?"

"It's still early. I'm sure that we won't be alone. Too nice a day for fishin'."

In addition to the rods that Bryan already had on the boat, Dave had brought his two. One was a six-foot bait rod with a 4/0 Penn reel loaded with fifty pound monofilament. This was rigged with two single hooks, one above the other, about twenty inches apart, with a weight hanging about six or eight inches below the lower hook. Jack knew it could be lowered until the weight rested on the bottom, leaving the hooks, baited with clam strips, to become an irresistible dinner offering.

"Grab that rod and take it out," Dave said to Jack, motioning to one of Bryan's rods, which was in a holder on the rail. After replacing it with his rod, he said, "All set—just needs to be baited. As soon as we're on his marks, it's bait, drop, and catch fish."

As soon as Dave set his bait rod in the rail, they felt *Miss Cookie* begin to slow. "Must be close," said Dave.

Jack watched as Dave went to work on his eight-foot jigging rod. Not quite as stout as the shorter rod, it was still substantial. It too had a 4/0 Penn reel, but instead of monofilament, it was loaded with fifty-pound Dacron line, with only the final fifty feet being monofilament. Dave attached one of his cod jigs to those final fifty feet.

The jig was a heavy weight about the size of a large banana, only thinner, and shiny. Two hooks were attached to it. At the lower end hung a large treble hook. From the top end a single hook protruded out the bottom of a four-inch piece of blue tubing that had been trimmed like fringe to hide the hook. When the jig was lowered to the bottom and then jerked continuously, the blue tube would flutter and the shiny weight would spin, making for a delectable temptation for their quarry.

Jack went in to look at the GPS. Their speed had dropped by half, as had the water depth, going from over five hundred feet to under one hundred and fifty feet.

"We're close," Bryan said. "Now I'm looking for fish."

Jack glanced at the fish finder. Pointing at it, he asked, "What exactly am I looking at?"

The contour of the ocean's bottom was scrolling across the screen, recording their forward progress. Above that were smaller blips and marks that looked like toenails. Jack assumed they probably represented fish or—more possibly—schools of fish.

"There. That's what I'm looking for," said Bryan, pointing at the screen. "Those're fish. The newer finders will give much more detail, almost like a photo. Might get one if I get real lucky."

Bryan pulled the throttle back and *Miss Cookie's* forward movement slowed until all that remained was the slow, gentle rocking of the nearly flat sea. Without the breeze from their forward movement, the temperature jumped immediately, and Jack could feel sweat beginning to form on his upper lip as he watched his two companions go to work.

Bryan left the helm, went outside, and joined Dave by the back of the boat. Dave had already begun hooking clam strips on to his bait rod, and after dropping the line over and waiting to stop it when it hit bottom, he began baiting the next rod, one of Bryan's.

"C'mon Jack, give a hand," Bryan called.

With Bryan and Dave baiting and setting fishing lines, Jack decided to untie the patio umbrellas and push them open. He grinned. They were bright and multicolored, with fringed edges that hung limp and lifeless, but the circles of shade that they created covered most of the back deck.

Jack watched as Dave picked up his jigging rod and set its lure on its way to the bottom. Bryan, after doing the same with another rod, began adjusting the positions of the chairs and umbrellas until circles of shade covered all. "Just about all set," Bryan announced. Then he opened a cooler and took out three beers.

"Gentlemen, here's to a great day of fishing." He cracked his beer, tipped it back, and took a long gulp.

Following his lead, Dave and Jack cracked their beers, returned his toast, and also drank.

"Now, we fish," said Bryan as he settled into one of the plastic chairs.

Nothing happened for what seemed like forever. They sat and then cracked second beers. They adjusted the positions of chairs and umbrellas and then they sat some more. Finally, near the end of this second beer, the first fish of the day hit. Dave grabbed the rod and began working whatever had taken the hook to the surface. It was only a matter of minutes before he pulled aboard a small cod. Too small to keep, it was released, and this went on for several hours. They were catching fish at about the rate of one per beer, or so it seemed, and most were too small to keep. Jack had been the first to pull up a keeper, and from Dave and Bryan's reaction he could tell that his "rookie luck" rankled them, especially after he pulled in several more. Finally, he was ready for a break.

"I don't know about you guys, but all this fishing is making me hungry," teased Jack. "Lunch?"

Dave continued jigging his rod. "I won't dignify that with an answer," he said. "*I* am in it for the Big One."

"Sounds good to me," said Bryan. He reached into the cooler for another beer.

Jack pulled out sandwiches and chips and passed a few to Bryan. They sat in the shade eating, but Dave moved to stand by the rail, jigging his rod in search of his great white whale.

Suddenly the tip of Dave's rod jerked and line began running off the reel. "Okay, this is it," he said. "Come to Papa."

Carefully and methodically, he began working the fish, and with each passing minute more line was wound onto the reel. Jack could feel his determination, and an air of collective excitement began to fill the boat.

Bryan put down his beer and stood by with a gaff, peering over the side of the boat, watching for the first sign of what had to be the "mother of all fish." Jack grabbed a camera to document the great victory.

"Easy, easy," coached Bryan. It had to be close. "There it is."

Jack joined them at the rail and peered into the water. For a moment he thought he saw something, but then he wasn't so sure. Dave, his neck red from the effort, cranked on the reel with one last burst of energy and finally brought his adversary to the surface. In silence the three men stared at what was probably the smallest fish they had caught all day.

Bryan was the first to laugh, followed by Jack. Dave's embarrassment and disappointment were obvious, and the hoots and hollers from Jack and Bryan seemed to amplify his mortification.

As Dave attempted to lift the fish into the boat, the tip of his rod remained bent from the weight of his catch. That's when they saw that a rope was caught on the treble hook. Bryan grabbed both sides of the rope below the hook and heaved. It was covered in sea slime and the doubled up thickness made it easier to hold on to while Dave freed it from the hook and swung the fish into the boat.

Dropping the rod with the flopping fish still on the hook, he moved to help Bryan with the rope. While Bryan and Dave pulled and worked to secure the rope to a cleat, Jack took the fish off the hook. He was about to toss it overboard when Bryan shouted, "Throw it in the cooler!"

Jack looked at the fish again and then he looked back at Bryan. The fish was the smallest they had hooked all day and obviously should be released.

"Put it in the cooler!" Bryan said again, this time a bit more forcefully. Jack shrugged and put the fish into the cooler. After all, Bryan was the captain.

By the time the rope was securely attached to the cleat, Bryan and Dave were breathing hard and sweating profusely.

"What the hell did you catch?" said Jack as he looked at the rope hanging straight down over the stern. Whatever it was, it was heavy enough that even the motion of the boat felt different.

Instead of replying, Dave wiped the sweat off his brow and moved to the cooler. "I need a beer!"

"Grab me one too," said Bryan.

"Make it three," said Jack. He looked over the side again.

Bryan tipped his beer back and swallowed what must have been half the can. Then he went into the deckhouse without a word. "Need to use the head," he finally called out behind him.

"Ahh, that's good," said Dave, taking a long swig and punctuating his satisfaction with a loud belch.

Jack belched in response then said, "But what the hell is still on the line?"

Dave turned his attention back to the stern of the boat, reached over, and tugged on the line. "Damn. Whatever it is, it's heavy. Let's see what we have."

Together, Jack and Dave heaved on the doubled up rope. Slippery with sea slime, they left it attached to the cleat while they pulled, in case they couldn't hold on. When they had retrieved maybe twenty-five feet of the doubled-up rope the first end appeared. By the way it was frayed, it looked like it had either chafed against something or had been cut. With all the weight on the remaining end of the rope, the retrieval became much more difficult since all they had to hold on to was a single slippery line.

"Sure hope it's not a body," said Dave.

"Not funny, man."

Suddenly the rope went slack and Jack and Dave nearly fell just as Bryan reemerged from the cabin.

"What the hell?" said Dave, still holding on to the rope.

"Whatever it was, it either let go or fell off," said Bryan.

"Ya' think?"

"What else?" said Bryan in a serious voice, "But, hey, it'll be a great story." He winked and all three laughed as Dave continued to pull the now light line in.

Their laughter stopped abruptly as a large, grappling hook broke the surface. Dangling from one of its tines was a piece of black neoprene.

CHAPTER 5

NO ONE SAID ANYTHING as Dave dropped the hook on the deck.

Jack spoke first. "Holy shit! Is that a piece of a wetsuit?"

Dave pulled it off the tine and studied it.

"Don't know. Never seen rubber like this."

"Let me see," said Bryan, taking it from Dave. "Not wetsuit. Probably just some garbage that someone dumped overboard." His pronouncement, said with much certainty, was punctuated with a flick of his wrist as he threw it back overboard.

"What'd you do that for?" said Jack.

Bryan gave him a withering look. "It was a piece of trash." Then he began to coil the rope that was attached to the grappling hook. When he finished coiling it, he put the hook and the rope in a corner by the deckhouse. Next he pointed to the seaweed that was now all over the deck. "Jack, throw a few buckets of water on this before it sticks—and stinks."

As Jack washed the deck off, Dave prepared his cod jig again. Glancing up, Jack saw Bryan take a long slow look, first all around the boat and then at the empty ocean. Looking satisfied, Bryan stepped inside the deckhouse. As he did, Jack said, "Shouldn't we call someone? Coast Guard or something?"

Bryan turned back and gave Jack a look.

"Hey, I was just asking."

Bryan reappeared as Jack was stowing the bucket he had been using to wash the deck. Dave was watching his line as it disappeared into the depths. "Who needs a beer?"

As they cracked another round of beers, the mood lightened. Jack pulled more sandwiches out of one of the coolers, and there was no more mention of the grappling hook in the corner.

Suddenly, a mischievous grin broke out on Bryan's face. "Who wants to have some fun? Jack, grab me that last little cod."

Jack looked at Dave, who simply shrugged. Then Bryan added, "I'll be right back."

He disappeared into the deckhouse, returning a few minutes later with another rod. It was short, like the bait rods, but it looked to be much heavier, and the reel was larger than what they had been using.

"What's that?" Dave walked over to Bryan.

"My shark rod."

"Let me see that." Bryan passed it to Dave. The rod was significantly thicker and heavier than any of his rods. The reel was a Penn Senator, model 115L2, with hundred-thirty pound test and a piano wire leader.

"Nice."

"Jack, give me that fish." Bryan took it and hooked it onto a ridiculously large hook. Next, he walked to the stern and cast it out. Before the bait disappeared from sight, Bryan attached a balloon to the line. Then he continued to feed line out. The balloon allowed the line to drift away from the boat. Once he had enough line out, he set the reel.

He turned back to Jack and Dave. "Now, if a shark takes the bait, the line can run out freely."

As Bryan moved to place the rod in one of the holders on the stern rail, Jack caught Dave's attention. Quietly, he said, "Is this actually kosher?"

Dave glanced over at Bryan. In a low, conspiratorial voice, he said, "Not actually." He paused and then added quickly, "Let's say he's a bit independent. What happens on his boat stays on his boat. But he's a very good fisherman."

Bryan walked back toward them. "There. All set. If we're lucky maybe we'll get a mako. They're really good eatin'."

Dave asked, "You still work with that Thai guy?"

"I do," Bryan said. "If we get one, I'll cut some steaks for us, and

I'll sell him the rest. He pays extra for the fins. I make the call, he meets us back at the dock—cash, no records—and no one knows any different."

"Sweet. Another beer?"

"Sure."

"Jack?"

He nodded. Dave opened the cooler and took out three beers. He passed them around and then sat down in the only chair that was still in the shade. He cracked his beer open, stretched his legs out, and announced, "It doesn't get any better than this."

Before opening his beer, Bryan moved the umbrellas around. Keeping Dave in the shade, he created some shade for the other two chairs and he and Jack sat down.

Little was said for that beer. They opened another round, and Jack was the first to speak. "What d'you think was on that rope?"

Bryan answered first. "Don't know. Don't care."

Jack didn't believe him, but he held his tongue.

Dave looked over at them. "You know what I think? I think that someone was trying to retrieve something and when the rope chafed through, he lost whatever it was. If that's the case, he'll be back."

"I suppose," said Jack. Then he asked again, "What d'you think it was?"

"No idea," said Dave. "Could be anything: a body, garbage, something being smuggled . . . Oh, I don't know. Could be most anything."

"What do you think, Bryan?"

"Sure."

"Sure what?"

"I agree that it could be anything, but now it's gone and we'll never know."

Jack was still sure the captain was hiding something, but he didn't know what.

Bryan continued, "Over the years I've seen a lot of funny things happen out on the water. Some even pretty unbelievable." Looking directly at Dave he added, "Remember that time back in Florida?"

Dave chuckled. "Which?"

Bryan just winked at him.

"Oh, yeah." Then he grinned.

"You guys gonna' fill me in?" asked Jack.

They looked at him silently. Then, simultaneously, they started laughing. "No!"

"If we did, we'd have to kill you," said Dave. He was still laughing.

"You guys are such assholes."

With that, Jack got up and went inside the deckhouse. A few minutes later he returned with binoculars. Ignoring the other two, he began scanning the horizon.

"Do you guys realize that there's no one out here today?" asked Jack. "Not another boat anywhere."

Dave looked around without getting out of his seat. "You're right. You'd think that on such a hot day on shore and with the ocean so flat, it'd be like a parking lot out here. What's your take, Bryan?"

"No idea."

"So, you're not curious?" Jack continued to hold the glasses to his eyes.

"Nope."

"So, you guys gonna' tell me about Florida?" Jack asked again. Before either could answer, he stopped and stared at the horizon. "Wait! Guys, I think I see—"

CHAPTER 6

JACK WAS INTERRUPTED BY THE SOUND of line being stripped off a reel.

"—smoke." Jack finished his sentence as Bryan and Dave jumped.

The shark rod's tip was bent over. Bryan grabbed it first. Immediately he began to apply a bit more drag to slow down the rate of speed at which the line was going out.

"Oh yeah, we've got a good one," he shouted. He pulled back on the rod while applying a bit more drag on the line in an attempt to make sure the hook was set and to get a better feel for what they might have.

"Guys, can you get those other lines in?" Even though Bryan posed it as a question, Jack had no doubt that it was an order.

Dave grabbed his jigging rod and cranked furiously on the reel. Jack did the same with the bait rod. They were only in about a hundred fifty feet of water, but it felt like it was more than three hundred based on how long it seemed to take.

"Done," cried out Dave.

Then, a moment later, Jack called out, "All set."

"Dave," Bryan said, without turning his head or breaking his concentration, "I need you to go start the engine. Jack, you stand by and relay my instructions to Dave. He'll drive. And get those umbrellas down."

"Got it," said Dave.

He disappeared into the deckhouse while Jack collapsed the umbrellas. The engine roared to life and Jack stuck his head inside the deckhouse and said to Dave, "So, is this where we need to get a bigger boat?"

"Funny. How's he doing?"

"Jack looked out, "He's working hard. I'll check. Be right back."

Before leaving the deckhouse to check on Bryan, Jack grabbed the binoculars. He was still concerned about the smoke. Back outside, without their shade, it didn't take long before Jack was sweating as much as Bryan, and all he was doing was watching. Other than occasionally relaying instructions into Dave, he mostly just watched as Bryan struggled with the fish and whenever possible stole a look out at the smoke.

CHAPTER 7

BRYAN'S FIGHT WITH THE FISH lasted nearly an hour. The entire time, Dave manned the helm and kept the boat in the best position for landing the fish. Jack alternately relayed instructions between Bryan and Dave, gave Bryan whatever aid he could, and kept an eye on the smoke.

"Okay, Jack. Time to finish this."

Jack looked over the side at Bryan's prize.

"Holy shit!"

"Yeah . . . mako . . . seven footer . . . big bastard." Bryan was grinning from ear to ear. "Go inside, down in the forward cabin. In a drawer under the lower bunk you'll find my gun. Go get it."

That wasn't what Jack was expecting, but then it hadn't occurred to him exactly how this would end.

"Jesus," he exhaled when he found the gun. It was huge. The only time he had ever seen a pistol that big was in *Dirty Harry*, and now he had one in his hand.

Dave was no longer driving the boat when Jack came out with the pistol in hand. He had joined Bryan out on the rail. There was lots of splashing and banging about. The rod was still bent over from the strain, and Dave was trying to loop a rope around the shark's tail that they would use for lifting the beast. The shark, tired from the fight, stilled for a moment and Dave called out, "Got it."

Bryan turned his head toward Jack. "You got my gun?"

"Yeah." He held it up to show the captain.

"Then shoot it!"

He wasn't prepared for that either. He hesitated a moment while his brain caught up with his ears.

During that moment, the shark began to thrash about again. Bryan strained to hold onto the rod and his catch and shouted,

"Goddamn it, Jack, will you just shoot this mother fucker!"

Jack moved to the rail, cocked the pistol, carefully aimed at the center of the shark's head, and squeezed the trigger. The sound and the kick were startling, but that one shot was all that was needed. All the splashing and thrashing stopped, and the water began to turn red.

"Nice shot. Now put the gun inside, and let's get this guy in before his friends come and eat him."

By the time Jack returned, Dave had already hung a large open block from the end of the lifting boom on the mast. He watched as Dave ran a heavy rope with a large hook over the block and handed the hook to Bryan.

"Here, take this," said Dave as he handed Jack the other end of the rope before releasing the lock on the boom and swinging it toward the side of the boat.

"Wrap it around the winch while I help Bryan."

Jack put several turns around the winch.

"Those are the up and down switches," Dave said looking back and pointing to two round black rubber circles on the deck. "Wait until Bryan gives you the word."

"Got it."

"Take 'er up."

Jack stepped on the rubber circle that was marked *up*, and the electric winch began to hum while he pulled on the rope. Soon the shark's tail appeared above the rail. At first the pitch of the motor was easy and high, but as more and more of the fish came into view, that sound became deeper and more strained. Jack could actually feel the boat start to tip toward the shark.

As soon as the shark's head was clear of the water, Bryan signaled for Jack to stop. He held on to the rope, awaiting instructions, and looked at the shark. The shark's back was a beautiful blue, a stark contrast to its bright white belly. Hanging there, suspended over the water, its mouth full of teeth served as a stark reminder that in the ocean, sharks are the alpha.

Jack watched as Bryan reached under the rail of the boat and pulled out a knife with a twelve-inch blade. He swung the belly toward him and, in a single, efficient motion, split the shark open. The guts spilled out, creating a slick of chum. Instantly the sky filled with birds vying for the floating scraps.

"Bring her up some more," called out Bryan, "so I can swing her on board."

The winch groaned and Jack pulled. When the shark's head was clear of the rail, Bryan signaled to stop pulling, and with Dave's help they swung the shark inboard.

"Holy shit, look at those teeth!" said Jack.

"Ain't they somethin'. Wouldn't want her chewing on me. Let'r down now."

Jack stepped on the down button and played out the rope until the shark was lying on the deck. Bryan looked at Jack. "Dave tells me you know how to drive a boat. While he and I begin carving up this beauty, how 'bout you take the helm and begin heading for home?"

"No problem." Secretly, Jack was relieved for the chance to step back from this experience for a while.

* * *

As *Miss Cookie* began to turn for home, her bow swung past the column of black smoke that Jack had been watching earlier. He picked up the binoculars and watched it again. He slowly turned his body in one direction to keep it in sight while *Miss Cookie* turned the opposite way. By the time the smoke was nearly astern, they were on course for home.

Jack stopped watching long enough to set the autopilot; then he picked up the glasses again. He knew that out on the deck, Dave and Bryan were busy carving up the shark. He could hear them tossing the scraps overboard, oblivious to both the column of smoke and the swarm of squawking birds that were now vying for the remainders.

"Hey, guys," he called. "I think someone is in trouble."

Bryan looked up. "What?"

Jack pointed. "There. Remember that smoke I saw just before you caught the shark? It's still there."

Dave and Bryan both looked astern at the smoke and then back at Jack.

Bryan spoke first. "Looks to me like someone spewing out a lot of exhaust,"

Then he added, "Diesels can do that, especially when under load. Probably someone who had a good catch and is pushing to get back home."

"I don't think so. That's definitely smoke from a fire," countered Jack, the binoculars still at his eyes.

"Let me look."

Jack handed the glasses to Dave.

Bryan stood up and threw another scrap overboard. A gull grabbed it before it even hit the water. He then held his hand above his eyes and stared as well. "Maybe."

"We've got to go see," said Jack.

"No. We don't," said Bryan. Then he paused, reached toward the glasses in Dave's hand, and sighed. "Fine. Let me see."

Jack knew that the captain simply wanted to get back as soon as possible now. He had a buyer who would pay well for such a fish—and even more for the fins. Even if they ignored the smoke, it would still be another four hours before they'd be back at Hampton Harbor. No wonder he had sighed.

While Bryan stared at the smoke, Dave turned to Jack. "I think you might be right."

Bryan lowered the binoculars and then handed them back to Dave. It was clear from his sour expression that he didn't want to spend another moment thinking about it.

Dave, on the other hand, now looked fully committed. He said, "Bryan, we should go back and check it out."

The sour expression on Bryan's face became even sharper. Playing Good Samaritan was obviously not on his list of things to do.

"C'mon, Bryan. You know we have to," said Dave.

The captain stared at them for a minute. Then he mumbled, "Fine, suit yourselves. It'll cost you extra for the fuel *and* time. I don't care, it's your money. I'm gonna' finish this fish."

Jack thought he heard him mumble, "Fuckin' goody two shoes" under his breath as he resumed his work cutting on the shark.

CHAPTER 8

JACK WENT INSIDE AND RETURNED *Miss Cookie* to a course for the mysterious smoke while Dave kept it in sight, watching through the binoculars.

"Hey, Jack, either it's heading straight at us or it's still in the water."

"Let me see." They swapped places. Dave took over driving the boat while Jack, standing next to him, studied the column of smoke. "I don't think it's moving. I'm going to go up topside; maybe I can get a better look from up there."

"Go." Dave nudged the throttle up a notch and frowned.

Jack said to Dave before leaving the cabin, "You know, this far from shore, it's hard to think that whatever is going on out there could possibly be any good."

He kept the glasses trained on the smoke as *Miss Cookie* chugged steadily on. He was still searching for the actual source of the smoke when suddenly it changed from black to gray to white. Then it was gone. He pounded on the cabin top and then headed for the ladder.

As he hit the deck, he shouted, "Dave. Bryan. Did you see that?"

Dave had, and he was trying to explain what he had seen to Bryan.

"Let me have those," Bryan told Jack, motioning to the binoculars. There was just a wisp of smoke remaining in the distance.

This time, Bryan took only a cursory look through the binoculars. "No idea," he said. "I'm going to finish with the shark." He handed the glasses back to Jack and left the deckhouse.

"What's with him?"

"Bryan?"

"Yeah, Bryan. Who did you think I meant?"

"No need to be snippy." Dave continued to look straight ahead.

"So, what's with him?"

"Bryan's got some issues. He's had some bad experiences in the past, and he doesn't like to get involved with things that are not his business."

"What kind of things?"

"Can't say."

"Can't or won't?"

"Both."

"C'mon, Dave, we've known each other too long. What?"

"I'll just say that he doesn't have the best track record with the Coast Guard or the fisheries people."

Jack thought a minute about that. "The shark?"

"Catching it wasn't a problem. His choice of bait and keeping it, yeah, those would be problems."

"Fine. You keep driving. Now that we're this close, might as well go on and check it out. I'm going back topside."

* * *

Shortly after climbing up to the top of the deckhouse, Jack looked down to see how Bryan was doing. It looked like the deck had been washed down, and a hatch was now open, exposing several large, ice-filled coolers.

Bryan looked up and, seeing that Jack was watching, called out, "Hey, Jack. Give me a hand?"

"Sure. What d'you need?"

"Help me get this fish down into the ice."

Next to him, on the deck, lay the two large halves of the shark's body, jaws, fins, and tail, the remains of the carcass having been tossed overboard. He told Jack that the fins and body halves would be going to his Thai buyer. The jaws he would boil clean and sell to some tourist, and the tail he would dry and preserve. It too would become a souvenir for some sucker. The few steaks that he had cut for themselves were already packed in ice in another, smaller cooler.

"Thanks," Bryan said, after the shark was stashed below. "Beer?"

"Yeah." Bryan grabbed three, handed one to Jack, cracked his open, and took a sip before taking the third in to Dave.

Jack took one more look forward and saw nothing but a flat empty ocean.

* * *

Beer in hand, Jack returned to the top of the deckhouse. The sun, even though it was going down, was still hot on Jack's neck and back, giving him a deeper appreciation for the cold beer. Between sips he scanned the ocean between their bow and the horizon. He was most thankful for polarized sunglasses. Without those, it would have been impossible to see anything. They had to be getting close. Even when he had watched the smoke from the top of the cabin, it had always been over the horizon.

He calculated that at a 10-foot height, the horizon would have been 3.6 nautical miles away. Doubling that, he decided that at first sighting, they were 7.2 nautical miles away. Then they steamed away for maybe 30 minutes at 5 knots before turning back; that added another 2.5 miles, which made the first sighting 9.7 nautical miles away. They had now been steaming at closer to 7 knots for at least 45 minutes. That would leave maybe 4.5 nautical miles to go. Best guesses all, but at least it gave him some comfort. Taking into account all the variables and assumptions, it seemed reasonable that they should see something pretty soon.

At least, Jack hoped so. The only definite was the forthcoming sunset, which would not change, and once the sun had set, he knew they would head for home if nothing could be found. Bryan had made that perfectly clear. It was only because of his long-time friendship with Dave—and the fact that they had agreed to pay the extra expenses—that he had agreed to humor them until sunset in the first place.

Jack lowered the binoculars and looked back. Their wake was straight and true. Then, before turning back to resume his search, he looked down and saw Bryan, who was sitting in one of the lawn chairs, sipping his beer. Bryan looked up and tipped his beer toward Jack.

"What an asshole," thought Jack. He made a mental note to find out the real story from Dave some time, but for the moment, Bryan was just an asshole.

Less than five minutes had passed before Jack thought he saw something in the water. He stared. And the more he stared, the more convinced he was that there was something floating in the water ahead. When he saw a second object near the first, he was certain. He knocked on the top of the deckhouse, shouted, and then scrambled to get down as fast as possible. His shout got Bryan's attention, and the captain looked up from his chair.

"Got something?"

Jack didn't answer; he just ran inside to tell Dave. He still needed the glasses to see it, but they were close enough that the binoculars did make it clear.

"Here. Look," said Jack. He handed the binoculars to Dave and pointed. While Dave was searching for the object, Bryan joined them. Jack pointed again. This time he thought he could see it even without the glasses.

Bryan spotted it at the same time that Dave did. "There's a lot of stuff," said Dave, as he swept the area with the binoculars.

"Shit," mumbled Bryan.

Then he added, "I'll take it," and gave Dave a nudge. Replacing Dave at the helm, the captain disengaged the autopilot and pulled back on the throttle.

CHAPTER 9

AS THEIR SPEED DECREASED, the amount of debris increased, and they began to see traces of oil on the surface. Then Jack spotted a piece of charred wood. Only the soft purr of the near-idling diesel broke the stillness as all three men silently took in the scene.

Dave spoke first. "We gotta' call the Coast Guard." He reached for the radio's mic.

Bryan grabbed his wrist. "I'll call. You go outside and see if there are any survivors."

"C'mon Jack. Let's go."

Once the friends were back out on the deck, Dave turned to Jack. "You okay?"

"Uh, yeah. I'm fine. Look, do you think he'll really call the Coast Guard?"

"I do. I don't think he wants to, but he'll do it anyway."

Jack took another quick look at the ocean, but now his legs felt weak. "I'll go up and look from there," he said, motioning toward the ladder.

"Okay. I'll stay down here and see what I can pick up."

As Jack sat down, he began to shake. He closed his eyes and tried to force those memories away, but they wouldn't go.

The fire, the stench of diesel, and the feeling of hopelessness as he watched his beloved Irrepressible slide below the water overwhelmed him. "Jack! Jack!" he heard Max's voice calling to him. She called again. "Jack!"

It wasn't Max. He looked up, startled to find that he was back in the present and it was Dave shouting up at him.

"Over there," Dave shouted, pointing off toward the sun. "There," he gestured. "I think I saw something."

The urgency in Dave's voice snapped Jack out of his funk. He lifted the glasses and began searching in the direction where Dave had been pointing.

At first he didn't see anything, but then, far off, there was something. He thought he saw a splash. But staring hard at the spot, he began to have doubts. Had he really seen something, or did he only want to see something? He wasn't sure until he saw it again. It *was* a splash, and even as far off as it was, and how small, he was certain that it wasn't a fish.

"I see it," he called back to Dave, never lowering the binoculars.

Rushing to the deckhouse door, Dave shouted, "Bryan, over there. Go that way. There's something in the water."

"That way!" Dave pointed again, and Bryan turned the wheel, pointing *Miss Cookie* in the direction that Dave had indicated.

Jack began climbing down from his vantage point on top of the deckhouse as Dave shouted again to Bryan, "Have you called yet?"

"I was about to. I wanted to get the coordinates first and have a better idea what to report."

Jack, as he reached the deck, could hear Dave muttering under his breath, *"Bullshit. You don't want to call. You son of a bitch."*

"Bryan, make the call," he yelled again.

Bryan looked at Dave and picked up the mic.

* * *

That evening, the call came in to the Search and Rescue (SAR) center in Portland, Maine at about 7:15. They relayed Bryan's information to the Small Boat station in Portsmouth, New Hampshire, who then dispatched their twenty-five-foot fast response boat. It would take less than an hour for them to get there, especially since the sea conditions were so flat. *Miss Cookie* was advised to remain on station until they arrived.

CHAPTER 10

JACK MOVED TO THE RAIL and peered forward around the deckhouse so he could keep whatever was in the water in his sight. He was sure he saw another splash.

"Dave," he shouted, "I think someone's there. Get Bryan to speed up."

He could hear some shouting back and forth and then felt the increase in vibration as *Miss Cookie* picked up speed.

The sun was a constant reminder that time was not on their side. It continued to get lower in the sky, making it increasingly hard to keep their target in sight. Fortunately, the surface of the ocean had remained mirror flat or they might not have seen anything.

Jack held his hand over his eyes. The binoculars were now useless because he was looking almost directly into the sun.

Dave had remained by the deckhouse door. "How're we doing?" he called over to Jack.

"Okay, I think. I saw a couple more splashes, but then I lost it."

"Well, Bryan finally called the Coast Guard. They should be here within an hour. We're supposed to stay put 'till then."

"Yeah, okay," Jack replied. Then, "What the hell?"

"Do you see something?"

"Yes. . . . Looks like a body."

"Where?"

"About three points off the starboard bow."

Dave disappeared into the deckhouse while Jack kept his eyes on what he had seen.

"He seems to be more on board with the operation now," said Dave as he returned to join Jack at the rail.

Jack pointed again. "See. There!"

"I think you're right. Holy shit."

Bryan began to throttle back and shouted out that he was going to come up starboard side to. Since the sea was flat the approach could be from any direction, and the starboard side would give him a better view.

"I've got him in sight," shouted Jack.

Dave, with boat hook in hand, joined him at the rail. "Easy now," he shouted as Bryan brought *Miss Cookie* close to the body and came to a stop.

Bryan came out and joined them at the rail. "Son of a bitch."

"That's no fisherman, and that's no *he*," said Dave under his breath.

No one moved for what felt like an eternity. They just stood and stared.

"She alive?" Bryan was the first to speak.

"Can't tell," Dave whispered.

The woman was being kept afloat by a couple of boat cushions. They could see that one was underneath her body, her arms through its straps, as if she were wearing a backpack, only on her chest. Her head lay on the other cushion, one hand clenched in a fist as it held on to a strap. Long blond hair mostly hid her face, and the strands that were out of the water were plastered to her skin, while other tendrils floated gently back and forth in the water. She was wearing tan shorts, the ones with lots of pockets, with a light blue shirt that had been partially torn away, revealing a white tank top underneath. It, too, was torn and stained. The backs of her arms and shoulders, which weren't completely submerged, revealed well-tanned skin, but the parts of her that were in the water had taken on a pallid, lifeless look. The scrapes and cuts on her arms and legs, while not actively bleeding, still had the potential to attract sharks.

"Can you reach her with the boat hook?" asked Jack.

His question was answered by a splash, as Dave thrust it out toward her.

"I'll bring the boat closer," Bryan said. He returned to the helm and began to shift from forward to reverse and back again to bring *Miss Cookie* closer.

Dave thrust out the boat hook again. This time it hit her leg, which caused her to kick.

"She's alive!" Jack shouted. "Quick, pull her over."

Bryan joined them as Dave carefully pulled her closer to the boat.

As Jack soon discovered, a wet, slippery, limp body is not an easy thing to haul out of the water. The lifting boom they had used on the shark would have made it much easier, but adrenaline seemed to be their only real option. When the woman was within reach, Jack and Bryan grabbed onto her and gave an enormous heave. With that she seemed to practically fly out of the water, landing on the deck, face down, nearly causing her rescuers to lose their balance and fall on the deck as well.

The impact revived her, and she began coughing and wheezing. As she tried to push herself up, Bryan moved to help, but when his hand touched her arm, she looked up for the first time. Her eyes grew wide as panic and confusion flashed across her face. She recoiled, struggling to back away from him. "No," she snarled, keeping her eyes locked on him.

The three men froze. But as they watched, her face began to soften, as if she was finally realizing they were even there. Slowly she took her eyes off Bryan and looked first at Dave and then at Jack. In the next split second, time seemed to stand still, while her conscious mind caught up with what her eyes had seen.

"Jack?"

CHAPTER 11

JACK'S LEGS FELT WEAK for the second time in less than an hour.

"Sylvie?"

Dave and Bryan looked at each other. "What the fuck?" said Bryan.

"What the fuck?" echoed Dave.

Never taking his eyes off the woman, Jack said, "Someone go get a blanket or something."

Sylvie remained still, staring at him, as if ready to flee. In a quivering voice, she whispered, "How? What? Who?" As she said this, she began to shiver uncontrollably.

Jack knelt down beside her, gently put his arm around her shoulder, and slowly pulled her in close. As warm as the day was, the ocean could never be called warm, and she was so cold. The sun, ever closer to the horizon, began to cast a pink hue over everything as she buried her face into his chest.

"Here." It was Dave. He unfolded a blanket and draped it over her shoulders. Jack then stood and gently reached for her arms to help lift her to standing. Sylvie held the blanket close and, with Jack's assistance, stood and leaned into him. He could feel her shivers—heavy, rolling tremors that welled up from deep inside. He wrapped his arms around her and stroked her back in an effort to warm her. "It's okay. You're safe," he whispered to the top of her head. It seemed that all she could do was shiver and shake.

"Was there anyone else?" he asked softly.

She shook her head and mumbled, "No."

"There's some dry clothes down below," said Bryan. "Don't know how they'll fit, but they'll be dry. I'll go put some water on for coffee."

Jack relaxed his arms and whispered, "Let's get you below and find something dry to put on."

* * *

Water on, Bryan returned to the cockpit while Jack guided Sylvie below. As they passed, Jack thought he saw her shoot the captain a quick look, but no one else seemed to notice.

Behind them, Jack could hear Dave and Bryan quietly talking together. "Fuck," they said at the same time.

"How long before the Coast Guard arrives?" Dave asked.

Bryan answered, "Soon. I'm going back to take the helm."

CHAPTER 12

JACK FOUND THE CLOTHES, checked the kettle, and gave Sylvie one last squeeze of encouragement. "I'll let you get dried off and changed."

Sylvie remained silent, but she smiled at him before he headed out to the deckhouse, closing the companionway door behind him. He heard it latch shut.

Bryan, at the helm, looked at Jack. "You know her?"

"I do." Jack paused and thought about how best to answer. "She's an old friend."

"An old friend."

"Yes."

There was something in the way Bryan had posed the question that stuck in Jack's ear. Only a feeling, but he got a sense that maybe Bryan knew her somehow. Maybe he hadn't imagined that look after all.

To the west, the sun was nearly below the horizon, and the sky was a brilliant red. Looking east they could see the purples and blues of night creeping toward them. It wouldn't be long before they would be overtaken by the darkness.

An uneasy silence filled the cabin, and before either said anything else, Dave stuck his head in. "I think I hear something."

"Good," said Jack. However, the expression on Bryan's face confirmed that the captain did not welcome this bit of information.

The latch on the companionway door rattled and the door opened. All heads turned at once to see Sylvie standing in the opening, holding a cup of coffee. She was a sight in the clothes that Bryan had said were down below. The old, red sweatshirt was large enough that another person her size could have fit inside with her. The same size issue existed for the dungarees, which she had rolled up several times so she wouldn't trip. Her hair was still wet and badly in need of brushing. The strain of her ordeal could be seen in her face, but now her eyes were clear and defiant.

"Did I hear you say the Coast Guard is on the way?" There was an edge to her voice.

"We did," said Jack.

"Why?" Her eyes bored into him.

"What do you mean *why*?" said Jack. "We had to call the Coast Guard. A boat burned and sank."

"Did you tell them about me?"

"No. We called when we first found wreckage. They told us to stay here until they arrived."

"Then don't."

"Don't what?" asked Jack. He was pretty sure he knew the answer, but he asked her anyway. "Don't stay, or don't tell them about you?"

"Don't tell them that you found me. Leave it that you found no one. It'll be simpler that way."

Dave and Bryan had remained silent throughout this exchange. Bryan spoke up first.

"Fine by me. What they don't know, won't hurt them—or us."

"But—"

Sylvie cut Dave off. Looking straight at him she said, "It'll be for the best." Her tone made it clear that there would be no further discussion. She glanced out the window. "I'll explain later."

"What's going on?" Jack asked Sylvie.

"I've got to hide." She ignored his question and backed down into the forward cabin.

CHAPTER 13

AS SYLVIE DISAPPEARED BELOW, they finally heard clearly the pulsing sounds of a high-powered boat skipping over the water.

"Shit," mumbled Bryan as he rushed out of the deckhouse.

Dave and Jack followed.

"Problem?" asked Dave.

"Yeah, it's a problem. They sent a fuckin' boat. I had hoped they'd send a chopper."

Dave gave him a puzzled look.

"What if they decide to be dickheads and board us?"

"What?"

"Worst case is—think about it—they board, find the shark, Sylvie comes out and tells them who-knows-what, and we have to deal with a world of shit."

"I see."

"So let's hope they decide to stay focused on finding that boat that sank and leave us alone."

Dave and Jack watched as the Coast Guard boat rushed toward them while Bryan went back inside the deckhouse and turned on the deck lights..

The radio crackled to life. "*Miss Cookie. Miss Cookie. Miss Cookie,* CG25565. Over."

Sylvie pulled the companionway door shut as Bryan came in and reached for the radio's mic. "CG25565, *Miss Cookie* here. Over."

Almost before they could exchange information, the Coast Guard boat was alongside. Jack took a bow line and Dave a stern. Once the boats were secured together, the officer in charge requested permission to come aboard. As much as Jack knew it must have killed him, Bryan emerged from the deckhouse and cheerfully invited the officer on board.

Jack was impressed with how professional Bryan was during the interview. He answered questions efficiently. With corroboration from Jack and Dave, their captain gave a close account of what had transpired—at least in terms of finding the wreckage itself.

"No survivors?" asked the Coast Guard officer.

"None that we could find," said Bryan.

He looked back and forth between Bryan, Jack and Dave. After an interminable moment, he said, "Thank you. We'll stay and continue to search the area in case there were any survivors you didn't find. You may go on and head home. If we need anything else, we'll be in touch."

Jack and Dave handed the lines to the crew on the Coast Guard boat while Bryan went into the deckhouse. The two boats separated and the Coast Guard craft pulled away and began its search while Bryan shifted *Miss Cookie* into gear. Immediately the distance between the two boats increased. Bryan killed the deck lights, and save for the red glow inside the deckhouse, their world went dark and silent except for the steady thrum of *Miss Cookie's* engine.

When the lights of the Coast Guard boat were nothing more than dots in the darkness, the men gathered on deck. Bryan spoke first.

"That was too close."

"But we're all good?" asked Dave.

"I think so. Fortunately, they were full-on rescue mode and not interested in anything else."

"So you think they bought it?" asked Jack.

Bryan shrugged and turned. "We're outta' here. I'll be inside at the helm."

CHAPTER 14

WITH THAT HE WENT BACK INSIDE and took his seat at the helm. Sylvie came out of the cabin. "Thank you," she said to Bryan, touching his arm, then, she sat down at the table. Bryan ignored her at first; then he turned and faced her. "You gonna' tell me what happened?" he asked.

Before she could answer, Jack and Dave walked in.

They had remained outside watching the lights of the Coast Guard boat fade into the darkness before following Bryan back into the deck-house. Jack was surprised to see her sitting so calmly at the table, considering her reaction to Bryan when they first dropped her on the deck. Based on some of the more disturbing aspects of his previous run-ins with Sylvie, he began to seriously wonder if there could be some sort of secret connection between them. After this crazy day, and especially given their past, nearly anything seemed possible.

Dave's voice interrupted Jack's thoughts. "How're you feeling?" Dave asked their new passenger.

In a voice barely above a whisper she replied, "I'm okay."

"You were very lucky. You know, it was Jack who made us turn back to see what that smoke was from."

She looked up but didn't say anything. Then, focusing on Jack, she took a deep breath. "Thank you."

"Sylvie," said Jack softly. "What's going on?"

Finally, she said, "I know it's not fair. You all deserve more, but all I can say is that I need to be dead."

Stunned, Jack repeated those words slowly and one at a time. "You – need – to – be – dead." He wanted to be perfectly clear.

"Yes."

"Do you care to explain?"

"Not now."

"Later?"

She didn't answer that question. "Is there anything to eat?"

＊ ＊ ＊

"Bro. Good job on those steaks," said Dave.

Since their supply of sandwiches had been devoured long before Sylvie had been fished out of the water, Bryan had fired up his grill on the back deck and cooked some of the mako steaks that he had cut for them.

Jack nodded in agreement.

Looking at Sylvie, Bryan said, "You know, you could very easily have been that guy's dinner."

"I know. I wonder if I would have tasted as good to him as he tasted to us."

Awkward laughter filled the deckhouse, followed by silence. The deckhouse's red lighting, which distorted their expressions, didn't help dispel the awkwardness of the moment. Then Bryan lifted his can of beer and said, "A toast."

They each raised a can, and then he continued. Looking straight at Sylvie, in a beer-fueled voice he said, "To sharks and women. They'll both devour you if you're not careful."

Cans clanked, and then that awkwardness returned. This time it was Sylvie who broke the spell.

"I need some air." As the three men watched, she slid out from the table and walked out of the deckhouse and into the dark.

CHAPTER 15

ONCE SYLVIE SEEMED TO BE OUT OF EARSHOT, Bryan turned to Jack.

"What's the story with your 'friend'?"

Jack hesitated a moment, wondering how little he could disclose. "We met several years ago, at a race. She fell, hurt her ankle, and I helped her. That's about it."

Bryan looked at him. "I see."

Jack could tell he wanted more, but he wasn't giving, so he turned the question back to Bryan.

"She had quite the reaction to you when we pulled her up. I also can't help but notice the way she keeps glancing at you. What about it? You two know each other?"

Jack could see that he had completely caught Bryan off guard. The captain's denial contained too much vigor.

"No. No. I've never seen her before. I don't know where you'd get that. She's easy on the eyes, and I'd be lying if I said I wasn't interested. After all, to catch a good shark and a blonde on the same day is quite a piece of luck."

As the tension continued to build, Dave changed the subject. "Another beer, anyone?"

"Sure," said Bryan.

Jack said, "I'll go with you."

"Be right back."

* * *

Once outside, Dave hissed at Jack, "What was that all about?"

"What?"

"Cut the crap. You just helped her at a race? And what's with you going at Bryan?"

Before Jack could respond, Sylvie's voice came out of the shadows. "Hey, guys."

Jack had actually forgotten for a moment that she was out there. How much had she overheard?

"Oh, um, Sylvie. We came for more beers—you want one?"

Dave gave him a slight whack on the arm.

"No, thanks." Her tone gave no indication that she had heard anything.

Dave rummaged through the nearly empty cooler, pulled out three beers, handed one to Jack, and said, "I'll see you inside."

Jack went over and sat down next to her. As his eyes adjusted to the dark, he could see that she had pulled her arms close. In the oversized clothes, she looked totally pitiful.

Neither said anything right away, and the only sound besides the drone of the engine and the hiss of the water was the *psht* of the tab on his beer can as he pulled it open. Behind them, barely visible in the dim light of the stars, a thin ribbon of phosphorescence trailed on the surface, stirred up by *Miss Cookie's* movement.

"Cold?" asked Jack.

On top of her experience, the night had finally brought some relief from the heat of the day.

"No, I'm fine." She didn't look at him, but rather continued to stare astern. "How're you doing?"

"Good. I'm good. Yourself?"

"I've had better days."

"You gonna' tell me what happened?"

"I can't."

"Can't or won't?"

"Probably both."

"Beer?" he asked again.

"I'm all set."

He left her sitting alone and returned to the deckhouse.

* * *

Bryan was again in the helmsman seat. He was looking out into the blackness with a glance every now and again at the chart plotter. Dave was back at the table, sitting sideways, legs stretched out on one of the benches, leaning against the wall. Jack couldn't tell if he was asleep or not.

"You ever had a trip like this?" he asked Bryan in an attempt to defuse the tension between them.

"Never."

"Will you get much for the shark?"

"I'll do all right."

Jack wondered what extent Bryan would go to in order to make a buck.

"Hey, listen, I didn't mean to imply anything before about you and Sylvie."

"No problem. I was pushing a bit myself." The captain held up his fist. "We cool."

They bumped fists and Jack echoed, "Cool."

CHAPTER 16

IT HAD BEEN OVER FOUR HOURS since sunset and their rescue of Sylvie, and it would be at least another hour before they would be tied up at the dock. Bryan had remained at the helm while Dave dozed, and Jack, restless, alternated between sitting inside in silence and then outside, where in spite of his minor attempts at small talk, Sylvie had remained silent. Now he returned outside again.

"Sylvie?"

She turned her head toward his voice. "Jack," she said. Then she returned her gaze to the dark sea behind.

"Can we talk now?"

She said nothing as he sat down next to her.

"You know, you have to say something. We'll be back soon and someone will be asking questions. The Coast Guard will probably be contacting us again."

"It's simple. Don't say anything. I never existed. It's for the best."

"But you're not dead. Even if we say nothing to the authorities, we know you're alive. *I* know you're alive. C'mon, Sylvie. Talk to me."

She looked at Jack and then turned away again. Several more long moments passed in silence. Finally, she said, "All right. But, you must understand: *I don't exist.*"

"Fine. You're dead. And if I tell anyone otherwise you'll have to kill me."

"It's not funny, Jack. I won't kill you, but others may if they think I'm alive and that by harming you it will help them find me."

Her tone and the urgency in her voice convinced him that she was not kidding around. "Understood."

She said it again. "No matter what, you can't let anyone know that you found me. If you have to talk about the sinking, fine, just leave me out of it. All hands were lost. No survivors. Nothing."

"I got that part of it. Sylvie. What's really going on? What kind of trouble are you in?"

"I never said I was in trouble."

"Sure looks like it to me."

"Look Jack. I never thought I'd see you again. You have Max and that's good. Keep it that way."

"You're not making much sense."

"Can't you just trust me?"

"I do. But I also care about you, and if you need help, I want you to know I'm here."

"I know."

She looked at the sky one more time, took a deep breath, and then reached for Jack's hand. "Let's go inside. I need to talk to all of you."

* * *

Dave was definitely asleep this time, legs stretched out on the bench, and Bryan was still at the helm. Ahead, the glow of civilization could finally be seen. Jack gave Dave's legs a push. His feet thumped onto the cabin sole and he looked around, obviously trying to get his bearings. "Hunh?"

"Pay attention," said Jack, nodding toward Sylvie.

Sylvie had sidled up to Bryan and was alternately looking out the front window and at the chart plotter. "Those the Isles?" she asked, pointing.

"Yeah. We'll be back soon. So what're we going to do with you?"

"First, I have to thank all of you again for saving me. You didn't have to do that." The men remained silent.

"I asked you to keep the fact that you found me a secret. I'm serious when I say I need to remain dead."

Dave seemed fully awake now. "Okay, you're dead. We get it. But what about the boat you were on? What's the story? Whose boat was it and what happened to them? Why did it burn?"

"You've got to trust me." she said, looking at Jack for reassurance. He nodded.

"Why not just answer the questions?" pressed Dave. "What does the fact that Jack trusts you have to do with anything?"

"If Jack trusts me, and I'm assuming you trust him— you do trust him, don't you, Dave?"

"Of course I do." Jack noticed that Dave's voice was beginning to sound a bit testy.

"Then trust me." As the three men watched, Sylvie took a deep breath and then started her story.

"The boat I was on picked me up in Newburyport." She spoke quickly, as if she hoped to stop them from interrupting with any questions. "There was just the captain and myself on board. Turns out, he was not a very nice man, and I don't think he intended for me to return. Shit happened, the boat burned, he's gone, and I'm here. That's all you need to know. You three are the only people who know I'm alive, so I'm asking again, can we keep it that way?" She looked from one to the other.

Jack had been watching Dave and Bryan as she talked. He had already made up his mind and would keep her secret. He was also sure Dave would go along, if for no other reason than out of respect for their friendship. Bryan, on the other hand? He had no idea.

"No problem with me," said Jack.

"Fine," said Dave, before adding, "because of Jack."

Then Sylvie looked toward Bryan.

"I'm cool."

"Great, now that that's settled, I need to get back to Newburyport as soon as possible. Ideas?"

Bryan spoke first. "I'll take you."

Jack stared at him, surprised at his sudden cooperation. The captain continued, "I've already called my friend to meet us in Hampton and take the shark. You guys go home. I'll take Sylvie down and then come back. Probably be back shortly after sunrise."

No one said anything for a few minutes. Then Jack spoke. ""Why would you do this?"

"Does anyone have a better idea?"

Dave shrugged, and shook his head. "Sounds like a plan to me. A while back I called Patti to say we'd be running late. She sounded relieved to hear me at first, but then she sounded a little pissed off. She and Max are at my place, and with a bit of luck they won't be on the dock waiting for us."

At this, Jack's thoughts suddenly jolted back from Sylvie to Max. Before he could give either woman further consideration, however, Dave's voice broke in again.

"The sooner we get rid of the shark—and Sylvie—the better off we'll all be."

"So it's settled?" asked Bryan, looking at each one of them in turn.

CHAPTER 17

FOR THE FINAL MOMENTS OF THE JOURNEY, Bryan remained at the helm, Sylvie hid in the forward cabin, and Dave and Jack stood in the back, next to all their gear. As *Miss Cookie* slid under the bridge and back into Hampton Harbor, the water was as still and glassy as when they had left some twenty or so hours earlier. With no moon, the harbor had once again become a mass of dark shapes.

"Ohh!" Jack ducked and then swiped at the back of his neck. The humid air condensing against the cold steel of the bridge created droplets of water, and one had certainly found its mark. As he looked up, it ran down his back and he shivered.

Normally the hours just before dawn were the coolest, but the humidity still hung like an invisible curtain. There was no indication that the heat wave would be stopping anytime soon. As Jack looked to the southwest, the sodium vapor lights that illuminated the nuclear power plant created an otherworldly scene.

Ahead, and to the right, a single dim security light lit one end of the dock. The halo of humidity around that light formed eerie shadows and pockets of darkness. As Bryan steered *Miss Cookie* to the dark end of the dock, the slow thrum of her engine was the only sound to break the night's silence.

Bryan, as he had nearly twenty-four hours earlier, laid his boat gently alongside the empty dock and brought her to a stop. Jack and Dave stepped off *Miss Cookie,* lines in hand, and secured the boat.

"Where's Bryan?" A deep, raspy voice startled Jack as two figures moved out from the shadows.

In the dim light he could see that the slight, wiry Asian men were dressed all in black like two ninjas.

Before Jack could reply, Bryan walked out of the deckhouse. "Hey,

Tran."

"Bryan. Thanks for the call."

Tran ignored Jack and spoke directly to Bryan. "You remember my cousin Lou."

"Lou, good to see you. Come on aboard."

Dave and Jack remained on the dock while Tran and Lou clambered aboard. Bryan opened the deck hatch, and Tran climbed down to inspect the fish. Then Bryan called over to the men on the dock.

"Hey, guys, could you give Lou a hand while Tran and I take care of business?"

As Tran followed Bryan into the deckhouse, Dave and Jack climbed back aboard *Miss Cookie* to join Lou, who was already waiting down in the hold. Looking down, Jack could see that there was barely enough room for the two coolers, let alone a man, even a small man. However, Lou signaled for Dave to join him and, when Dave hesitated, hissed and waved his arms for Dave to hurry up. Finally, Dave lowered himself down, while Lou wriggled out of sight. Together they somehow managed to manhandle the cooler containing the shark up to a point where Jack could grab one of its handles. It was heavy and awkward, but as Jack pulled and they pushed, the cooler finally made it onto the deck. The second cooler was a bit easier for them to maneuver out.

Just then, Bryan and Tran reappeared on deck. "Tran, it was a pleasure," said Bryan as he stuffed a wad of bills into his pocket.

"Any time, man."

Jack and Dave watched as Tran and Lou hefted the coolers onto the dock and then disappeared into the night. The whole transaction had taken less than ten minutes.

"Let's get your stuff off so I can get going," Bryan said. With that he began grabbing their pack and rods.

Jack jumped onto the dock and took their gear from him while Dave grabbed their cooler and handed it over to Jack.

"Bryan," Dave said, "That was a great day. You gonna' be all right?"

"No problem. I'll just take her down to Newburyport and we'll be done."

"Thanks. Let me know what happens with the Coast Guard."

"I will. Shouldn't be a big deal. We really didn't see or find anything."

They shook hands, and Bryan turned to wave curtly at Jack. Then the captain returned to the red glow of the deckhouse while Dave climbed onto the dock and helped Jack untie *Miss Cookie*. Seconds later she was moving away, heading back to sea.

CHAPTER 18

"WELCOME TO MY WORLD," SAID DAVE.

"Bryan is quite the character."

"He is. Good man, but best to just accept him and not ask too many questions."

"I'm surprised the girls weren't waiting here for us." Dave lived right around the corner from the marina; they had taken Jack's truck down to the dock earlier only to avoid lugging the heavy cooler.

"Me too. Glad they weren't, though. Tran and Silent Lou might have been a bit much to explain."

As they loaded their stuff back into the truck for the brief ride back up to Dave's place, Jack wondered if he should mention Sylvie again or not. But before he could give it much thought, a voice called out from the shadows, "Tran and Silent Lou who?"

A second voice quickly followed. "Explain what?"

"Shit," said Jack under his breath. He turned toward the voices, trying to hide his surprise. "Max, Patti, you're here!"

Max said, "What did you expect? We were worried."

"There was nothing to worry about," said Dave.

Patti's voice chimed in. "Easy for you to say, but I know your friend Bryan." She paused and then added, "By the way, where is he?"

"He had to get going, so it was pretty much a dump and run."

"A dump and run. Right. Probably up to no good is more like it."

"We got some nice fish."

Patty simply gave him The Look and followed after Max, who had already started walking back up to Dave's.

* * *

Later, as Jack and Max drove north through Hampton Beach, the pre-dawn air felt like the atmospheric version of sweet-and-sour candy. It was still really warm, but the warm humidity against bare skin made it feel cool. With dawn still a couple of hours off, the beach had finally gone to sleep save for a few late-night souls.

"So, what really happened?" asked Max.

"Nothing. It was pretty much a long, hot day. No breeze, only a few fish, took us over four hours just to get out."

"Stop, Jack." She cut him off. "I know it was hot. I know you went pretty far out. I know you drank a lot of beer. I know you caught some fish. What I don't know—what I want to know—is why you were so late and why you had such a quick drop off." Then she added, "And who were those two skeevy-looking guys we saw leaving?"

"Max, I don't know what you want me to say. We did all those things you said. Bryan did catch a big shark, and I've got some steaks. That really slowed things up because he hooked it just when we were going to begin heading for home. Those two guys were friends of Bryan's who bought the shark."

There was no response. He glanced over at her and saw that she was staring out the side window. She seemed to have accepted his explanation, but he had a feeling that she wasn't completely satisfied. He turned the radio on to blunt the silence in the truck. By the time they made the turn off Route 1-A onto Harbor Road and then crested the small bridge just before Ben's, the first hints of a brightening sky could be seen to the east.

"This heat ever gonna' end?" asked Jack. He had to work to suppress a big yawn.

"I hope so. Work was brutal yesterday."

Yes, Max seemed to be relenting in her anger at him.

As the truck crunched to a stop in front of the place they shared, he looked over at her and said, "I'm sorry. I should have called, but too many things were happening."

As soon as he said those words, he knew they were a mistake. Not the "I'm sorry" part, but the "too many things" part. Maybe he wouldn't pay for it now, but he'd probably pay for it later.

Before Max could reply, he leaned over, kissed her, and quickly whispered, "I know, next time I'll call. Now let's go in. I'm tired."

* * *

"Mrowh!" Cat greeted them at the top of the stairs, not at all pleased to have been disturbed. However, when she got a whiff of the fresh fish as Jack unloaded the cooler, her tone changed. Seconds later she began working him: purring, rubbing against his leg, talking in a small voice, and doing everything in her power to let him know how special and deserving of a treat she was.

"Here you go, sweetheart," he said as he gave her a few kitty treats.

She looked up at him and mrowhed her displeasure at the wholly inadequate offering.

"I'm sorry; that's all you're getting now," said Jack. "I'm tired, so go back to bed."

He could feel Cat's eyes boring a hole through his back as walked toward the bedroom. When he turned to close the door, he saw her look down at the treat. She had made the insult clear. Now she could swallow her pride and eat it.

* * *

"You working today?" Jack said softly as he tiptoed into the bedroom. Then he realized he shouldn't expect a reply. There was just enough light coming into the room through the skylight and windows for him to see that Max was already in bed under a thin sheet, and—from her steady breathing—asleep. A small fan in the window created just enough breeze that, for the moment, the room was almost cool.

As tired as he was, when he lay down, he couldn't fall asleep. He stared up through the skylight at the ever-brightening sky while the day's events replayed over and over in his head. The most troubling images involved Sylvie floating in the water and her subsequent reaction to Bryan.

He was convinced that they knew each other. Why and how he couldn't imagine, but lying there, looking up, he decided that he had to find out.

"Jack?" Max's sleep-tinged voice brought him out of his thoughts.

"Yeah."

"I was really worried about you."

"I know."

Then she rolled onto her side and began breathing deeply again. He wondered if she would even remember that short conversation, and then he too closed his eyes.

CHAPTER 19

AFTER A QUICK WAVE GOODBYE to Jack and Dave, Bryan cleared Hampton Harbor and put *Miss Cookie* on a southerly course toward the mouth of the Merrimack River and Newburyport. He checked his watch. The ocean remained a dark charcoal blue, but the inky blackness of night, made all the more so by the lack of moonlight, was beginning to lighten. Soon the stars, already dulled by the haze of humidity, would disappear as the sun rose, signaling the start of a new day. For Bryan, that day was already many hours old, and he needed a cup of coffee.

The companionway door opened and Sylvie stepped up and into the deckhouse. Gone were the oversized clothes that she had been wearing. Now that her own clothes were dry she had changed back into them. As Bryan looked her over, he didn't care if she noticed, and he liked what he saw. "I need some coffee. Want some?"

"That would be nice."

She moved away from the companionway while he engaged the autopilot and then went below to put water on for coffee. When he came back up, she was standing in the doorway to the deckhouse, arms crossed, leaning on the frame, looking astern. Her shorts, while not overly short or tight, accented her form perfectly, and even though her white tank top had several tears and was stained, he didn't care. In fact, a little voice in his head gave thanks that she wasn't wearing her blue shirt over it.

"So now are you going to tell me what happened?" he asked.

Sylvie stood silently, continuing to stare aft.

Then in a soft, matter-of-fact voice she said, "He was going to kill me."

"Who? Why?"

She shook her head and remained silent.

"So you killed him instead, and burned his boat."

"Yes."

"What are you going to do?"

"I'm not sure, but for now, I'm just going to be dead."

* * *

"Here you go." He handed her a cup and returned to the helm.

They were just over halfway to Newburyport as day overcame the night. The ocean's surface was no longer mirror-like. The first traces of a breeze were creating tiny ripples on the surface. He tuned in the marine weather forecast on the VHF radio. A front was expected later in the day accompanied by thunderstorms and strong west winds. He heard all he needed and turned the VHF off.

When Bryan had first moved to the area, he'd discovered that the Merrimack River is considered to be one of the great rivers of New England. Originating at the confluence of the Pemigewasset and Winnipesaukee rivers in Franklin, New Hampshire, and running for one hundred seventeen miles to the ocean, it was the engine that drove many of the great old mills in New England, creating cities and opportunities for the many waves of immigrants in the nineteenth and early twentieth centuries.

After he had taken a few trips to and from Newburyport, he'd quickly learned that the mouth of the Merrimack still earns its reputation for having the potential of being one of the most dangerous places for boaters on the East Coast. In fact, it commands such respect that the Coast Guard located one of its Surf Stations in the mouth of the river on Plum Island. Firsthand experience over the years had reminded Bryan that with the right combination of wind and tide, steep, powerful seas can develop at the mouth of the river, and those seas can be further exacerbated at low tide by the existence of sandbars.

Now a quick check of a tide table told him that they should arrive at nearly high water. Water depth would not be an issue. Also, since the front was still hours away and the ocean had long since overpowered the river's natural outflow, they would be moving with the current on relatively flat water.

"Hey, Sylvie."

She turned her head in the direction of his voice, and he signaled for her to join him.

Uncrossing her arms, she left the steadying influence of the door-frame and walked toward him.

"Where am I to leave you when we get in?"

"The town dock will be fine."

"Town dock it is."

CHAPTER 20

AS SYLVIE FINISHED HER COFFEE, they rounded the breakwater and began the run up river. With the current, Sylvie noticed that *Miss Cookie's* speed increased dramatically.

"It won't be long." Bryan's voice broke into her thoughts. "Anything else you need?"

She shook her head, left the deckhouse, and sat in one of the lawn chairs. She squinted as she watched the sun climb in the sky. Soon it was directly behind them, a yellowish-orange ball that shimmered through the haze.

At the sound of another motor, Sylvie turned her head and watched as a lobsterman on his way out passed close by. Both boats began to rock as they hit each other's wake. The lobsterman turned his head and waved. She waved back.

It wouldn't be long before she would be back on dry land. Her thoughts drifted back over the previous twenty-four hours.

Richie tried to kill me. Why? It was supposed to be a simple job. I was along for the ride, nothing new, just sent to make sure that everything went as planned. What happened? Why did he try to kill me? The more she thought about it, the more convinced she was that he had only been following orders from above.

She could feel the heat from the newly risen sun on her face, and sweat began to bead on her upper lip. As hot as yesterday had been, this morning was even more uncomfortable. "Gross," she thought as a bead of sweat slid down her face. She wiped it with her hand. At least yesterday the air had been clear. This morning the sky was so heavy with humidity it actually felt dirty.

"Hey," Bryan's voice snapped her out of her thoughts. She got up and walked to the deckhouse door and looked in.

"I'm just gonna' come alongside and let you jump off, okay?"

"Sure. Thanks."

"You sure you'll be all right?"

She turned away without answering.

CHAPTER 21

SYLVIE STOOD ON THE DOCK in Newburyport and watched as *Miss Cookie* headed back toward the mouth of the river. She looked around warily. Other than a few early morning runners she was alone. She had no reason to be worried. After all, she was dead. But she wasn't, and she wanted to keep it that way.

Her stomach grumbled. As hot as it had been in the boat, now it was worse. Her arms glistened, sweat beaded on her forehead, and her clothes started to cling. Sweat stained the edges of her tank top around her neck and arms. She decided to slip her blue shirt on over the tank top, hoping that by covering the tears and stains, she might gain some degree of anonymity. The less attention she could draw to herself, the safer she would be.

That's when the smells of baking pastries and freshly roasting coffee hit. Had it only been about twenty-four hours since she'd gripped that convenience store coffee? How good it had tasted then. But now, these new smells were even more intoxicating. Looking around, she could see that Plum Island Coffee Roasters was but a short walk from where she stood. Located next to a large marina, across from a boat yard, now empty save for a few derelict boats, it was on the main walking thoroughfare along the waterfront, and clearly enjoyed a thriving business from both tourists and locals alike. Thank goodness the cash in her pocket had dried out along with her clothes.

Despite the early hour, the coffee shop was already busy. At first she remained cautious and simply watched as people disappeared inside. Sometimes they reemerged just a few moments later, taking quick sips of their coffees as they hurried away. She didn't care if they were locals, tourists, or boaters. What mattered most was that no one seemed interested in her.

74

Satisfied, she went in. As she waited in line, she realized that every conversation around her seemed to be about the weather.

When Sylvie finally had her dark roast and chocolate-filled croissant in hand, she went outside and chose a table that overlooked the marina. Fortunately, the wedge of shade from the table's umbrella made it possible for her to watch both the marina and the steady stream of people and cars that moved past.

During the course of her breakfast, the breeze continued to increase, as did the heat and humidity. She realized that even with the benefit of caffeine and chocolate, the longer she sat, the more she wanted to curl up and sleep. Sleep wasn't an option yet, but it certainly was time to leave.

The day before, she had parked several blocks away, and now she braced herself to hike back to the car in the unbearable heat. By the time she reached that spot, she was carrying her blue shirt and no longer cared how she looked. All she wanted to do was get into her car, turn the air conditioning on high, and drive away. Then she could figure out what she was going to do next.

CHAPTER 22

IN JACK'S APARTMENT, the phone rang once. Then it rang a second and third time before Jack became conscious enough to realize that it wasn't a dream. He glanced at the clock as he reached for the phone. He had been asleep for far too few hours.

"Hello."

What he heard jolted him awake.

"Who is it?" asked Max. She sounded as groggy as he had been.

"Dave," he lied. "Go back to sleep. I'll take it in the other room."

"*God*," he thought as he stumbled toward the living room, phone in hand. "*I'm lying about this already. What have I gotten myself into now?*"

He put the phone to his ear. "Okay, go ahead."

"Jack. I'm so sorry. I'm in Newburyport. I just borrowed a phone from the parking lot guy. My car is gone. Everything is gone. Can you help me?"

He paused for a moment as he let what he had just been told sink in.

"Jack? You still there?"

"Yes, yes, I'm here."

"Did you hear me? Can you come get me? I can meet you at the coffee place near the marina."

"Plum Island?"

"That's the one."

"Sure. Give me a couple of hours. I'll meet you there."

He didn't hear Max as she entered the room. He was too intent on the call.

"Who's that you are meeting?"

When he heard Max's voice, he jumped slightly and hit the *off* button on the phone.

"Damn," He thought. From Max's reaction, he was sure that the guilty expression on his face had sealed his fate.

"Who was it?" Max's tone demanded an answer.

"No one." He knew that was the wrong answer, but he couldn't help himself.

"Jack!"

He turned away, and as softly as he could he mumbled, "Sylvie."

"Did I just hear you say *Sylvie*?"

"Yes."

That was met with a withering silence.

Shit. He knew that things were about to go from bad to worse.

"Speak." She wasn't letting him off the hook.

"I'm sorry. What do you want me to say?"

"What do I want you to say? What I want you to tell me is the truth. You can do that, can't you?"

Jack told her the truth, from the smoke to the phone call. When he finished, she looked at him and said, "And you expect me to buy that?"

"You can check. Dave'll tell you. Call the Coast Guard. But right now, I have to help her."

"Fine. I'll go with you."

This was becoming a perfect storm of shit, and all he really wanted was to go back to sleep. Not an option, apparently.

CHAPTER 23

THE DAY WAS GETTING MORE and more uncomfortable by the minute. The heat and humidity had continued to build, and by mid-morning a hot wind was blowing but gave no relief. The sky, which only twenty-four hours before had been clear and blue, now seemed dirty and ominous.

As uncomfortable as the heat was outside, even without the air conditioning, the mood inside the cab of Jack's truck was decidedly chilly. Little had been said before they left Rye Harbor, and now they rode south in silence. It wasn't until they had crossed over the Merrimack River and headed into Newburyport that Max finally spoke.

"So where do we find this cadaver?"

"She told me she'd be hanging out by the Plum Island Coffee Roasters."

"Where's that?"

"Down behind that boat yard next to Michael's. I've heard of it, but I've never been there."

Sylvie had told him to turn at the sign for the Windward Yacht Yard and then right at the end of the drive. Jack parked his truck across from the coffee shop, but he left the engine running so the air conditioning could stay on.

"So where is she?"

"Don't know. Maybe inside—I'll go check."

"I'm coming with you."

Before turning off the engine, Jack took a quick look around. There was a sailboat, on stands, near a large building, and he could see several workmen. They were standing on ladders with power sanders, smoothing her topsides. As hot and miserable as they looked, a wave of melancholy swept over him. He missed *Irrepressible*. He missed all the hours of hard, tedious work that she had required before launching each spring.

"We going in?" asked Max.

"Uh, oh, yeah." He removed the key from the ignition and they walked over.

The door had a small bell, just like Ben's, which clingled as the door was opened. Several people looked up, curious about who had walked in, but just as quickly they looked away, curiosity satisfied.

Jack didn't see Sylvie. "We should look outside again," he said to Max. "But before we go, I'm gonna' get a coffee. Want one?"

Looking at the line she knew it was going take a while and as much as she wanted to get this whole thing over with, she wasn't going to begrudge Jack a badly needed coffee. She shook her head. "I'll wait for you outside."

About ten minutes later, with a small regular in his hand, Jack left the shop. He looked to the left of the building but saw no sign of either Max or Sylvie. Turning his head to the right, he still didn't see them, but he paused a moment to again watch the men working on the sailboat.

A gust of hot wind hit from the west, stirring up such a swirl of dust that he was forced to squint and shield his eyes. High, thin clouds were already forming. There was no doubt they would see a storm before the end of the day.

Jack surveyed the area again. No Sylvie, no Max. He decided to stay by the truck and wait for Max to return. Otherwise, they might end up chasing each other around for hours. Besides, by staying he could sit in the cab with the engine running in air-conditioned comfort and enjoy his coffee.

He was about halfway through the cup when the knock on the window startled him.

"Jack. Thank you so much," Sylvie said as she climbed into the cab.

He said nothing for a few moments. He could only stare. She was wearing the same ripped and torn clothes that she had been wearing when they fished her out of the water. Her skin glistened from the heat outside. Her tank top clung to her like a second skin, and her body's reaction to the cold air in the truck left little to the imagination. He had to force himself to return his eyes to her face.

"Jack. Are you all right?"

He realized he must have looked like a fool. "Yes. Yes, I'm fine. Did you see Max?"

As soon as Max's name rolled off his tongue, some of the sparkle in her eyes seemed to dim.

"No. No I didn't."

"She's looking for you."

"I thought you would've come alone."

"She insisted."

Just then he saw Max come around the corner of the coffee shop. He hit the horn.

Max looked up and waved. Then, as she got halfway to the truck, she suddenly froze in her tracks. Clearly she had just noticed that Jack wasn't alone.

CHAPTER 24

MAX SIGNALED FOR HIM TO GET OUT OF THE TRUCK.

"How long has she been here?"

"Just a few seconds. I was about to come looking for you."

The look she gave him made her feelings perfectly clear. Then she said, "She's not riding in the middle next to you."

Jack had no chance to respond as Max went to the driver's door, yanked it open, and climbed in. She immediately turned to Sylvie and said, "Push over." Then she placed herself firmly in the middle, forcing Sylvie over against the passenger door. No other words were needed for this message: "He's mine. Back off."

Then she turned back to the driver's side. "Jack. You coming or not?"

As Jack took his seat behind the wheel, Sylvie said, "Jack. Thank you, but this was a bad idea. I'm sorry," and began to open her door.

"No. Stop. You said your car had been stolen, right?" said Jack.

She stopped and looked at him. Max whipped her head around and glared at Jack.

Sylvie nodded.

"Close the door. Sylvie, where can we take you?" asked Jack.

Both women remained silent. Finally Sylvie said, "I have a place I use sometimes in Gloucester. If you can leave me off there, I'll be gone."

"Gloucester it is."

He started the truck, shifted into gear, and glanced over at his two passengers as the truck began to roll forward.

"Jack!" Max shouted.

He slammed on the brakes. Had she not shouted, he probably would have hit the car that was passing by. It was a large, late model black BMW, and in spite of all the dust in the air, it shone.

81

"Thanks. I don't think he would have appreciated a dent in that baby."

"Pay attention to where you're going," said Max.

Sylvie kept watching the car as it drove out of sight.

"You all right?" asked Jack.

In a distant voice, she said softly, "Yes. Yes, we should get going." But the whole time she was speaking, she continued to watch the path of the BMW.

* * *

About a dozen miles later, Jack asked, "Is anyone hungry? Coffee can only take me so far, and I've reached my limit."

Neither woman said anything, so he made the call. "Lunch is on me. The Agawam is just ahead."

The Agawam Diner, practically a fixture on Route 1, was one of Jack's favorite lunch spots. It was always busy, with a healthy mix of locals and tourists. During those rare times that Jack had the chance to stop for a meal, he would.

Between the body language and the silence in the cab of the truck, Jack knew his passengers wanted him to believe that they couldn't care less. However, he was hungry, and he knew they were as well, even though hell would be freezing over before either would break down and admit it.

Once they were seated, Max ordered a garden salad with chicken. Sylvie asked for a cup of chowder and a garden salad, while Jack had the chicken pie. A round of large iced teas washed down their lunches, which were eaten mostly in silence.

As they left the diner, Jack said, "You realize we're not too far from Willowdale where we ran that trail marathon—The Rockdog Run."

As soon as those words left his mouth, he knew he had made a mistake. That was where he had first met Sylvie. They had been running together, and when she had tripped and twisted her ankle, he had helped her. If only it had been that simple. There were many other fit and talented women running that day. Many wore similar, equally sexy, skintight black running clothes. But she was different. It was her strength and the freedom with which she ran that had first caught his attention. She had encouraged him through that first icy stream crossing and then they ran together until she tripped and fell. She had looked so small and helpless lying beside the trail, but the look in her eyes as he helped her up, and the way that she felt as he held her were forever locked in his brain.

"I remember," said Sylvie. He looked at her, not sure whether something in her voice indicated that she shared the same memories in the same way as he did.

All Max said was, "And you remember how that turned out."

He did. Neither had finished the race since later that day, it had been his turn to trip and fall, landing on a dead body.

Silence returned to the cab. There was a steady stream of traffic, so their progress was slow. Near the turn for Crane Beach, slow became "stop-and-go" as many of the locals and tourists sought relief from the heat.

Jack said, "You know, by the time some of these people make it to the beach, I'll bet that front will arrive. It feels like it's going to be nasty."

"You're probably right," said Sylvie, leaning forward to look up through the windshield.

Once past the beach, they began to make progress again. Sylvie gave directions, and soon they were winding their way through the edges of Gloucester. At several points, Jack could see the open ocean and wished that he still had *Irrepressible.* Sylvie pointed out the Annisquam Yacht Club, adding that they had guest moorings available.

The house that Sylvie directed them to was up a small side street. A row of tall arborvitae planted on the edge of the road hid the small yard and long, narrow house from view. On the right side of the lot, a drive with barely room enough for Jack's truck provided the only access to the house from the road. He pulled in.

The heat and humidity were now so oppressive that as soon as Jack shut off the engine, killing the air conditioning, they could feel the temperature begin to rise in the truck.

"Thanks, Jack," said Sylvie. "But I can't get out."

The passenger door was so close to a fence between the properties that she couldn't open it. They would all have to get out on the driver's side.

He began to sweat the moment he stepped out of the truck. The combination of his fatigue, the heat, and the dull glare of the sun made his eyeballs ache, even with sunglasses on.

Max slid out next. She stepped away from the truck and stood in the front yard looking at the withered flowerbeds on either side of the door.

"I'm not much of a gardener," said Sylvie.

Max shrugged. "So I see."

"You guys want to come in? Cold drink? It's the least I can do considering . . ." Whatever else she said was lost as she pushed the door open.

"I'm good," said Max too late. "We should get going."

* * *

Jack heard Max sigh heavily as she followed him into the house. The house was air-conditioned, and the relief was immediate and welcome. Max was surprised. She wasn't sure what she expected, but it definitely wasn't what she saw. The house was one room wide and on one side of the door was a fireplace and on the other, stairs led up, to what she assumed would be bedrooms. Straight ahead through the living room she could see the kitchen. That was it except for a small bathroom set in between.

"I'm going up to get changed," said Sylvie, "Water's in the fridge."

"Can you get me a water?" Max said to Jack while she continued to look around.

He handed her one. "She's not so bad, you know."

Max twisted the cap off the bottle of water and took a sip.

"She was almost killed yesterday."

"So you said."

"Max, you gotta' cut her some slack."

"We'll see."

Max was having a hard time remaining mad at Sylvie. She had obviously been through a lot in the last day or so, and yet hadn't played the victim card.

Footsteps coming down the stairs announced Sylvie's return. There was a strange look on her face. "Everything okay?" asked Jack.

"No. Someone's been in here."

She was now wearing navy blue shorts similar to her tan ones and a white polo shirt, the collar flipped up She had brushed her hair, and while it was an improvement, it was obvious that it needed a good washing.

"What do you mean 'someone's been in here'?" said Jack.

"Things have been moved around in my room. I didn't notice anything missing."

"You're sure?"

"Yes." Sylvie brushed past Jack and got a bottle of water from her fridge. "Listen, you two need to leave."

That was obviously fine with Max, who quickly moved toward the door. Jack remained motionless, looking at Sylvie.

"I'm serious, Jack. You need to leave."

Max stopped with her hand on the door knob. She shot Jack a look that said, "NOW!"

He moved toward the spot where Max was waiting but then turned back toward Sylvie. "What about your car?"

"Doesn't matter. I'll get another and I still have my motorcycle."

"Okay, but remember that if you ever need help, you can count on us." Just for good measure, he added a little extra emphasis on *us*.

A blast of warm air rushed into the room as Max opened the door and stepped out. When Sylvie touched Jack's arm, he turned and she pulled him close. Wrapping her arms around him, she gave him a hug. "Thank you," she whispered before letting go.

Then, pulling away, she said, "Go. Get out of here. Take care of Max. Tell her I'm sorry and that she has nothing to worry about." She gave him a slight push toward the door.

He wanted to say something, but he couldn't.

"Jack, toss me the keys. It's too hot." Max's voice snapped him back. He tossed them to her. Just before Sylvie shut the door he repeated, "Remember, we're here for you."

CHAPTER 25

JACK AND MAX WERE ABOUT HALFWAY HOME on a fairly empty stretch of Route 1 before either said a word. Only the sudden arrival of the storm caused them to break their silence.

The sky had seriously darkened. The ugly, mustard-gray-green clouds now had black edges. The first giant raindrops splatted against the windshield, while others bounced off the hood of the truck and still others tap-tapped on the top of the cab, each one leaving a distinct crater in the dust covering the truck. Steam began to rise from the road's surface as the raindrops vaporized upon hitting the hot pavement. An instant later, a loud clap of thunder exploded nearby, like a starter's pistol, and the heavens opened up. Lightning flashed, thunder crashed, and the wind shook the truck.

Max jumped.

"Holy shit!" said Jack.

Max slid across the seat until she pressed against his side.

In an instant it was nearly impossible to see out the windshield, even with the wipers running as fast as possible. He pulled off onto the shoulder of the road.

As wild and intense as the storm outside was, the cab felt quiet and intimate. They spoke in voices just louder than whispers.

"I'm sorry, Jack," Max said, as she pressed closer to him.

He looked at her.

"I can't help it. She has something for you, and I won't let her have you."

"Max, she doesn't."

"She does. You just won't admit it."

"Okay, what if she does. She doesn't hold a candle to you."

"I know." It took a moment before he saw the edges of her mouth begin to twitch. Then she giggled.

"You are such a brat."

"Am not. You . . ." Her words were cut off by his kiss. She responded in kind. The intensity of their kisses was matched only by the intensity of the storm.

The front moved by in less than five minutes, although it felt much longer. It left behind a steady rain that fell from still-dark rain clouds onto a road now littered with leaves and small branches.

As the storm subsided, Max pulled away from Jack and said, "I just want you to know that I do trust you. She's the one I don't trust. How much do you actually know about her?"

Jack thought a moment. "You know, I really don't know all that much about her. One thing I'm sure of—she's tough and a survivor."

"So, what do you think she's up to? I mean, she said someone tried to kill her. But she survived, sank the boat, and then decided to swim twenty miles back. Really? Why get rid of your ride back? Not too bright if you ask me."

"When you put it that way . . . ." He paused.

"Did you notice how un-lived in her house was?"

Jack looked at her, she continued, "I mean I didn't see anything personal, did you? A hotel room would look more lived in. I bet she's a contract killer."

"Max. Stop. Now you're being silly. What makes you think that, except that you've watched too many bad cop movies?"

"Jack! Think about it. She's been nothing but trouble from the day you met."

CHAPTER 26

WHEN BRYAN LEFT SYLVIE at the town dock, he headed right back to Hampton. The wind continued to pick up and, glancing at the sky, he knew that he wanted to be back in the harbor before the weather hit.

The tide was turning, so again he had an easy time navigating the Merrimack. This time, instead of the tide pushing him in, the wind pushed him out.

As he cleared the mouth and began the course for home, he pulled out a bottle of rum that he kept on board for medicinal purposes and took a healthy drink. He began to relax. His thoughts returned to the previous night and he smiled. After all, he did make a pretty penny on the shark.

Dave was a good guy, solid. He enjoyed fishing with him. Jack turned out okay, but as he wondered what the deal was with Sylvie, he began talking to himself.

Me and him pull her out, mostly dead, and she reacts like that? I mean, I just saved her ass, but she takes one look at me, freaks, and grabs on to Jack. What was with that? He had no answer now, but he'd get one.

Back in Hampton, he secured *Miss Cookie* to her mooring and went below for some much needed sleep. Sylvie had left the clothes he had loaned her folded neatly on the lower berth. He smiled. Even in that getup she was still one of the hottest women he had ever known. He picked them up, and as he did, he held them to his face and imagined that he could still smell her lingering scent. With a rum-induced slur he said, "Oh, Sylvie. What have you got yourself into?" Then he tossed them aside, fell into the berth, and was asleep almost before his eyes closed.

The front passed through. *Miss Cookie* swung back and forth on her mooring as the wind tried to rip her free. She shook with each clap of thunder, and waves of rain lashed at her. Through it all, Bryan slept. Memories came and went, each a chapter of his dream. And like all dreams, they were vivid, and made perfect sense, until you woke up.

Sylvie. He'd never forget that day, sitting at the bar in the Wok, self-medicating after what had been a most taxing day. The guys he had taken fishing had been complete idiots of the worst kind. They didn't listen to his instructions, knew everything, drank too much, and in a word were—at best—complete assholes. As he sat there drinking a large Mai Tai, he began reconsidering his life. When he was well into his second large Mai Tai, she came in. For a noticeable moment the bar quieted as all heads turned and watched as she sat at the end of the bar under the television. After that initial checkout, she was mostly ignored. She also ordered a large Mai Tai and he alternately watched her and the television. She was more interesting.

When the chair next to her opened up, he left his vantage point and moved next to her. She was on her second and he was on his third. Hello turned to small conversation to deeper topics. Then she invited him to join her for dinner, and eventually they ended up back on Miss Cookie. *Morning came with no awkwardness, no embarrassment—just coffee and the short row ashore. It wasn't that taking a woman back to* Miss Cookie *hadn't ever happened before. It was just that this time, there was something different.*

Every now and then, they would run into each other. She said that some time she wanted to go out on his boat, fishing. She was always interested in everything and seemed especially curious about the Fingers area of Jeffreys, that same area where Dave had hooked that rope.

The rain had eased to a drizzle when Bryan finally woke. The sun was about to set, its rays shining below the low clouds at the back edge of the storm. To the east, the sky was dark, and only the tips of white-caps, lit by the setting sun, made it possible to separate water from sky. Tomorrow would be a good day.

His stomach growled. It had been a long time since he had last eaten, and now, after some sleep, he was ready for food. While he bailed out his dinghy, bits and pieces of his dreams flashed through his head, alternating with what had happened in the last day and a half. He was still trying to make sense of it all as he rowed in and walked to the Wok.

The storm had quieted the crowd, and it was near closing time when he sat down at the bar. "Hey, Mel," he said to the bartender as she placed a cocktail napkin on the bar in front of him.

"Bryan. You out in that storm today?"

"Nah. Slept all day. Overnight trip yesterday. Didn't get back here until late morning."

She nodded. "What would you like?"

Of course, she already knew. He always ordered a large Mai Tai, but she asked anyway.

"I think I'll have a large Mai Tai."

She smiled. As she turned to make his drink, she pushed a dinner menu in his direction and asked, "Something to eat?"

"Thanks."

When she set the drink in front of him, he took a sip, looked at her, and said, "That's good. Yes. How 'bout the blackened scallops."

Mel smiled again. "I knew it! Two for two. I'll put that right in."

As Bryan sipped his Mai Tai and waited for his scallops, his thoughts returned again to the trip just completed.

CHAPTER 27

THE STORM THAT HAD PASSED took with it the oppressive humidity of the previous days, leaving behind a perfect late summer's day. Max still wanted to talk about Sylvie and their trip to Gloucester; Jack didn't. Fortunately for him it was a Sunday, and he knew that the weekly reggae party at Ben's would keep Max and her team of bartenders so busy, he'd be spared those conversations. Courtney, the owner of Ben's, had also asked Jack to help out, and from the moment the doors opened, Ben's was even busier than usual. By the time the day was over, all that either one of them wanted was sleep.

Jack let Max sleep in on Monday morning since she wasn't scheduled to work until the evening. He decided to go down to Paula's for some breakfast.

"Mornin', Jack," said Beverly as she poured his coffee. "'Nother beautiful day in paradise."

"Mornin', Beverly. It is."

He glanced around before opening the newspaper that he had grabbed on the way in. Paula's was mostly filled with summer people who got to sleep in late. Most of the locals would have been in earlier, and because he didn't really feel like talking, that was fine with him. Then he saw it, page three, near the bottom in a sidebar of local news stories: COAST GUARD LOOKING FOR INFORMATION ABOUT MISSING BOAT.

"Hey, Jack." It was his friend Tom Scott, the town's Chief of Police.

"Tom. When did you get here?"

"Been here a while. You must have had a rough day yesterday. You looked right at me when you came in. Never saw me."

"It was a long weekend. Started on Friday with a fishing trip with Dave. All day turned into all night, too. Got in early on Saturday, spent most of the day sleeping, then yesterday at Ben's."

"I drove by a few times. Looked pretty busy"

"It was beyond busy. Max is exhausted, so I left her sleeping."

Tom nodded his head in understanding. "So how was the fishing trip?"

Before he could answer, Beverly returned, topped up their coffees, and took Jack's order before walking away.

Jack looked at Tom. "You're not eating?"

"I had just finished when you arrived. You were saying?"

"Oh yeah, the trip. Dave arranged it. We went out to Jeffreys with his friend Bryan."

"Bryan? What's his boat's name?"

"*Miss Cookie.* Why?"

Tom didn't answer right away. "No reason. Just curious."

Jack looked at him, then continued. "It was to be a day trip and we expected to be back before dark. Only, as we were about to head back I saw smoke on the horizon, which then abruptly disappeared. Long story short, we went to check it out, found wreckage in the water, called the Coast Guard, and had to stay there until they arrived."

"A boat sank?"

Jack nodded.

"Survivors?"

"None that we found. I just saw this in the paper." He folded the paper open and pointed to the article, which noted that the Coast Guard was looking for any information on overdue boats.

Tom quickly scanned the article. "Does this Bryan keep his boat in Hampton Harbor?"

"Yeah. Why? What aren't you telling me."

"Nothing I'm sure you don't already know. He's a bit of a sketchy character. Knows his stuff. But I've seen his name come up before with regards to some incidents. Nothing serious—no arrests that I know of. Mostly just seems to be around when something happens."

Jack suspected as much. "I'll have to talk to Dave, see what he knows. All I can say is we had a really good time out fishing."

"Well, sounds good. Nice to see you, Jack. Gotta' go."

As Tom walked out the door, Beverly brought Jack his French toast, topped up his coffee, and picked up the money that Tom had left on the counter. "Did I hear you talking about a missing boat?"

"Yeah. On Friday it seems like one sank out on Jeffreys, just as Dave and I were about to head home from a fishing trip. We called it in to the Coast Guard, and now they're trying to find out what boat it was."

"Oh, that makes sense. I think some of the guys from down at the harbor were talking about something like that, but I only heard bits and pieces. It was so busy in here just then. Maybe it was that."

Jack made a mental note to stop by the harbor on the way home.

CHAPTER 28

BY THE TIME JACK LEFT PAULA'S, the sides of the road were filling up fast with beachgoers. It looked like the trend in nice weather was going to continue for a while. While not officially retired, he helped out at Ben's often enough that it felt like a job, but without the formality or responsibilities of an actual job. Today there was nothing pressing to do so he decided to see if Dave was up for a late afternoon run followed by a few beers while Max was at Ben's working.

His mental note kicked in on the way home and he pulled in at Rye Harbor. He parked by the commercial pier, hoping to catch Art as he returned from his morning of lobstering. The *Sea Witch* wasn't back yet, so he walked over to the public docks.

One of the whale watch boats was at the dock, and a line of cars, each filled with excited children and parents trying to remain calm, were waiting for their turn to pay the fee and park. Adding to the mix were a few late-arriving boaters, whose intention no doubt was to spend a leisurely day on the water—if they could ever get there.

Jack knew that most of the more serious and experienced boaters arrived really early, sunrise early. These later arrivals tended to be less sure of themselves, and the stress and dread of backing a trailer down the ramp and launching their boat without looking foolish could be seen on their faces. Like the whale watchers, most of them had a full complement of excited kids, which would make the ordeal that much more difficult.

"Jack. What're you doing here?"

Ever since *Irrepressible* sank, he didn't spend much time over at the harbor. There was no reason to. He turned. Facing him was Eleanor, the short, vibrant woman who worked for the Port Authority and, with the Harbor Master, reigned over all the chaos.

"What do you mean, what am I doing here? I came to see you."

"You are so full of it. Now really. What brings you by? I miss you, you know."

"I miss you too, Ellie."

They were standing by the snack shack. "Woah, slow down!" Jack held out his hand to slow down a nine- or ten-year-old boy with an overstuffed backpack who was being chased by his older brother.

"Sorry," said the kid. He began walking away, keeping a wary eye on his big brother.

"How do you put up with this?" asked Jack.

"Oh, it's not all that bad, and besides, they'll get out there, the boat'll be rockin', and he'll pay for that breakfast burrito he just ate."

"There's a mean streak in you, Ellie."

"Nah, I just love them all. So, you didn't answer my question."

"I did. But I came down for another reason. You hear anything about a missing boat?"

"We got a call from the Coast Guard this morning. Apparently there was a sinking out by Jeffreys Friday night, and they're trying to identify who it was."

"I know. Dave and I were out on a day trip with his friend Bryan and we're the ones who called it in."

She looked directly up at him, about to say something.

"We didn't find anyone or anything other than some wreckage. Looked like it burned and sank."

"You were out with Bryan? As in, *Miss Cookie*?"

"Yeah. He's a friend of Dave's."

"I'd stay away from him if I were you."

Now it was Jack's turn to look surprised. "Why's that?"

"Oh, I don't know. I just hear stories. Stories, mind you, but he has a reputation for skirting around things and . . . well, let's just say that trouble seems to follow him, but he somehow stays clean."

This news wasn't anything that he hadn't figured out for himself after spending a very long day on the water with Bryan. "I'll keep that in mind. So, no idea on the lost boat?"

"Nah, lots of talk. You know those brothers who fish outta' here, Richie and Lewis? Some folks said it might be Richie. On the one hand, it wouldn't surprise me. Lewis isn't so bad, but Richie has always been the bad seed in that family. I've even heard rumors that he's had some dealings with Bryan. But Richie disappears for days on end all the time, so really? I don't think it's him. We'll see."

"Richie?" Jack thought. From his own dealings with the guy, he knew that Ellie's description was spot on. Over the years, Richie had had run-ins with just about all the fishermen in the harbor. One of those altercations had escalated from accusations to actions and retaliations. Guns being drawn, and Richie had even ended up in jail for a while.

"Bad seed is an understatement," Jack thought. "But why would Sylvie ever go out with him, and why would he try to kill her?"

While Jack tried to digest these questions, a boat honked its horn. The *Sea Witch* had returned. One of those just-launched boats was drifting into the channel with the owner frantically trying to restart the engine while his panicked wife divided her attention between watching him floating out to sea, three kids clambering over the rocks near the launch ramp, and glares from the next boater in line waiting for her to pull the trailer off the ramp.

"Gotta' go!" Ellie shouted as she scampered off to help the woman. All the while the line of cars waiting to pay and park continued to grow.

Jack smiled as he watched Art skillfully maneuvered *Sea Witch* alongside the wayward boat and return it and the embarrassed skipper to the dock.

CHAPTER 29

"MORNIN' ART," Jack said later as he took a line from him. "How's fishin'?"

"Not bad. Price could be better, but what's new."

"You hear anything 'bout the boat that sank out by Jeffreys Friday night?"

"I heard about it, but that's all. You know what happened?"

"Sorta'." Jack tied the line to a cleat. "I was out with my buddy Dave, fishing. We saw some smoke so we went to investigate. Found some wreckage. Nothing to say what boat, and no survivors."

He watched Art carefully. He didn't like lying, but he had promised Sylvie. "We called the Coast Guard and had to wait until they arrived. Made for a really long day."

"Any ideas who it was?"

"No, but Ellie told me that rumors say it was Richie."

Art's voice hardened. "That little prick. If it was, it'd serve him right."

"Well, that's the rumor. Was he involved in anything specific that you know of?"

"Nothin' comes to mind, but if I hear anything, I'll let you know."

"Thanks."

"So, who'd you guys go out with?"

"A guy Dave knows down in Hampton. Bryan. Has the *Miss Cookie*."

Art's eyes opened wide. "Bryan? You're kidding! He went to somebody's aid?"

"We had to kind of push him, but yes."

Art was obviously stunned. "He's another sketchy one. I don't think he'd lift a finger to help his own mother. I'm surprised."

"That's the feeling I'm getting from everyone. All I know is that we had a good day fishing, and we did go to see what was up."

Art lowered his voice. "If you ever go out with him again, just be careful."

* * *

"Mrowh." Cat greeted Jack as he climbed out of his truck.

"Hey, Cat. Max up?"

"Mrowh." She rubbed against his leg, looked up, and demanded a head scratch. "Mrowh."

Once Cat was satisfied that she still had total control over her human, she sauntered off. No doubt, she had far more important things to do than sit around all day having Jack doing her bidding.

"Hey, Max," he called out as he went upstairs. As he cleared the top stair, he called out again.

"In the bedroom," Max called back.

As he walked toward her voice, a grin began to form on his face and an idea began to form in his brains. She was folding some towels with her back to the door. Her curly red hair still looked damp, so Jack knew she had only recently showered. "Too bad I spent so much time at the harbor," he thought. She was barefoot, wearing a pair of fitted tan shorts that hit just below the tops of her thighs. She had on one of her white, thin-strapped tops that he knew required no bra underneath.

Now grinning, and not really thinking, he walked up behind her and wrapped his arms around her, pulling her close. She dropped the towel she was folding and held his arms. Without turning, she leaned back, and he could feel her sag against him. He nuzzled her neck. She squirmed away and turned to face him, and they kissed.

* * *

"I'll help you refold everything," he said later, still grinning.

"You better. I'm hungry."

"Me too. That was a great way to work up an appetite."

CHAPTER 30

"HOW FAR TODAY?" Jack asked Dave as they headed out for their run.

"I was thinking eight."

"Sounds good to me. Which way?"

"I thought we'd just go north along the boulevard, turn around the mansions, and come back. Should be somewhere around eight, and it'll be a bit cooler by the water."

The first two miles along Hampton Beach were slow since they had to deal with the early evening evacuation of beachgoers, so conversation was limited. However, by the time they had reached the North Beach seawall and could run on the wide sidewalk next to each other, they were able to talk.

Jack was the first to speak. "Have you heard anything about that boat?"

"Not really, but I was pretty busy at work today. You hear anything?"

"I stopped down at the harbor and talked with Ellie. She thought it might've been Richie."

"Richie?"

"You know, the brothers. Richie and Lewis, fish out of Rye. Lewis is okay, quiet, minds his own business, but Richie is always into something."

"Oh, him. Yeah, now I know who you mean. Trouble with the guns and all that. Not too many folks would be missing *that* guy."

"But if it does turn out to be him, then what was Sylvie doing with him, and what did he do to make her kill him?"

"No idea. She'd be the one to ask!"

Further conversation became limited as they ran along Route 1-A. They had to wait for the left turn that would bring them behind the mansions before they could run side by side again.

"Can you imagine being this rich?" said Dave.

"No."

"But wouldn't it be fun to find out!"

"Maybe . . . I suppose. But you know, Max sees some of them down at Ben's and she tells me stories."

"What kind of stories?"

"Oh, the usual. Some are nice and others are complete dickheads. They have a subtle way of letting you know just how rich and important they are— at least in their eyes. Doesn't Patti ever talk to you about Ben's?"

"I guess. She gets going sometimes. I don't pay much attention." Then Dave chuckled. "I can just see Max, working hard to be nice when someone is being that kind of a jerk."

Jack grinned in agreement and then changed the subject. "Ya' know, this morning down at the harbor, whenever I said we had gone out fishing with Bryan, everyone said the same thing: *Be careful. Don't trust him.* It was strange."

"Well, like I said, I only know him from fishing, and I haven't had any problems."

"Ellie seemed to think that Bryan and Richie may have had some dealings together."

"Not that I know of. I mean, I only know Bryan to fish with. I know he's not adverse to bending the rules, especially if there is a buck to be made, but with Richie, I don't know."

"Did you notice Sylvie's reaction to Bryan? I got the sense that seeing him both startled and spooked her."

"Ya' know, I did too. But I was more interested in the way she glommed onto you. You not telling me something?"

"C'mon man. She did not glom onto me."

"Bullshit. What's the story?"

"There is no story. We're just casual friends who met at a race."

"You are so full of shit. What about in Rye? You're going to try to tell me that she isn't hot for you? She was practically stalking you."

"Where'd you get that from?"

"Where do you think? Patti told me, 'cause Max told her all about it."

"So for that you listen to her? Asshole."

"What can I say?"

Jack picked up the pace a bit, making conversation slightly more difficult. "They're wrong and that's all I'm gonna' say about that."

"Touchy, touchy," teased Dave.

Jack stepped up the pace again. The sooner this conversation ended, the better off he'd feel.

* * *

"Good run."

"Yeah, I needed that," said Jack as he took a long sip on his beer.

"Cheers." Dave wasn't ready to give up on Sylvie just yet, "So you're not going to tell me about Sylvie, are you?"

"What's to tell?"

"C'mon, you know what I mean."

"You still harping on that stuff on the boat?"

"You know I am. It wasn't all her. I saw how you looked at her."

"Give me a break. We pull this hot chick out of the water. Barely conscious, wearing that white, torn tank, and I'm supposed to look at her how? I saw you looking, too."

"That's different."

"I don't think so. End of discussion."

CHAPTER 31

"HEY, JACK, PHONE'S FOR YOU. Coast Guard."

Nearly a week had passed since the fishing trip.

"Yes, this is Jack Beale."

* * *

"What was that all about?" asked Max when he hung up.

"Some Coast Guard investigator with a few more questions. Sounds like they've decided that the boat did belong to Richie. Unless something changes, they're presuming that the boat caught fire, he died in the fire, and then he went down with the boat. So I guess that's the end of it."

"Is it?"

"I hope so."

"But what about Sylvie?"

"What about Sylvie? Richie was an asshole. Nuthin' but trouble. Probably got what he deserved."

"I meant, she's still around. She told you *she* killed Richie."

Jack looked at her, thinking about what to say next. "So? She said it was self-defense and I believe her. And if we're lucky, she's gone, and that's the end of it."

"But what if she's not?"

"Then we'll just have to deal with it. In the meantime, we say that all we know is what everyone else knows. Richie's boat burned and sank. A tragic accident."

He could tell that Max wasn't comfortable with that.

"Come here." As he held out his arms to give her a reassuring hug, he really hoped that Sylvie would remain dead.

* * *

"Hello, Bryan."

Bryan spun around from his stool at the Starboard Galley in New-buryport. He had just finished a meeting with the North Shore Charter Captains, and now, standing behind him, was the last person he would have expected to see.

"Sylvie. What are you doing here?"

"Just stopped by for a drink and some food, saw you, and thought I'd come over and say 'Hi'."

He didn't believe her, and he wasn't sure how to respond. She was complicated—no way could he trust her—but damn, she looked good. She was wearing tight, low-cut jeans and a female version of the classic wife-beater, which left nothing to the imagination. He noticed that he wasn't the only one staring.

"So, 'Hi'."

"What're you doing here?" The way she asked the question put him on guard, not because it was accusatory, but because he realized he couldn't resist her.

"What's it to you?"

She looked into his eyes and his voice softened. "I was here for a monthly meeting of charter captains. Good excuse to get out of Hampton. Also, I have a charter booked for the morning that's leaving from here."

Sylvie made no attempt to hide her surprise. "You what?"

"I can't belong to a group that has meetings? You know, there's a lot more to me than you give me credit for. Now your turn. What're you doing here?"

"I was hungry,"

He didn't completely buy that answer, but he couldn't resist the possibilities that her being there created. "Join me?"

She smiled and slid into the empty chair beside him.

Before either could say anything else, the bartender came over. Sylvie ordered a glass of red wine while Bryan ordered another Coors Light. Both were promptly served.

"Menus?"

Bryan nodded, took a menu, and then stated clearly, "We're going to need a few minutes."

Once the bartender was out of earshot, he turned to Sylvie again. "You seemed to have made it perfectly clear that you were dead. The dead aren't supposed to rise, and they don't need food."

"Okay. Think of me as the mostly dead. I need your help."

"I can't think of any reason why you'd need my help."

"It's not so much that I need your help, it's more that I think you know where something that I want is."

"What the hell are you talking about?"

"Don't play stupid with me. I know you know where it is."

"Sylvie, you must be delusional. I have no idea what you are talking about."

"Cut the crap, Bryan."

"Are you ready to order?" The bartender had returned.

They were, and they did, along with another round of drinks. They sat in silence for a few minutes, but once the second round of drinks was served, Bryan turned toward her again. "Where were we? Oh. I remember. You were asking me for help finding something."

"I saw your notes."

"What are you talking about?" Maybe she was bluffing. It was up to him to find out.

"Look Bryan. When we were on your boat, I saw the coordinates you had scribbled down on a scrap of paper. I know you found something out at Jeffreys when you were out with Dave and Jack, and I know that you must have written down exactly where you were located at the time. Very smart move. Don't even waste another breath trying to deny it. I saw the grappling hook. So, are you gonna' help me or not?"

Before he could answer, the bartender returned with their dinners in hand. "Okay, here we go. One grilled chicken Caesar salad and one grilled scallops. Can I get you both anything else?"

"No!" they both said so sharply that the waitress looked surprised. Bryan hastily added, "I mean, no thank you. I'm sure we're all set for now."

Then he turned to Sylvie. "We need to stop calling attention to ourselves, Miss I'm Dead. Let's suppose that what you're saying has a grain of truth in it. What's in it for me?"

She smiled and said, "Oh, Bryan. I think you know that answer. I'll let you live."

CHAPTER 32

"I'M OUTTA' HERE."

Sylvie eyed him. He slid off his barstool and headed slowly for the door. She watched him for a moment before following, only catching up to him outside on the sidewalk. "Hey, Bryan, where're you going?"

"To my boat. Wanna' come? We got a few hours before the sun's up." He never turned back; he just kept walking down the street.

"Maybe. Where is it? I have my motorcycle."

"In the marina by the coffee shop. See you there." He waved but again never slowed or looked back.

Sylvie knew there was no hurry. It would take him a while to get there on foot, and she needed a few minutes to think. She walked out back to where she had parked behind the Starboard Galley. They shared a parking lot with a different marina from the one Bryan was going to. She walked past her bike and over to the locked gate.

Why do they even bother? All they're keeping out are the honest people. With her background there were few locks that could keep her out. Pulling the gate shut behind, she decided to walk down onto the floats, working her way further and further out over the river. Nearing the outermost floats, the subtle shimmying and shaking underfoot became more pronounced, as boats gently tugged on their lines in response to the mighty Merrimack's efforts to coax them free.

The hinges holding the floats together squeaked and clanked while the river gurgled. A light breeze began to blow, and even though it was still warm, goose bumps covered her arms. A loose halyard, which slapped against its mast with a distinctive rhythm of alternately being fast then slow, added to her chill. She rubbed her arms and looked out over the water. Lights from the shore reflected off the river's surface, and if she listened carefully she could hear the hum of car tires as they passed over the Route 1 bridge up river. She felt alone and yet was comforted by that aloneness.

"Richie. That little prick," she mumbled under her breath. "Hopefully they think he was just collateral damage. Assuming I was the target, they'll think it was a success. He's gone and his boat is gone so they should be assuming the same for me, and that will be a big problem for them."

Her only problem now was that Bryan knew she wasn't dead, as did Jack, his girlfriend, Max, his friend Dave, and probably Dave's girlfriend. They would all be marked if it became known that she wasn't dead.

She shivered. Then, thinking of Bryan, she smiled and felt a rush of warmth wash over her. Bryan was waiting and with a little luck, she'd get what she needed.

CHAPTER 33

BACK ON HER BIKE, Sylvie discovered that the night was perfect for riding. It didn't take long for her to get to the marina. She found Bryan asleep in a plastic chair by the coffee shop where all her recent problems seemed to have begun.

"Hey, Bryan. Get up," she whispered in his ear, giving it the slightest touch with her tongue.

He jumped. "Hunh? Oh, hey, Syl. I was beginning to think you stood me up."

"Not a chance. Didn't you invite me for a nightcap out on your boat?"

He smiled. "C'mon."

As Bryan struggled with the combination lock on the gate to the slips, she brushed up against him. "Here, let me," she whispered.

Stepping aside he said, "Be my guest."

She could tell he wasn't watching her work the lock. Instead, he seemed to be focused on the way her body flexed and moved in those tight jeans and that tight white T.

Gate open, she walked through. Then she turned toward him. "You coming?"

"Sorry." He passed through and moved to her side, put his arm around her, and pulled her close.

Miss Cookie was tied, stern to, on the inboard side of the last float that ran parallel to the river. He climbed aboard and offered his hand to her. She stepped over and as she lifted her second leg over the rail, the river jostled *Miss Cookie* and she fell into him. He caught her, she wrapped her arms around him, and for a moment neither moved.

"Wait," she finally said, pulling away from him. "Let me get these boots off." She sat in one of his plastic lawn chairs.

"I'll be below."

A moment later a faint, flickering, yellow glow filled the forward cabin, spilling out into the deckhouse and his silhouette filled the companionway. "You coming down?"

Sylvie left her boots by the chair. The deck was cold on her feet and she shivered. The hairs on her arms stood up and she could feel her nipples begin to harden. She stretched, then rubbed her arms.

"Coming," she said as she stepped into the deckhouse. Immediately that chill was replaced by a completely different sensation. A warmth began to build and radiate out from somewhere deep inside of her. She could feel her cheeks flush and a sense of urgency overcame her.

She could feel Bryan watching as she stopped halfway through the deckhouse, lifted the white tank top, and pulled it over her head, dropping it on the floor. Then she heard him suck in his breath.

"Your turn," she whispered.

He seemed to become all thumbs as he fumbled to pull his shirt off and unbuckle his pants, all the while keeping his eyes locked on her.

Although Bryan nearly fell over trying to get out of his pants, her jeans slid off her body as effortlessly as a raindrop might run down a pane of glass. Now wearing only the smallest of black lacy panties, she stepped toward the companionway while Bryan retreated into the cabin. As she stepped down into the cabin, her body was bathed in that soft yellow glow of the single candle that Bryan had lit. The dancing shadows created by that one small flame, made her soft curves come alive and become that much more alluring and mysterious. Time seemed to stand still. She held his gaze, moved toward him, and slipped out of her panties.

Moving even closer, she took his face in her hands and gave him a kiss. Gently, she moved him backward until they had nowhere to go but the berth. She eased him back. Then slowly, she straddled him.

* * *

The first light of dawn found Bryan breathing heavily, having only just fallen asleep. Sylvie, satisfied, carefully slid away from him. She considered looking for her panties but decided that it was more important to get what she came for and leave than to risk waking him. "Besides," she thought with a smile, "they'll be a nice reminder for him of last night."

She slid into her jeans and left the cabin, carefully and quietly closing the companionway door behind. Her tank top was right where she had dropped it. The fabric was cold, causing her to inhale as she pulled it on.

She paused a moment and listened for any sound that might indicate that he was awake, but all she heard was the cry of a single gull announcing the new day. Quickly and quietly she looked through the papers in his nav station for the notes she remembered seeing. She found nothing. She sat in the chair and thought about what he could have done when it came to her: the GPS.

She pressed the *On* button, which responded with a low sharp beep. In the silence, it felt like a truck horn. She held her breath and listened again. Nothing. The screen came alive and she hit the waypoint button. She began scrolling through the list, jotting down several coordinates. If he refused to help her, at least now she had the information and could find another way.

Satisfied that that was all she'd get this day, she left the deckhouse, picked up her boots, climbed off the boat, and disappeared into the dawn.

CHAPTER 34

VOICES. BRYAN TRIED TO OPEN HIS EYES. The lids felt as if they had been glued shut. Next he tried lifting his head, but all that got him was a violent, spinning head rush. He dropped his head back down and draped his arm over his eyes in an attempt to calm the demons that were assaulting his senses. His mouth was dry, his bladder full, and images of Sylvie flashed in and out of his head. He didn't move, and as the spinning subsided, he slid his arm off his eyes and slowly forced them to open. Bright sunlight drilled into his brain and he covered his eyes with his arm again. That was the moment when everything snapped into place.

He sat up sharply, ignoring the resultant head rush. He fought to focus on his watch. *10:30! How could it be 10:30?* He looked around, trying to get his bearings. *Didn't he have a charter? Shouldn't he be well offshore by now?* As he struggled with these thoughts, other things flashed through his head. First, he was absolutely certain that he had drunk too much last night. He was also pretty sure that he had seen Sylvie and that she had returned with him to his boat. That's where things began to get fuzzy. *What happened? Where was she? Where was his charter?* The only certainty was that he had to piss.

Relieved, he searched for a bottle of water. His mouth was dry, and he was still trying to make sense of the memories rolling around in his head. Finding the bottle of water was easy. He had downed half of the bottle before he realized it and paused to take a breath. That's when he saw the panties and all those jumbled memories began to come into focus. *Sylvie had been there.* He smiled. Holding the pair of small, black lace panties in his hand was all the proof he needed to confirm that it had been a night of unrestrained pleasure.

That pleasant memory abruptly ended when he once again remembered his charter. He threw the panties onto his berth and rushed up into the deckhouse, sprinting though and out into the day. Standing in the back of his boat, he heard gulls crying, cars singing their way over the bridge that spanned the river, and a powerful engine roaring to life. He was beginning to panic. There was no one on the docks, no sign of his charter group, and he began to imagine the worst: They had come down to the boat and—because he was unresponsive—they had left, perhaps finding another boat to take them out fishing.

"Shit!" He exhaled and then, as he turned to go back into the deckhouse, he saw the note.

Bryan,
Your charter called and said they would be unable to make it today. They'll be in touch.
Jane

As he read the note, he was both pissed and relieved. He needed the job, and coming from Hampton to Newburyport had cost fuel and time. Considering how he felt, though, he was actually glad that they had cancelled. Now, as the adrenaline rush of the last few minutes began to wear off, he knew he needed coffee and something to eat.

CHAPTER 35

THAT EVENING, DAVE GOT HOME from work before Patti. It was a nice night, so he went for a walk down to the marina. He missed those days when he fished for a living, but now he had a steadier job with a small surveying company. Besides, commercially, fishing wasn't so lucrative any more. As he stood on the pier looking out over the boats, he saw Bryan coming in on the *Miss Cookie*, so he went down to the float to say hello.

"Hey, Bryan," said Dave. He took the dock line from Bryan and tied *Miss Cookie* to the dock. "How've you been?"

"Good, man."

"What'cha been up to?"

"Not much."

"You know, I never really got a chance to thank you for that fishing trip last week."

"Don't worry about it."

"Well, thanks."

"Want a beer?"

"Sure."

Bryan motioned him to come aboard, and Dave climbed over the rail and accepted a beer. They each sat down in one of the plastic chairs.

"Thanks," Dave said. Then they sat in silence and listened to the squawking of the gulls.

"This was a wasted day," Bryan finally said. "I had a charter scheduled down in Newburyport for this morning. So I went down last night. Stayed over, and then the guy didn't show."

"That sucks."

"On the bright side, it wasn't a complete loss. At least I got his deposit. And last night, you'll never guess who I saw."

"You're right. I'll never guess. Who?"

"That chick, Sylvie. The one we hauled out of the ocean who wants to be dead. You want another beer?"

Dave said, "Really! I may need a second beer. Sounds like you have a lot to tell me."

Bryan finished the one he had and grabbed two more.

"So?"

"I was at the Starboard Galley, having dinner. She walked in, came over, and joined me."

"And?"

"And what?"

"And what else happened?"

"Not much, really."

Dave got up and turned toward the deckhouse.

"Where're you goin'?"

"Head. I'll be right back and when I get back you can tell me what you're not telling me."

* * *

When Dave returned he was twirling a pair of scanty black lace panties around on one finger.

"Not mine."

"Whew! That's a relief. . . . Really? C'mon give."

"Obviously someone left them behind. It can happen."

"Cut the crap, Bryan. Tell me."

"Fine. What do you want to know?"

"These hers?"

"Whose?"

"Bryan, you are such an asshole. You know who I mean."

Bryan just smiled. "A gentleman never kisses and tells."

"Bullshit. You're no gentleman."

He shrugged and took another long sip of beer.

"They're hers, aren't they?"

Bryan still wouldn't say anything, but his smile gave Dave all the answers he required.

"Jesus, Bryan. So what happened? She didn't seem too happy to see you when we pulled her out of the water."

"It's complicated."

"Complicated? How 'bout you tell me."

"Look, Dave. I don't think that would be a good idea. She's trouble. Here's all that I'm going to say. I don't know what's up with her and Jack, but you might want to tell him to be careful."

CHAPTER 36

"YOU BEEN DRINKIN'?" Patti asked as Dave walked in the door.

"Not really. I was down on the dock and Bryan came in. We got to talkin' and had a couple, but drinkin' . . . nah."

Patti gave him The Look. "Well, I hope you're all right, 'cause I invited Jack and Max over. We're gonna' get pizzas and eat here. I hope you don't mind."

"Mind? Why would I mind? When are they coming?"

"Should be here any time."

"I just need a shower first."

* * *

When Dave came out of the shower, Jack was in the living room with no sign of the girls. "Hi, Jack. Where're the girls?"

"The girls went to get the pizza. I brought a growler of Throwback Dippity Do. You ever had it?"

"No."

"Try some?"

"Sure."

Glasses filled, they moved out on to the back porch. The sun was starting to set.

"So what's up?" asked Jack.

"Funny you should ask. I just saw Bryan. Had a few with him just before you got here."

"What's he up to?"

"Well, I'm not exactly sure. "

"He ever hear anything from the Coast Guard?"

"I didn't ask but, he didn't say, so I'm guessing not."

"You heard that they think the boat that sank was Richie's, right?"

"Fishes out of Rye? Has a brother, right?"

Jack nodded.

"I hadn't heard, but that could explain a lot about what happened to Sylvie if she was out with him. A woman might need to use self-defense with a slimeball like him."

"I suppose, but why would she even have been out with him in the first place?"

"Well, get this. When I was down on Bryan's boat this afternoon, I found a pair of black lace panties lying around in the cabin."

"He's not . . ."

Dave cut him off, laughing. "That's what I said to him, too. No, he's not. But I think they were Sylvie's."

Jack had just taken a sip of beer when Dave said that and he all but spit out the beer as he began coughing. Finally, he managed to croak, "What?"

"Yeah. Apparently last night he was down in Newburyport, having dinner, she showed up, and they ended up back on his boat. I'm guessing it was quite the wild night, because he wouldn't talk about it. Only thing he said for sure was that he saw her at dinner. Actually, he also said to tell you to watch your back."

Still recovering from his choking spell, Jack wheezed, "What the fuck?"

"Food's here!" Patti's voice came from downstairs, followed by a great deal of thumping and giggling as they walked up the stairs.

"Don't say anything," said Dave. "I haven't told Patti any of this and . . . well, you know."

CHAPTER 37

"MROWH." CAT GREETED THEM at the door. She had been out hunting mice, or maybe just enjoying the late summer's night, but now she was ready to come in and retire. "Mrowh," she said repeatedly, obviously annoyed that the door wasn't being opened quickly enough.

"Take it easy, Cat," said Jack as she dashed by and bound up the stairs the second he opened the door.

He held the door open for Max, but she didn't rush in the way Cat had. Rather, she turned and faced him. It had been a fun night over at Dave's, and she was buzzed. She pressed up against him, wrapped her arms around his waist, and pulled him close, burying her face in his chest. He released the door and wrapped his arms around her.

She was warm, and her warmth made the night air seem that much cooler.

"Jack?" she whispered.

"Mmmm."

"Everything's okay, isn't it?"

He considered the question, but the feel of her body pressed against his had him focused on other things. "Yes, everything's fine." The urgency of the moment overwhelmed them, and they stumbled up the stairs, ignoring Cat's demands for her share of attention.

CHAPTER 38

EVER SINCE THE HEAT WAVE HAD BROKEN, the weather had been glorious. Warm, sunny days followed by cool nights and even though it was still summer, there were times that felt fall-like. Bryan shivered and smacked his lips. His mouth was dry, his neck stiff, and the lights from the nuclear power plant hurt his eyes, forcing him to look away. Turning his head, he saw that the night sky was dark, and as his other senses awakened he realized just how quiet everything was. Lifting his arm to check his watch, he thought he felt something fall. Looking down, he saw, on the deck, amongst a half dozen empty beer cans scattered around the plastic lawn chair in which he was sitting, a pair of black lace panties. He picked them up and even in his rough hands he could feel their silky smoothness. Lighter than a feather, they were more illusion than substance, and he smiled. It was all coming back to him, well, most of it.

He remembered tying *Miss Cookie* to the dock when Dave stopped by to say 'Hi'. He came aboard for a beer, which turned into several, and after a visit to the head, Dave returned twirling them on his finger. He remembered denying that they were Sylvie's. Then they talked about his new fish finder and after that, it was a blur, he didn't remember driving *Miss Cookie* back to her mooring.

"Shit," he mumbled as he pushed himself out of the chair. His head began spinning and he fell back into the chair. His second attempt at standing was more successful, even though he had to hold on to the chair to steady himself. Turning, he stepped towards the deckhouse, kicking one of the beer cans in the process, sending it clattering across the deck. The sound, amplified by the silence of the night, seemed much louder than it really was. He froze, half expecting to hear someone yell for him to be quiet. Instead, the only sounds he heard were his own heavy breathing and the pounding of his heart in his ears. Satisfied that he hadn't disturbed anyone, he made his way below and collapsed into his berth. He fell sound asleep, the black lace panties still in his hand.

"HUNH?" BRYAN SAT UP QUICKLY. Someone had been shaking him awake and now, as he looked around, his brain fought to comprehend the fact that no one had shaken him awake, that he was alone.

His head dropped back onto the pillow and he closed his eyes, arm draped over, in an attempt to block out the beam of sunlight that was focused on his face. *Miss Cookie* was still rocking gently, water slapping against her side, and the fading drone of a diesel engine made him realize that it had all been part of a dream. No one had awakened him. It had only been one of the other fishing boats in the harbor, sailing past, heading out for the day.

His head hurt, his mouth was dry, and even though he was conscious enough to understand what had really awakened him, he continued to lie there, eyes shut tight, trying to remember the dream. His thoughts drifted. "Was it really only two nights ago?" He lifted his arm to cover his eyes from the bright sun when something brushed against his face. He opened his eyes and saw in his hand the black lace panties and it all came back. It wasn't a dream and he smiled.

He needed coffee. His first sip burned his tongue, making the cup of instant tolerable. As he settled into the helmsman's seat, he looked up at the black lace panties which were now hanging on a hook above the nav station where he usually hung his hat. He smiled again as he remembered what he could of that night. He had a vague recollection of hearing her say that he was going to help her find something kept echoing in his head. What it was, and why, he couldn't remember.

Looking down at the chart spread out in front of him, he turned his GPS/chart plotter on. Scrolling through the digital record of the fishing trip with Dave and Jack, and fueled by a second cup of coffee, it came to him. Clearly she must be after whatever it was they had hooked and lost. "Okay, Sylvie, I know what you want and now I'm going to find it," he said out loud.

The weather forecast was favorable, so he decided that tomorrow he would begin his search. It would also be a great time to test out the new fish finder he had picked up with the cash he'd gotten from Tran. Decision made, it was time for some food.

* * *

After securing his dinghy, he walked over to Inga's, a small breakfast and lunch place favored by locals. It was nearly empty since it was already mid-morning. The commercial fishermen would have been in really early, and the lunch crowd, made up of people going out for an afternoon of deep sea fishing, had not yet started to arrive. He ordered three eggs over easy, home fries, bacon, toast, and a third cup of coffee. The coffee came first—hot and fresh which made what he had been drinking on his boat taste like shit.

"No, thanks," he said holding his hand over his cup when Inga came by for a top-up.

"Morning, Bryan." The voice from behind startled him. Déjà vu.

"Sylvie. What are you doing here?"

"What do you think?"

"I can't imagine." He could imagine, but he decided to play dumb and let her talk.

"Here you go." Inga put his plate down in front of him. "Coffee dear?" she asked Sylvie.

"That would be lovely." Sylvie smiled, and Inga turned for the coffee pot.

"So why are you here?" repeated Bryan.

"Oh, I think you know," Sylvie said with a wink and a smile.

Inga returned with the coffee pot, poured her coffee, and asked if she would like to see a menu.

"No, thank you."

Bryan kept his eyes on her throughout this exchange. As Inga walked away, Sylvie sat down next to him and took a sip of her coffee.

"Mmmm, this is good."

"Look, Sylvie, I don't know exactly what you're up to, and I'm not even sure I want to know."

Bryan reached for the salt and grabbed a forkful of eggs.

"So, when are we going out?"

He didn't answer her as he spread some strawberry jelly on his toast.

"I was thinking tomorrow," she continued. "I'll meet you down here, say three a.m., couple of hours before sun up. That way we'll get out there before too many other boats. Once we find what I want, you take me back, I disappear, and you don't have to see me again."

While she talked, Bryan continued to eat in silence. Finally, he wiped his plate with his last scrap of toast. "Do I have a choice?"

CHAPTER 40

3:01 A.M. BRYAN CHECKED HIS WATCH for the umpteenth time since bringing *Miss Cookie* to the dock. From the moment they had walked out of Inga's—separately—he had been on edge. His initial excitement of the challenge to find the mysterious object was still present, but now it was tempered with apprehension.

3:04. "*Where was she?*" He went into the deckhouse again to check that the course he had plotted was correct. He checked his watch again. 3:10.

He went out on deck and looked down the floats toward the ramp that connected them to the pier, then up toward the parking lot. Still no sign of her. This time, the soft purr of *Miss Cookie's* engine as it idled soothed him. He looked down at the grappling hook. After breakfast, he had rigged it with three hundred feet of all new line, which was neatly coiled in a basket and ready to deploy.

He was about to check his watch again when he thought he saw movement up on the dock. A dark shape was moving quickly toward him and *Miss Cookie*. He breathed a sigh of relief that she had arrived and then noticed that she made no noise at all as she hurried down the ramp and along the dock. How did she do that?

"Let's go," was all she said as she tossed her bag into the boat and moved to untie the bow line.

"Well, good morning to you, too."

She tossed the bow line onto the foredeck and moved efficiently to the stern line, which she also untied. Then she climbed on board. "Well?" she said to him.

Her meaning was clear and Bryan didn't say anything. He turned and walked into the deckhouse, shifted the engine into gear, and eased the throttle forward. While he guided *Miss Cookie* under the Route

1-A bridge, Sylvie made her way to the foredeck. He watched as she retrieved the bow line and coiled it. As they cleared the bridge, there was enough light from the streetlamps for him to study her. Dressed in dark, form-fitting clothes, she was a shadowy silhouette, her movements efficient and sure, unaffected by the rising and falling of the bow as *Miss Cookie* met the ocean's swell. For Bryan, for that moment, all felt right with the world.

With the bow line coiled, she made her way back to the cockpit, tossed it onto the deck, and did the same with the stern line. When she finished, she joined Bryan in the deckhouse.

"Three, four hours? Sunrise in two?" she asked.

"'Bout that. Looks like it'll be a nice day."

Sylvie didn't reply as she focused her attention on the chart plotter. Satisfied, she said, "I'll be below. Call me when we've got an hour to go." Her tone cut off any chance of conversation or discussion.

"Sure," was all he could get out before she disappeared into the forward cabin and pulled the door shut.

CHAPTER 41

BRYAN ALWAYS LOVED WATCHING THE SUNRISE, especially out at sea, and today was no exception. First the sky brightened a few shades, from inky black to a bluish gray. Then it took on more silver hues as clouds began to appear. In that early lightening, it always looked bleak and stormy, but soon the clouds began to change from tarnished silver and gray to rust and orange. As the sun rose nearer to the horizon, the clouds took on silver edges tinged with pink, and then, in the blink of an eye, the first rays of sunlight tracked across the water, blindingly bright. Then, with each passing second, the sun got larger and the world got brighter. When the sun was fully sitting on the horizon, the explosion of color announced the start of another new day. He could almost feel the earth spinning toward the sun.

A quick glance at the GPS/chart plotter told him that they should arrive within an hour or so. He remembered Sylvie's last words and was just getting ready to pry himself out of the helmsman's seat when he heard the companionway door begin to open. He settled back.

"Really?" she said. She was pointing at the black lace panties hanging on the hook above the nav station. In the dark when she boarded she hadn't seen them.

Bryan smiled. "Souvenir."

"They're yours; go nuts." Her expression seemed to add the word, "*Pig.*"

"I will. We're about an hour away. You want some coffee?"

"That'd be nice."

"Stove's down below. Go put some water on."

This day she wasn't his guest and he wasn't trying to seduce her, although that would be nice. Instead, she was his employer, or perhaps partner, depending on whose view you took. Regardless, he was driving the boat, so she could make the coffee.

When she reappeared with two cups of coffee in hand, the black pants, shirt, and shoes were gone. She had changed into navy blue shorts, boat shoes, and a white t-shirt that said "Save the Whales." The shirt was loose fitting, and the way it shimmied as she moved hinted that she wore nothing underneath.

She made better coffee than he did, but he didn't offer any comment.

"So are you going to tell me exactly what we're looking for?"

"I would if I could."

"What do you mean by that?"

"Exactly what I said. I don't know what it is. The job had been to go out with Richie, retrieve a package and return. I never knew what it was and he never told me."

"So what happened?"

Sylvie stared at him silently for a moment. "When we got there, we rigged the grappling hook and began to drag it back and forth. We caught onto something and began pulling it up. It was almost up when he came at me with a knife. As he swung it at me, he hit the rope and the package went to the bottom."

"And that's when you killed him?"

"Yes."

"So why sink the boat?"

"Because at that moment I knew I hadn't been put there to help him, I had been put there so he could kill me. The only way I would be able to survive would be to sink the boat with him in it. If nothing was found, they'd presume that I was also dead."

"Who's they?"

"That I can't tell you."

"Fair enough, but why burn it?"

"There wasn't a life raft or anything on board. If I burned it, my hope was that someone would see the smoke and come find me."

"That was a crazy idea."

"It worked."

"I suppose."

As they sipped on their coffees, he showed her where the coordinates were on the chart where they had lost the package and explained how they would do it. Having searched for lost traps in the past, he knew that it had to be done methodically, carefully following a predetermined grid. He would drive the boat and have to trust her to properly handle the grapple.

"Check this out," he said as he pressed a button on the depth/fish finder. The display changed and now looked almost like a video of the bottom. The level of detail was incredible and she was fascinated. "I'm hoping that this will make it easier to find. If we spot it, the trick then will be to catch it with the hook. With a little luck it won't take us long once we find it."

"Where'd you get this?"

"Remember that shark I caught just before we landed you?"

He could see her thinking about this and then she nodded indicating that she understood. "I'll be outside."

"I'll give you a shout."

Bryan remained focused on the GPS until she showed up on the foredeck. He had assumed that she was going to remain in the cockpit, but she had made her way around the deckhouse and was now standing near the bow. The sun was still low enough in the sky that all he could see was her silhouette. With nothing to hold on to she stood with her legs spread slightly, each alternately bending and straightening, like shock absorbers, as *Miss Cookie* gently rolled with the sea. There was a gentle breeze blowing and the ocean was not as flat as the day all this had started. Her balance was superb and watching her as she swayed in sync with the motion of the boat was mesmerizing. Had she gone on top of the deckhouse, the view for her would have been better, but his wouldn't have been. He shot another look at the panties and smiled.

He began to slow the boat. The coordinates on the screen ticked closer to their destination, and he watched the fish finder more closely, hoping that their prize would suddenly appear. She looked back at him when *Miss Cookie* slowed. He could tell that she was chilly, and that elicited another smile. As soon as they were on the mark, he rapped on the front window and waved her back.

"Anything?" she asked.

"No, but we're at our starting point," he said. He pointed at the chart plotter. "It's definitely drifted since there's nothing showing here."

CHAPTER 42

SLOWLY, METHODICALLY, BRYAN began guiding *Miss Cookie* back and forth. He kept each pass parallel to the next, about a mile in length. After completing a pass, he would shift the boat no more than a hundred feet and do it again. During their fifth pass an image popped up on the screen.

"There," she said.

Bryan hit the waypoint button on the GPS so they wouldn't lose the spot. Now it was just a matter of passing back and forth around that spot while dragging the grappling hook until they caught it.

He said, "You want to get the grapple ready to drop over?"

It took her a few minutes, but then she called back, "Ready."

"Okay, I'm coming up on it again. When I say to, drop it."

Bryan watched the screen for another minute before shouting, "Drop it!"

He heard the splash and, glancing back, saw her paying out the line.

"Okay!" he shouted. "I see it! We're close."

The first pass missed, but on the second Bryan saw the hook hit the object.

Then Sylvie shouted, "I think we've got it!"

He took the boat out of gear and headed out to help her. Now that they were hooked on, drifting wouldn't matter. Sylvie had taken a turn on one of the cleats, but she was still having a hard time holding on, particularly since the boat still hadn't fully stopped. Bryan took the line from her, put another wrap on the cleat, and waited. Slowly, gradually, the strain eased as the boat lost way. When *Miss Cookie* was dead in the water, he pulled the slack out of the line and tied it off on the cleat.

"Well, we've got something," he announced.

"So let's get it up."

"Hang on. Let's get set first. Then we'll pull it up." He turned to ready the lifting boom. As before, he hung an open-sided single block onto the end of the boom. After unlocking, then pushing the boom toward the side of the boat and locking it in its new position, he uncleated the grappling hook's line, led it over the block and back down to the winch.

Holding on tightly he looked at Sylvie. "Ready?"

She nodded and he stepped on the switch. Even with as many wraps around the winch drum as he could fit, the winch strained as he pulled with both hands.

Sylvie stood watching over the side while slowly, foot by foot, the line came in.

"I can see it," she finally called out. "It's almost at the surface."

Bryan just kept pulling. His arms ached, but stopping wasn't an option.

"It's out," she announced.

Bryan kept pulling until a large black bag was hovering above the water. About the size of a large man, it sagged to either side of the hook and water dripped from where the hooks had punctured the bag. As soon as he felt it was high enough to clear the gunwale he tried to unlatch the boom's locking pin, but because of the strain on the boom it was jammed. "Sylvie, come over here. I need you to help me release this pin so we can swing this mother onboard," he said, motioning with his head.

After several unsuccessful attempts to wriggle it free, Bryan told her that she would have to hit it and where she could find a hammer. It required several raps before the pin came free. As soon as the pin released, the weight of the package hanging off the end of the boom instantly caused it to swing even further out and away from the boat, causing *Miss Cookie* to list.

"Grab the boat hook and see if you can get hold of the bag and pull it in."

This proved to be more difficult than Bryan thought it would be. After several tries, she managed to catch it and began pulling it toward the boat.

"C'mon, pull it in."

She flashed him a look, which he ignored. Then he added, "Move further back. You'll get a better angle."

"Look, asshole, I'm trying!"

As she moved back she had to lean further and further out, and by the time she had sufficient angle to pull, she was bent over the coaming, stretched out as far as she could reach.

Bryan just stood and watched. It wasn't that he couldn't have helped her. He could have cleated off the rope, but he was enjoying the show way too much. Stretched out as she was, her shirt was getting splashed, which meant the wet fabric alternately stuck to and released from her dangling breasts.

She glared at him. "Bryan! A little help over here!" Her look told him that she knew exactly where his mind was.

Snapped back to reality, he cleated off the hauling rope and moved to help. He could see more clearly that the grappling hook had snagged one end of the bag, leaving the other to hang down at a precarious angle. Covered with slime and bits of seaweed it appeared to be bound with rope and it was that rope that the boat hook was caught on. He leaned out next to her and took the boat hook, careful to preserve its hold on the rope.

"I've got it."

Sylvie pulled back into the boat and stood up, leaving Bryan now extended out over the water, holding on to their prize.

He said, "When I pull it in, go back and try to get the boom pinned again."

He pulled, she got the pin back in, and with that, they were right back where they had started with their prize still hanging out over the water. Keeping the boat hook attached, Bryan stood and studied their catch.

"We won't be able to pull it on board until we raise it a bit more. This time I'll hold on to it while you work the winch and pull it a bit higher. With a bit of luck, we'll get it high enough to clear the gunwale. Then we can release the pin and swing her aboard without doing too much damage."

"So I have to uncleat it first, then press the winch switch and pull, right?"

"Right."

She was about to uncleat it when Bryan stopped her. "Hold it. Something's hanging down into the water." He leaned over the rail and looked under the bag, "What the hell is this?" Another rope was dangling down into the water.

Bryan twisted the boat hook until it was free, which allowed the package to swing more freely, occasionally hitting the side of *Miss Cookie*. Trying to stabilize it with his left hand, he used the boat hook in his right to reach under and fish for the dangling rope.

"Got it," he said. "Come over here. Can you steady it while I pull it in?"

Whatever he had hold of, it was heavy, but he thought he'd be able to grab it, and if he could get close enough, pull it in. He pulled in about ten feet of rope before he saw the end.

"Looks like a block of concrete or something," he said. "You got any problem if I cut it free?"

"Go for it."

He reached under the gunwale, grabbed the same knife he had used to gut the shark, and cut the rope. Instantly *Miss Cookie* rocked in relief as the weight disappeared from sight.

Standing, he grabbed the rope that bound their prize.

"I've got this. Go on and uncleat the rope. Hold on tight and begin to haul it up."

Now that the extra weight had been dropped, everything became much easier, and in just a few minutes the bag was on the deck. Bryan looked at Sylvie. "So what is it? Drugs?"

She stared at it but didn't answer.

Bryan alternately looked at the package and then at her. Finally, sensing that he wasn't going to get any more information, he said, "I need some more coffee. Want some?"

CHAPTER 43

BRYAN RETURNED TO THE COCKPIT with two cups in hand and offered one to Sylvie.

"Blah!" she spit out her first sip. "What did you do?"

"I added a little something." He grinned.

"Well, it tastes like shit."

He shrugged and took another sip while she tossed her coffee overboard. Bits of seaweed and sea slime were everywhere, and the deck was a slippery mess as water continued to drip from the package.

Sylvie reached for the knife and began to cut the ropes that bound their prize. When her task was complete she stopped, stood, and stretched, but Bryan noticed that she never took her eyes off it. She was about to start unwrapping the object when he stopped her.

"Before you start doing that, let's get this mess cleaned up." While Bryan had his faults, a messy boat wasn't one of them. "Better yet, I'll hose it down. You go get cleaned up and find some dry clothes. You're beginning to stink." Without giving her time to reply, he picked up the hose.

By the time she came back out from the cabin, he had washed the cockpit clean and was standing at the stern.

Sylvie looked surprised to see the fishing pole in his hand.

"What are you doing?"

"Fishing."

"Why? We have what we came for. Let's get back!"

"No."

"What do you mean, 'No'?"

"Look, Syl. The day is young. It's beautiful out and we're sitting on top of a school of fish. There's no rush, and besides, if we head in now, we'll just draw attention to ourselves." He pointed out other fishing boats, which could now be seen in all directions. "I'm assuming you don't want that, do you?"

"No. You're right."

"So, you ready to cut this puppy open?"

She nodded.

Now cleaned off, their catch looked like a large black bag. Sylvie knelt next to it, ran her hands over it, and then looked up at Bryan.

"Give me a hand. I need to roll it over."

He knelt opposite her and pulled as she pushed. They nearly knocked heads in the process, but grudgingly it moved. Whatever was inside seemed to be made up of several parts, and as one began to turn, they had to begin rolling the next before the first could go all the way over. As the package rolled, more water dripped from the punctures made by the grappling hook.

"Here," he handed her the knife.

"Thanks."

Carefully, she pressed the point into the fabric and then pulled the knife horizontally the length of the bundle. Together they pulled the cut sections apart; this step exposed another layer of what seemed to be the same fabric.

Before attacking this inner layer, Sylvie made several more cuts in the outer layer until it lay flat on the deck, exposing a second bag, which was intact. The tines of the grappling hook hadn't penetrated it. Sylvie began running her hands over it, prodding and poking in much the same way a doctor would first examine a patient.

Bryan watched and bit his tongue. He would have just slit it open.

Sylvie finally picked up the knife. With the same practiced efficiency that he possessed when gutting a fish, she picked her spot, pressed the knife in, and slit the bag open. Inside he could see there was some kind of packing material that further protected whatever was in the bags. Carefully, she pulled at the material before removing two black plastic cases each about the size of a large briefcase and a third that was longer and flatter.

"That your electric guitar?" he asked.

"That's not your worry. Help me get these down into the cabin." Her voice was cold and commanding. He knew from their time in bed that she liked to control things and wasn't afraid to say what she wanted and how she wanted it, but this time her tone took her power to a whole new level. She grabbed the "guitar case" and he followed with the other two. "You're not going to tell me what's in them, are you?" he asked when they were down below.

"No."

Then she turned her back, gestured for him to leave, and shut the door firmly behind her.

* * *

Bryan shrugged and returned to the deckhouse, topped up his cup again, looked at the fish finder and went back out to the cockpit, where he gathered up all the material that they had cut away and put it all into a plastic garbage bag. Even for him, it was just too much to throw overboard. He checked his line and settled into one of his plastic lawn chairs.

The day was getting nicer by the minute. His "coffee" was kicking in and he really didn't care if he caught anything or not. It was just good being out on the boat, and besides, Sylvie was here. "Maybe she'd want to "celebrate" their find," he thought to himself, knowing full well that that wasn't going to happen.

He was just beginning to doze off when the fishing line began to rip off the reel. The tip of the rod bent and when he got it under control, he looked up to see Sylvie standing there.

CHAPTER 44

HOURS LATER, AS *Miss Cookie* chugged back toward Hampton Harbor, Sylvie kept conversation to a minimum. She had spent most of day with the packages down in the forward cabin.

"At least the fishing was good," Bryan thought. He had a cooler with at least a dozen beautiful filets as proof.

"We'll be in soon. What do you want to do?" he asked.

She looked toward the coast and up at the darkening sky. The pinks were turning more red, the reds were getting darker, and lights were coming on along the beach.

"Once it's totally dark and I can get the cases to my car, I'll disappear."

It wasn't the answer he had hoped for.

"You still haven't told me what's in the cases. What's the big secret?"

"Bryan, you're a nice guy. You've helped me out, and I appreciate that. But, there are some things that don't concern you. Can we just leave it at that?"

"But—"

She cut him off with a wave of her hand.

"Fine," he mumbled. Then he turned his attention away from her and concentrated on driving the boat.

* * *

By the time *Miss Cookie* was heading under the bridge, the sun had set, leaving only a faint glow in the west. The sodium vapor lights that lit the nuke plant reflected off the water, and a steady stream of cars hummed over the grid deck of the bridge. Sylvie stood next to him in the deckhouse.

"I'm serious, Bryan. It will be best if you just forget that today ever happened."

Before Bryan could reply, his attention was caught by loud voices coming from a boat tied near the floats. As best as he could tell, a large group was celebrating a wonderful day at sea.

Sylvie instantly retreated to the forward cabin. In a low but commanding voice she called, "Tie up as far from them as possible."

When he started to reply, she cut him off. "Just do it."

Not about to challenge her command, Bryan laid *Miss Cookie* up against the dock without any fuss or fanfare.

"We're going to sit here a while," said Sylvie from inside the shadows of the forward cabin. "We'll wait until they're gone."

"Sure, but I'm hungry," he said. "How 'bout I go up to the Wok for some takeout. You stay here."

For the first time since they had recovered their prize it seemed that her voice warmed. "Okay."

* * *

The Wok was busy. Pushing his way in, he reached the register and ordered dinner. He needed a drink. At the bar, all the seats were taken, and there was at least one person standing for everyone seated. Mel was behind the bar, and he managed to get her attention and signal her for a Mai Tai. He didn't specify the size, but he wasn't surprised when she handed him a large one.

"Bryan." Over the din in the restaurant, he thought he heard his name, and a waving hand from one of the tables down by the windows caught his attention. He signaled Mel to add his drink to his order, pointed out to the hostess where he'd be, and made his way down to Dave's table. Jack was there also.

Dave saw him looking at the two extra drinks on the table and said, "Patti and Max are in the bathroom. Long day at Ben's so we're treating the girls. What're you up to?"

"Just got back in."

"Good trip?"

He hesitated a moment before answering. "Yeah."

"Who'd you take out?"

Again, he hesitated, and looked around as if about to divulge a great secret. Then, in a low voice he said, "You wouldn't believe me if I told you."

Both Dave and Jack looked at him. Before either could say anything else, Max's voice cut in. "Believe what?"

They hadn't seen her and Patti returning. Bryan turned, and Dave and Jack began sliding out of the booth to let the girls slide in. In the commotion, the hostess caught his eye and signaled that his food was ready. Saved from having to answer, Bryan whispered to Dave, "Tell you later. Gotta' go. Food's ready."

CHAPTER 45

"SMELLS GOOD!" One of the guys from the noisy boat called and waved as Bryan walked past with the food.

He paused. "It does. Have a good trip today?"

"We did. How was yours? Find anything interesting?"

"Any day on the water is a good day." With that, Bryan tightened his grip on the twelve-pack of Coors Light he'd grabbed at the convenience store next to the Wok and continued on down the dock toward *Miss Cookie*.

He climbed on board, went into the deckhouse, and put the food and beer on the table. He was about to turn on the lights when Sylvie said, "Leave them off."

"What?"

"No lights."

"Are you nuts? How are we going to see to eat?"

"We'll eat down here."

Bryan liked the sound of that. He considered the possibilities, smiled, and picked up the bag of food and the beers.

"Close the door."

As soon as he did, she lit a candle. It wasn't much, but it was more than enough, and in the flickering light, his imagination began to work overtime.

He put the food on the counter by the stove. He opened two beers and passed her one.

"Did I hear you talking to those guys?"

"Hunh?"

"Those guys on the other boat. Did I hear you talking to them?"

"I wouldn't say talking, more of just a passing 'Hi'."

"What did they say?"

"Nothing really. Guy asked if we caught anything."

"Is that all?"

Her questions were beginning to make him uneasy. "Yes, yes, that's all."

That seemed to satisfy her, but now his mind was churning, and as he began unpacking their dinner, it occurred to him that the guy had asked if they had found anything, not if they had caught anything. He decided he was too hungry to worry about it, so he began to scoop their dinner onto plates.

Aside from small comments on how good the food was, little else was said. However, Bryan could feel a subtle shift in the atmosphere in the cabin. Maybe it was the closeness of that small, tight cabin. Maybe it was the feeling of mystery created by the ever-changing shadows from the flickering light of that single candle. It could have been the Chinese and beers or the sound of the water as it gurgled past the hull. Whatever it was, there was no denying the feeling of intimacy between them now.

"Syl, what's going on?"

"Let's not ruin this moment."

He sat silent. "You worry me."

"Bryan. Stop. You need to understand something. You're a good time. I like that we can get together, enjoy each other, and then go our separate ways. That will not change. So please, just accept it for what it is. Now, no more questions."

He couldn't think of anything else to say that wouldn't make him seem pitiful. Better to be silent and enjoy what might come.

His hopes were dashed, however, when she suddenly said, "Shhh. Are they leaving?"

"Who?" he whispered. Then he realized what she meant. Gone were the voices from the other end of the dock. He heard an engine start and then a boat leave.

"I'm going to change into what I had on this morning, and then I'll check." She ducked into the head and moments later returned, all dressed in black.

"Why don't I go?" he offered. He tried to hide his dismay that their time might be over.

"No. I know what to look for."

Before he could say anything else, she slithered over the rail and moved up the dock. She had already disappeared up the ramp by the time he realized that once again she had made no noise at all.

He turned on a light in the cabin and decided to open another Coors Light.

CHAPTER 46

AS BRYAN REACHED FOR THE BEER, he caught sight of the cases and did some quick calculations instead. Yes, his time was limited, but he had to know. He lifted the first case onto the berth. With his heart pounding in his chest, he tested the latches. To his surprise they weren't locked. He snapped the latches open and slowly lifted the lid.

All he could do was suck in his breath and hold it. "Shiiit," he finally exhaled. Then he began to panic that she'd return before he could open the other two cases, so he quickly shut the lid and put the case back and moved on to the next.

It was smaller than the first and weighed next to nothing. This time he moved even more quickly. The noise from the latches snapping as he pulled them open seemed louder than before. He stopped and looked around as if that action would ensure silence. Reassured that he was still alone, he lifted the lid. "What the hell?" he whispered. Then he closed the case.

Two down, one to go. The third one was the large flat case and it was the heaviest. Its latches seemed harder to pry open than the others. With each loud snap he froze and then immediately looked up and around to make sure he was still alone. Fear and paranoia gripped him, but he couldn't stop. His breathing was shallow and his hands were shaking more than before as he lifted the lid.

Time slowed as Bryan tried to comprehend what he was seeing. "Oh, my God!" He shut the case quickly and snapped the latches closed. It was as if that action would erase from his memory what he had just seen.

"Knock knock!" The words were accompanied with raps against the side of the boat.

Bryan's heart nearly stopped as he snapped his head around. He had been so focused on his discovery that he hadn't heard footsteps or felt the boat sway. Then he realized that the voice wasn't Sylvie's; it was too low to belong to a woman. Who the hell could it be?

Trying to still his shaking hands, he went up into the deckhouse. Through the deckhouse windows he could see that it was Dave, and he breathed a sigh of relief.

He waved his hand and called out, "Dave! Come!" He tried to make his voice sound as casual as possible.

"Hey, Bryan. What's up?"

"Sorry I took off so quickly up at the Wok."

"No biggie. What's going on?"

"Can I trust you?"

Dave looked at him a bit crossways. "Sure."

"Anyone know you're down here?"

"No. What's going on?"

"You're sure?"

"Bryan, what's going on? No one knows I'm down here." He began looking around as if curious about why Bryan was acting so queer. Then he added, "We just finished dinner. Jack and Max headed home. I needed a walk and Patti said she was too tired, so she went up. Tell me who you took out on the boat today!"

Bryan hesitated, still freaked out with what he had just seen in the cases. Then, moving in close to Dave, he lowered his voice so it was just above a whisper.

"I probably shouldn't say anything. Can you keep a secret?"

Dave nodded.

"It was Sylvie. We went after that thing you caught when we went out."

"Really? You found it again?"

"We did."

"So, what was it?"

"A big waterproof bag. Tethered to the bottom."

Dave motioned with his hands for more.

"We brought it up." Bryan stopped and nervously looked around.

"And . . . ?"

Bryan remained quiet.

"C'mon, Bryan. Spill it. What was inside?"

Relenting, he spoke in hushed tones. "Three waterproof cases."

"What was in them?"

"She wouldn't tell me."

"Is she here?"

"No. She got spooked earlier by some guys on the dock and now she's gone off to make sure the coast is clear."

"And you haven't looked?"

Bryan stopped. "I just did."

"And?"

"And you don't want to know."

"Jesus, Bryan."

Bryan was about to say more when he felt the boat sway slightly. Looking up, he saw Sylvie climbing back on board. "Shhh. She's back. I'll tell you later," he whispered.

Bryan grabbed two beers and handed one to Dave. As Sylvie came in, he re-introduced them. "Sylvie, you remember Dave?"

As Bryan watched, she masked her displeasure well, almost too well.

"Dave, of course. Good to see you again."

"I saw them at the Wok when I picked up the food."

"Who's them?"

"I'm sorry. Jack and Max, Dave and Patti. They were at a table having dinner."

"I see." Her voice sounded pleasant, but Bryan could hear the subtle questioning edge.

He continued, "Dave took Patti home and then decided to drop by. But he can't stay long."

Dave appeared to get the message.

"Listen," Dave said, setting down the unopened beer. "I'll have this another time. Patti will be wondering what's taking me so long. Good to see you, Sylvie. Bryan, I'll call so we'll set up another trip. Soon."

As soon as Dave was gone, Bryan asked, "Coast clear?"

"Yes."

Sylvie disappeared below, turned the light out, and passed up the large flat case to Bryan. Then she emerged, carrying the other two.

"Let's go."

Bryan's heart was pounding all the way to her car as he hoped that she didn't suspect that he had looked inside the cases. Once the cases were in the trunk, she turned and gave him a brief kiss. Then she said, "Bryan. Listen very carefully to me. I've told you once and I'll tell you again. You must understand that what we did today, *no one can know.*"

"Yes, of course," he said, even though it was already far too late for that. As he watched her taillights disappear down the road, he thought, *Just like you're dead.*

CHAPTER 47

PATTI HAD ALREADY GONE TO BED by the time Dave got home. After his interrupted chat with Bryan he knew that sleep would be impossible, so he turned on the television to blunt the silence. Sitting in his favorite chair, he surfed the channels and finally settled on a station that was showing news.

As the talking head droned on and on, his thoughts drifted and his eyes grew heavy. Sylvie and Bryan? Jack and Sylvie? How did she know both of them? He recalled that Jack had met her first at the Rockdog Run. Could she have set that up? No, it must have been an accident. But then she had showed up again, somehow involved in that real estate scheme in Rye Harbor. People had been killed, and some nearly killed, and Jack had confided how Sylvie had been coming on to him before she had vanished mysteriously. Who was she, and what did she want?

Then there was Bryan. First he had seemed reluctant to check out the smoke during their trip, and then it had seemed like Sylvie knew him. How? Why? And was her story about killing Richie in self-defense even true? And what about tonight? Bryan had taken her out to retrieve whatever they had snagged while fishing. Did Bryan recognize what it was at the time? Was it his idea to go after it, or was it hers?

Dave jerked his head up. The alarm in his watch was beeping, and his neck ached. As sunlight streamed in through his kitchen widow, he realized that the television was still on, and last night's talking head had been replaced with an overly cheerful young woman. The remnants of his dreams were fading fast. All he could remember was that they had involved Bryan and Sylvie, and that bad things had happened.

"Shit." He had to go to work. He clicked the television off. It was going to be another beautiful day. Patti was still asleep.

Rubbing his sore neck, Dave considered his options and decided that he'd call in sick. He hadn't slept well, and the combination of his dreams and his experiences on Bryan's boat was bothering him. He had accumulated enough time and he needed the break.

Decision made, he went to the bathroom and brushed his teeth, intending to start the day with a run. Then he noticed that the clothes that Patti had worn last night were in a pile on the bathroom floor next to the shower— all of her clothes. The thought of going for a run suddenly wasn't quite so appealing. There was a much better way to elevate his heart rate, and besides, he could run later. He smiled and his clothes joined hers on the floor.

* * *

"Dave!"

He had fallen back asleep after their early morning lovemaking. Patti must be getting ready for work. She had the lunch shift at Ben's, and he knew that she wanted to get in a little early. She had mentioned that Sunday had been extremely busy, and there were always extra things to do. "Dave! Come here!" The second time she called, he jumped out of bed. Maybe she'd seen a spider.

Instead, when he got to the living room, he found her pointing at the television.

"Look!"

He froze when he saw the screen. The reporter was standing next to Hampton Harbor. There were blue and red flashing lights everywhere, and police officers were stringing up yellow tape.

"What the hell?" He continued to stare at the screen as the reporter explained how the body of an unidentified male had been found in a dumpster on the pier. She seemed to drone on and on, speaking with great authority about what had happened, even though it was mostly speculation.

Patti grabbed her camera and headed for the door. "I've got to get to work, but I'm gonna' go down and see if I can get any good shots first."

Patti often shot crime scenes for Tom in Rye Harbor. Today's shots would be strictly freelance, but Dave knew that she couldn't help herself.

* * *

Jack was in his shop when the phone rang. Before he could even say hello, he heard Dave's voice. "Hey, Jack. Did you hear about the excitement down here this morning?"

"Yeah. I was over at Ben's helping Courtney earlier with some landscaping stuff when Patti came in and told us. You at work?""

"No. I took the day off. . . . Have I got something to tell you."

"What?"

"Did you know Sylvie was down here last night?"

Jack went silent for a moment. "No, I didn't."

"Remember when Bryan saw us at the Wok?"

"Yeah."

"He said he had something to tell me, so after you guys left I walked down to the marina."

"And?"

"Hey, you up for a run? I'd rather talk in person."

"Sure. How about Maudslay?"

"Great.

"See you there."

The phone went dead, and Jack was left wondering and worrying about what was going on.

CHAPTER 48

BY THE TIME THEY MET UP at Maudslay State Park in Newburyport to begin their run, it was well into the mid-afternoon hours.

"What do you think? Six?" asked Dave as they left the parking area and took their first steps onto the trails.

"Perfect."

During the first half-mile or so little was said as they settled into a comfortable pace. They were on one of the main trails, which was wide enough to allow them to run side by side. Jack knew that Dave, who normally had to deal with the traffic and distracted drivers of Hampton Beach, preferred running in the woods whenever he could manage to do so. Sunlight streamed through the trees and an occasional squirrel chattered, warning of their approach. Sometimes they could hear rustling in the underbrush just off the trail.

Unlike when they ran on the roads, the rhythm of their footfalls was less monotonous. The varying terrain caused them to shorten or lengthen their strides, slow or quicken, or even hop and jump as rocks and roots interrupted the path.

"Okay, Dave. What's this about Sylvie?" Jack had to know.

"Okay, so I told you, last night I went down to the dock after you guys left. His boat was there, all dark, tied down at the end of the floats. Only boat there. Couldn't tell if he was on board, but I went to check anyway. It was strange, didn't see any lights on, and you'd think there would be, at least inside the deckhouse. Anyway, it wasn't until I got right up to the boat that I could see some lights on in the forward cabin. I knocked on the hull. He came out and waved me on."

"Sylvie?"

"Oh yeah. Sylvie."

"I guess he had taken her out that day to look for that thing we had hooked."

"What?"

"I know. I don't understand it all, but it sounded like Bryan was planning to go out looking for it and she went along. They found it and then she went all secret and weird on him."

"What was it?"

"She wouldn't tell him. But just before I got there, she had stepped off the boat and he had looked."

"So what was it?"

"A bag or something. With three cases inside."

"And?"

"He wouldn't say. Seemed sorta' spooked. Then she came back and he clammed up. That was weird too."

"How so?"

"I don't know. She seemed all nice and friendly, but there was something. I don't know what. Just a feeling I got. That's when I left."

The trail turned to single track and required more concentration so they ran in silence for the next mile. When they returned to the main path and could run side by side, Dave picked up where he left off.

"Hey, Jack? You heard anything else about Richie?"

"Haven't. As far as I know, the Coast Guard thinks his boat caught on fire and he went down with it. End of story."

Dave said, "Okay, so we have Bryan, Sylvie, Richie, and the mysterious cases. What do you think is going on? They all related?"

Jack didn't answer right away. Then he said, slowly, "Don't know. Hope not. But my gut says that they are."

* * *

"That was great." Jack was huffing as he slowed to a stop.

Dave, a few steps ahead, had already stopped and looked back. "It was."

"You know, I was thinking—"

"That's never good," interrupted Dave.

Jack continued. "Hey, for shits and giggles, what if that guy they found in the dumpster this morning was also somehow part of it?"

Dave said, "What gave you that idea? And what's it?"

"No idea. But can we agree that Sylvie is the common denominator?"

"Okay— except for the dumpster guy."

"As far as we know. So forget about the dumpster guy for the moment." Jack paused a moment and then continued. "I hate to say it, but think about how bad things seem to happen whenever she's around. Back when that whole real estate scheme was happening in town and Courtney was in trouble, Sylvie mysteriously showed up and told me she was going to take care of things. Well, someone certainly took care of things all right! The body count went up, June ended up in her coma, and then Sylvie disappeared. Next thing you know, we find her floating in the middle of the ocean and we're supposed to pretend that she's dead."

"And then there's whatever's in those cases . . ."

"Right," said Jack. "So let's agree on one more thing. Until we can find out exactly what's going on, you, me and even Bryan—we make sure we're really careful."

CHAPTER 49

JACK GOT HOME FROM HIS RUN just after Max got home from Ben's. She had worked the day shift with Patti and was stretched out on the couch, asleep. He knew that working lunch the day after a busy Sunday was exhausting. Fortunately it happened only once or twice during the summer. He showered quickly and quietly so as not to disturb her and headed over to Ben's for a beer.

* * *

"Hey, Court. What're you doing here?"

"Covering for Alicia. She had to leave, some personal crisis."

"That sucks for both of you."

She nodded her agreement. "Beer?"

"Thanks."

As she placed the ESB in front of him, he asked, "Good day yesterday?"

"It was. Summer's too short. Could use more of those."

"I hear ya'."

"Hungry?"

"I'm good."

* * *

Jack was just finishing his beer when Art came into the bar.

"Hey, Jack. What's up?"

"Not much." He nodded for Art to join him.

"Coast Guard investigator came by again today, asking questions about Richie."

"Really. I thought it was pretty much settled."

"So did I. From what he said, sounds like there's no doubt that it was his boat that sank, and it seems they're satisfied that he's dead, but . . ."

"But what?"

"Well, it was the kind of questions he was asking."

"What do you mean?"

"I don't know. Things like how often he went out. Was he always alone or with anyone? Any new equipment on his boat? Stuff like that."

"What's so strange about that? Probably just trying to fill out a final report."

Art looked straight ahead and in a quiet, thoughtful voice said, "Wasn't so much what he was asking, but more the way he was asking." Turning toward Jack, he added, "You know what I mean?"

"I guess," said Jack. He took a long slow sip of his beer and tried to hold his expression in check. He understood more than Art would ever know.

When Courtney returned, she asked, "What's with the long faces?"

Jack responded first. "Oh, sorry Court. We were just talking about Richie's disappearance. Coast Guard was by talking to guys down at the harbor again. Art was filling me in."

A shadow came over her face and her tone chilled. It was common knowledge that she had banned Richie from the bar many years ago.

"Well, I'll agree, it's too bad—you always hate to have someone die—but he was bad news. I for one won't miss him in the least."

CHAPTER 50

ALL THE WAY HOME FROM MAUDSLAY, Dave kept thinking about their conversation, and by the time he neared the bridge, his mind was made up. If *Miss Cookie* was there, he'd stop and see Bryan before heading up for a shower.

As his tires hummed on the bridge's deck, he glanced down. *Miss Cookie* wasn't there, and he was surprised at the relief he felt, considering how concerned he had been. However, he was also really tired. Time for a beer and a shower. Tomorrow would be soon enough to talk to Bryan.

* * *

As he walked into the kitchen, he found Patti talking to an official-looking man.

"Dave, I'm glad you're here. This is Special Agent Alistaire Peeves from the Coast Guard Investigative Service."

Special Agent Peeves stepped toward Dave and held out an ID case in his left hand. Surprise, confusion, and a touch of concern washed over Dave's face as he looked toward the ID, over to Patti, and then back to Special Agent Peeves.

"Dave Wheeler," the agent said, as if making sure that he had the right person.

"Yes."

Nodding toward Patti, the officer said, "As your friend here said, I'm Special Agent Alistaire Peeves with the Coast Guard Investigative Service, and I'd like to ask you a few questions."

Patti interrupted. "It's about that boat that sank when you and Jack went fishing with Bryan."

Agent Peeves looked over at her.

In a sheepish voice she apologized. Then she asked, "Would either of you like a cold drink? Lemonade, a Coke, iced tea, beer?"

"No, thank you," said the agent. His voice was as stern as the look he gave her.

"Dave?"

As much as he wanted a beer, he said, "No. I'm all set."

Patti didn't say anything else, but she also didn't give any indication that she was going to leave.

"It's nice to meet you Special Agent . . . Peeves was it?" Dave offered his hand in greeting.

"Yes. That's correct."

"So, how can I help you?"

"A couple of weeks ago you were out on the fishing vessel *Miss Cookie*?"

"I was. Is this about what Patti just said, the boat that had sunk?"

"Yes. I'm following up on the original incident report that was filed by our responding crew. If I understand correctly, you saw smoke on the horizon, went to see if someone needed aid, and shortly thereafter you found a debris field."

"That's almost right. My friend Jack saw the smoke and convinced us to investigate."

"Us?"

"Bryan, who is the owner of *Miss Cookie,* and myself. There was only the three of us on the boat. But you knew that, didn't you?"

"So there was smoke on the horizon. What made you decide to go check it out?"

"It wasn't me. Like I said, my friend Jack first saw the smoke. Bryan and I were busy with our fishing lines when Jack spotted it."

"You didn't hear anything on your radio?"

"No. Nothing. We, Bryan and me, thought it was just another boat heading home, so we didn't really care. But Jack wanted to go check it out. We actually had to twist Bryan's arm and agree to pay for extra fuel and time."

Dave wiped a bead of sweat from his forehead and wished he had taken that beer.

"Soon after that we began finding debris. That's when we called it in to you. The Portsmouth Station told us to stand by until they could get out there. It was about an hour before they showed up."

"And while you were waiting, you continued to search the area for survivors?"

"We did, and all we found was debris."

"Just debris?"

"Yes."

"No sign of life, no one?"

Dave looked down and shook his head. Softly he said, "No one."

"You're sure?"

Dave hesitated just for a moment, recalling the urgent note in Sylvie's voice as she had emphasized her need to be dead.

"You all right?" asked Special Agent Peeves.

"Yes. Yes I am," said Dave. Then he added, "You know, thinking about it now, it was strange that we didn't see anything that even hinted that someone had been out there. But no, we did not."

Dave hoped that this last statement would satisfy Agent Peeves, because he didn't like the feeling he was getting.

"Interesting."

To change the subject, Dave suddenly asked, "Is it true that it was Richie Lowe's boat?"

It was obvious that Agent Peeves was not expecting that question. "Why do you ask?"

"That's just what I heard. You gotta' know that fishermen are as bad as women when it comes to gossip."

Regaining his official voice, Officer Peeves said, "You know, I can't confirm that officially at this time." Still, his expression said otherwise.

"But it seems likely," pressed Dave.

Peeves didn't say anything for several seconds and then he took over the questions again.

"Could you take me back to when the smoke was spotted? What was it exactly that made you go check it out?"

"Sure." Dave repeated the story again, minus a few small details like the shark, the way that Bryan was so reluctant to call the Coast Guard, and Sylvie. As he talked, he glanced in Patti's direction several times, hoping that she would catch his drift and not add anything to his narrative, and hoping that Special Agent Peeves wouldn't notice the looks exchanged between them.

Nearly three quarters of an hour passed before Dave finished. Looking straight at Special Agent Peeves he added, "And that's, as best I can recall, everything."

Agent Peeves had asked few questions, and taken no written notes. When Dave finished he said, "Just so I am perfectly clear on this, it wasn't until the smoke changed from black to white and then vanished that you became concerned enough to go check it out."

"No. We were already on the way when it changed from black to white."

"Thank you for your time and help. Here is my card. Please call me if you think of anything else."

"No problem."

Just as Special Agent Peeves reached the stairs, Dave added, "You know, Richie was a hard case. No one really trusted him, or would mess with him. There were always rumors about what he did outside of fishing. I don't think anyone will miss him. "

Special Agent Peeves did not respond and kept on going down and out.

CHAPTER 51

"WHAT WAS THAT ALL ABOUT?" asked Patti as soon as they were alone.

"What do you mean?"

"You know exactly what I mean. You didn't tell him everything. You didn't tell him about finding Sylvie. Why not?"

"You know about Sylvie?"

"Of course I know about her. Max told me that you guys had found her. Max also said that she was pretty mysterious. You—"

"Okay, that's enough, I get it. So then you also know that she asked us to keep her dead?"

She nodded.

"I gotta' talk to Jack."

"Well, I'm hungry. Why don't we go to Ben's? Maybe Max and Jack can meet us there."

Dave cracked his long overdue beer and said, "Give Max a call while I get cleaned up."

* * *

Max had joined Jack at the bar and was on her second drink when Dave and Patti walked in. After hugs and hellos, Dave and Patti ordered drinks, and Jack motioned to Courtney that they were going to sit out on the deck.

"Tell him," Patti said as they reached a table.

Jack looked over at Dave, who said nothing as he pulled out a chair and sat down.

Max handed her drink to Jack and said, "I'll be right back. I need the ladies room."

"I'll go too," said Patti.

"Long time no see," said Jack as he took a seat beside Dave.

"At least two whole hours." They laughed. Then Dave's expression turned serious. "I had the most interesting visitor waiting at my place when I got back this afternoon."

"Who?"

Dave took a card from his pocket, placed it on the table, and slid it toward Jack.

"Special Agent Alistaire Peeves, Coast Guard Investigative Service" Jack read aloud. "He was there waiting for you?"

"Seems he's looking into the sinking we had reported."

"You know, Art said they were asking questions here, too. I thought that was all set."

"So did I. But apparently, it's not. He was especially curious about when you spotted the smoke and what happened after. I kept getting the feeling that he knew something and was testing me to see what I knew."

"Did you —"

Dave cut him off before he could finish his thought. "No, I didn't tell him about Sylvie."

"What about Sylvie?" It was Max.

Before he could answer, Courtney walked over with their drinks. "Want to order some food?"

As soon as Courtney left with their orders, Max repeated, "What about Sylvie?"

Dave said, "This afternoon, when I got home after our run, an investigator from the Coast Guard was waiting for me."

"Patti just told me. What did he want?"

"He had questions about what happened on our fishing trip."

"Why?"

"He never really said. I think he was fishing—no pun intended."

"And you think he knows about Sylvie?"

"Don't know, but it wouldn't surprise me. Just something in the tone of his voice."

"Well, so?

As Dave paused, Jack could see that Max was getting anxious.

"Dave. Jack." She looked back and forth between them. "She is gone, isn't she?"

"Max, it's all right. She's gone now," Jack answered.

"What do you mean, now?"

Just then, Courtney returned with their dinners.

"Thanks, Court," said Jack.

"Well, enjoy. I'll check back in a bit."

"So, where were we?" asked Max. She picked up her fork and began moving food around on her plate.

Jack really didn't want to have this conversation, so he took a mouthful of food. Dave quickly followed his lead. Max looked at Patti, who shrugged.

"All right, all right," said Max. "I can see that I'm not going to get any more answers from you two tonight. But make no mistake, I will find out what's going on and if she's still around . . ." Max paused, "well, let's just say that it won't be pretty."

In an attempt to change the subject, Jack said, "So, Court's busy tonight. So who's Alicia?" asked Jack, while looking at her.

"Alicia's the one who's become such a pain in the ass lately. I think she has a new boyfriend and would rather spend time with him than work, if you know what I mean."

"She the cute one with the great rack?"

"Jack!" Max slapped him on the arm. "That's not very nice."

"I was just asking," he said, feigning innocence.

That took the edge off the conversation, and nothing else was said about Bryan, Sylvie, or fishing for the rest of the night, although the issue was far from resolved.

CHAPTER 52

JACK WAS UP EARLY. Sleep had come in fits and starts as thoughts of Sylvie floated in and out of his dreams. Who was she? At the time of the Rockdog Run, it had seemed like a one-time chance meeting with an attractive woman—end of story. But then she had reappeared shortly after the Francis House had burned, and things then had become even more complicated with the suspicious deaths that had accompanied that event. Elusive at the time to all but Jack, she had become a persistent temptation to him.

He made a cup of coffee and quietly slipped out. He needed some alone time to think. Often a run would suffice, but this morning it wasn't what he needed. Just a few years before, he would have walked down to the dock in front of Ben's, climbed aboard *Irrepressible*, and then, slipping her mooring lines, sailed out to greet the new day. But now, having lost her, the best he could do was walk down to the jetty to watch the new day begin. Once there, if he closed his eyes, the gentle shooshing of water against granite always reminded him of the sound her bow used to make as she cleaved the ocean. Sometimes, if he was lucky, he could even feel her gentle rise and fall as she slid over the swells.

This morning the air was cool, but judging from the sky he could tell that it was going to be another beautiful, late summer's day. Finding a niche in the jumble of granite that made up the jetty, he sat down and looked out over the ocean.

Sylvie, what have you gotten yourself into now? He thought back on how different everything would be around Rye Harbor if Giles Endroit and his development scheme had not been thwarted. He was convinced that Sylvie had played a role in stopping it. But, what kind of role? And how far had it gone? Jack suspected that she might have had a hand in putting June into her coma. Another case of "self-defense"?

And now Richie?

He imagined facing her, demanding answers to his questions, but he knew that was a fantasy at best. Even if they met in the future, he had no doubt that once again, it would be entirely on her terms. Everything with her was on her terms.

Damn you, Sylvie! What are you mixed up with this time

Still frustrated, Jack stood up, empty coffee mug in hand. He stretched and then began the walk home.

CHAPTER 53

AS HE OPENED THE DOOR, Cat dashed by, ran halfway up the stairs, turned, and glared at him, "Mrowh."

"Well, excuse me," he said to her. She turned her back to him and bound the rest of the way up the stairs.

"Where were you?" Max asked as he cleared the top stair.

"I didn't sleep very well last night. So I got up at sunrise and went down to the jetty. I needed to think."

"Well, I slept like a rock. Never even heard you get up. I was starting to get worried."

"Sorry."

"Thinking? About what?"

"Nothing really."

"Jack, if you didn't sleep, it wasn't nothing. Talk to me."

He didn't answer immediately. He knew that if he mentioned Sylvie, it would set Max off.

"You want to go get some breakfast?" he asked.

"That would be nice, but you know you're not getting off the hook that easily."

He knew that.

* * *

"Mornin', Jack. Max." It was Beverly.

"Mornin', Sunshine." Jack looked around Paula's for empty seats.

She gestured toward two empty places at the counter. "Coffee?"

Jack said yes but Max shook her head and mouthed "Tea."

By the time they had settled into their seats, Beverly was there with their drinks. "Late breakfast or early lunch?"

"Breakfast," they both said at the same time.

"Eggs Benedict, and Stuffed French Toast," repeated Beverly before turning away.

Sipping her tea, Max looked at him and asked, "So what's going on?"

"Nothing really."

The look she gave him made it clear that that answer wasn't sufficient.

"Okay . . . I was thinking about Sylvie."

She frowned and he added, "Stop. Not the way you're thinking."

"And what way is that?"

Ignoring her implications, he looked at her and said, "Bryan."

"Bryan what?"

"She and Bryan have been together."

"An affair?"

"I don't know if you'd call it that, but apparently they get together for booty calls."

"And you know this how?"

"Dave told me."

"Dave."

"Yes, Dave. Bryan told him."

"So why is this causing you to lose sleep?"

"Max."

"Don't Max me. So what if Bryan is having sex with Sylvie? Why should that bother you?"

"The sex part doesn't. But . . . ."

"But what?"

"Max, listen, ever since Dave told us that the Coast Guard was questioning him about our fishing trip, I've been thinking . . . ."

"Thinking what? About her?"

"No. Uh, yes. No. I'm just saying that whenever she's around, things seem to happen. She sinks Richie's boat and kills him in 'self-defense,' which, let's face it, it probably was. We find her out in the ocean and she tells us she has to stay dead. Her car gets stolen, her place gets broken into, the Coast Guard is still asking questions, she's banging Bryan, he helps her find some stuff out by Jeffreys, and then that body is found in the dumpster down in Hampton."

"Here we go." Beverly placed two plates in front of them. "Refills?"

"Thanks, looks delicious. Sure, I'll have some more coffee," said Jack.

"I'm all set. Thanks," said Max.

"What stuff out by Jeffreys?" Max asked while she began eating her Eggs Benedict.

"That's part of what's bothering me. Dave said that Bryan took her back out to where we had been fishing and they hauled up the mysterious package that we had found when we were out there."

"Back up. What package that you found when you were out there?"

"I didn't tell you?"

She shook her head. "Jack. Eat. Your food's getting cold."

As he started to eat his French Toast, Beverly stopped by to check on things. "This is really good," he said. "Walnuts?"

"Yeah. Walnut and cream cheese filling. Cook'll be glad to hear you like it."

Jack had wolfed down more than half his breakfast before he resumed his story.

Max listened, then said, "So what was in the package?"

"Don't know. Apparently Bryan looked while she was off the boat, but before he could tell Dave, she returned. Dave said that Bryan was spooked, but he didn't hang around."

They finished their meal in silence. After Beverly had picked up their empty plates, Max said, "This isn't your problem. It's Bryan's."

"I know it isn't my problem, but excuse me if I am a bit worried. I mean, I was on the boat when we first caught that package. Whatever was in there was enough to scare Bryan. Given Sylvie's past history and the body count when she was involved in the Francis House scandal, I don't think it's unreasonable to be worried."

"I suppose. What are you doing the rest of today?"

"Not sure. I'll probably go over to the Harbor and hang out. Maybe go for a run later. You?"

"Patti and I are going out to the malls shopping."

"Sounds like trouble."

CHAPTER 54

"HEY, LEWIS," CALLED OUT JACK.

Lewis stopped and turned, his face blank, emotionless. He had just climbed up onto the commercial pier and was walking toward his truck, an older model Chevy that looked as tired and worn as its owner. It was dark blue and well dented, and even from a distance Jack could smell the long- dead, sun-dried bits of whatever remained attached to mostly unrecognizable pieces of fishing gear that were piled in the bed. Its tailgate was missing and rust ate at its corners. Behind, Jack could see Lewis's boat tied to the floats.

As Jack neared, Lewis shuffled his feet as if he was in a hurry.

"Lewis, I just wanted to say how sorry I am about your brother."

He stared at Jack for a moment before replying. "What's it to you?"

"Hey, I'm just saying that I'm sorry we didn't get there sooner."

Lewis continued to stare at Jack in silence.

Not sure whether he'd reply, Jack said, "I'll let you go. I just wanted to say sorry." He began to turn away.

"Did you find her?"

Those four words stopped him in his tracks. "What did you say?"

"You heard me."

"Find who?" Jack's heart was beginning to pound.

"You know. That fucking cunt who killed my brother and sank his boat."

Now it was Jack's turn to stare. He almost felt dizzy. A jumble of thoughts flew through his head, and his vision tunneled down to where all he could see was Lewis's face. Gone were the sounds of gulls crying, gone were the cars driving past, pulling trailers, ready to launch their boats, gone were the crowds of tourists waiting to go on a whale watch. His stunned silence lasted but seconds yet it felt like an eternity.

"What are you talking about?" he managed to say when he found his voice.

"Look, Jack, You know exactly what I mean."

"I don't. You'd better tell me."

Lewis looked at Jack as if he had just been insulted. "I'm not wasting my time with you."

He turned and continued walking toward his truck, leaving Jack standing alone.

"Wait! Lewis!" Jack followed after him.

His hand was on the door handle when Jack came up from behind. "Lewis. Talk to me."

He stopped, turned, and faced Jack again.

"I don't really have anything to say to you."

"Lewis. I'm sorry about your brother. You said he was out with a woman and she killed him. I need to know what you meant."

"I meant exactly what I said. It was that bitch who was hanging around when the Francis House burned. The one that you were messin' 'round with."

"What!"

"You heard me."

"Lewis, talk to me."

"No." He began to pull his truck door open.

Jack pushed it shut. "Yes."

Lewis turned and faced Jack. The look on his face made Jack wonder if he had gone too far.

Jack took half a step back and relaxed his voice. "Forget what you think I was doing with this woman—that's all bullshit. Tell me about her and Richie. It's important."

"I don't think I can help you much. You know we weren't close."

"I know, but you were still brothers. Talk to me. C'mon Lewis."

Lewis yanked the door to his truck open, climbed in, and started the engine. But as he began to drive away, he leaned out the window and called back to Jack. "All right. Meet you back here after dark."

CHAPTER 55

THE DUST FROM LEWIS'S DEPARTURE hadn't even settled when Jack heard an unfamiliar voice call his name.

Jack turned and found himself fact to face with a man about his size. The man was wearing khaki slacks and a short-sleeved shirt. His face was tanned and clean-shaven, his bearing confident, and commanding.

"Jack Beale," he said again.

"Yes."

"I'm Special Agent Alistaire Peeves with the Coast Guard Investigative Service." He offered a leather badge case to Jack.

Jack examined the badge and handed it back.

"Nice to meet you, Special Agent Peeves. How may I help you?" He offered his hand and they shook. Peeves had quite a strong grip.

"I'll get right to the point. As I'm sure you know, I had a conversation with your friend Dave."

"Yes, he told me."

"Good. Then you know why I want to talk to you."

"I'm not sure what else I can tell you. We talked to the responding officer when we found the wreckage."

"Yes, your account was clear. However, I'm looking at some other aspects that I feel may have been—shall we say—less than apparent."

Jack knew where this was going, and he had no plans to divulge any more than what he had said during the initial interview.

"Buy you a lemonade?" he asked. It was about noon and the sun was hot. The line at the snack shack wasn't too long yet, and he motioned toward one of the picnic benches.

"Sure." The two men walked over to an empty bench. Special Agent Peeves sat down while Jack went for the drinks.

"Here you go." Jack handed him the bottle of lemonade and a straw before sitting down himself.

"So, how can I help you?"

"First, tell me what you know of Richie Lowe."

"Most of what I knew of Richie was anecdotal. I never really had much direct contact with him, but I know plenty of people who had trouble with him. A number of years ago he was banned from Ben's." Jack motioned toward Ben's.

"What was that about?"

"He was in the bar. He'd had a few too many and got into an argument. Let's just say he wasn't welcome after that."

"Who?"

"Who, who?"

"Who'd he have the argument with?"

"I don't remember."

"You don't remember. You're telling me that the incident was so serious he got banned from Ben's, but you don't remember who it was with?"

"Yes. I'm sorry, I don't. It was quite a while ago."

"I see." The two men stared at each other.

Jack looked away first. "Tell me. Why this interest in Richie? He in trouble for something other than being an asshole?"

Jack noticed that Special Agent Peeves nearly cracked a smile.

"Whenever something happens on the water that results in a death, we always take a closer look. What do you know about his brother?"

"Lewis? He's okay. A bit of a loner. Keeps to himself. Not an asshole like Richie was."

"You seen him around?"

"Haven't. Sorry."

"If you do see him, would you let him know I would like to talk with him?"

"Sure."

Special Agent Peeves stood and looked down at Jack. "Thanks for the lemonade."

"No problem. Sorry that I wasn't much help."

Jack stood and they shook hands, once again firmly, and then Special Agent Alistaire Peeves started to leave. After a few steps he stopped, looked back at Jack, and said, "I'm sure we'll be seeing each other again." Then he walked away.

CHAPTER 56

"WHO WAS THAT?"

Jack turned toward the voice behind him. It was Eleanor.

"Ellie, what's up?"

"Just got rid of the two whale watch boats. No one's launching, and I saw that officious-looking man talking to you, so I'm being nosy. What's going on?"

"He's an investigator for the Coast Guard. Looking for Lewis."

"Lewis, hunh?"

"Yeah. Said he was wanted to talk to him about Richie."

"I thought that was all taken care of."

"So did I, but apparently not."

"Ever since Richie's boat disappeared, Lewis has been kind of scarce."

"I know. Although I did see him just before that investigator showed up. I'm going to meet him later."

"Jack, you be careful. Even though I don't think Lewis is involved in any of the shit Richie was, I'd still be careful if I were you."

"I will. I've got to get going. See you soon."

"'Bye Jack."

* * *

Later in the afternoon, when he was sure Dave would be home from work, Jack gave him a call.

"Jack! What's up?"

"You know that Coast Guard guy you told me about? Well, he caught up to me down at the harbor around noon."

"What'd he want?"

"Asked a bunch of questions. Mostly the same things he asked you, but he was also looking for Lewis."

"Lewis?"

"Richie's brother. I guess he hasn't been around much since Richie disappeared. Funny thing was, just before the agent turned up, I actually spoke with Lewis. I'm going to meet him later tonight."

"Did you tell Peeves you're meeting with Lewis?"

"No. I want to see what Lewis might know about what Richie was up to and how Sylvie was involved. Lewis clearly knows something about her, but if the authorities get to him first, we may never know what they were up to. You seen Bryan?"

"Haven't. Let me know how your meeting with Lewis goes."

"Will do."

* * *

By the time Jack left Dave's, the sun was nearly down and it took him as long to drive through the beach area as it did for him to drive all the way from Rye Harbor earlier. The bumper-to-bumper traffic crept along, not much faster than a brisk walk, and sometimes was even slower. Driving down the strip, he felt out of place in his plain old pickup truck. Jack chuckled as the thought occurred to him that the scene he was witnessing was just like a nature documentary on the mating habits of some exotic species.

Loud, tricked out cycles, cars with too-dark tinted windows, convertibles with tops down, radios blaring, and jacked-up trucks with lots of chrome were the plumage of attraction for the young men driving, as they showed off for the throngs of young women walking along on the sidewalks. And the young women took notice in their too-tight, too-small and often colorful outfits.

A cacophony of sounds complemented this visual feast. Bells, whistles, and clangs from the arcades, music from the outdoor bandstand or the muted sounds of some band performing behind a club's closed doors filled the cab of his truck.

The crowds thinned, and his speed increased the further he drove away from the center of the beach. Soon, all he could hear was the whoosh of his tires on the road and the rush of air through the open windows. By the time the harbor was in sight, the sun had set completely and the moon was rising over the ocean. After taking the turn toward Ben's, he turned left just before the bridge and drove toward the commercial pier where he hoped to find Lewis.

CHAPTER 57

AS JACK NEARED THE PIER THAT EVENING, he could see several fishing boats tied up, probably awaiting an early morning departure. A single flood-light lit the pier, and he could see a lone pickup truck and a late model car parked next to each other on the pier. The truck didn't belong to Lewis. In fact, he didn't recognize either vehicle, although one of the men glanced his way as he drove past.

By the time Jack reached the harbormaster's shed, he was begin-ning to wonder if Lewis would show. A glance at the clock on his dash told him it was only a bit past 9:30. He decided to wait until 10:00.

Jack parked in the section of the parking lot that was reserved for the crews of the party boats. From his vantage point, he had a clear view straight down the launching ramp and out over the harbor. All was quiet. He could see silent headlights out on the boulevard as it snaked around the harbor. If he listened closely, he could hear muffled laughter, the murmur of voices, and the clinking of glasses. Another summer's evening on the deck at Ben's was coming to an end.

As the numbers on his dashboard clock clicked over from 9:59 to 10:00, a set of headlights moved slowly toward him from the direction of the commercial pier.

"C'mon, Lewis." He mouthed the words, but his anticipation turned to disappointment as the car turned toward the boulevard, its lights sweeping through his cab. It was the car he had seen on the pier, and a few minutes later the truck followed, its headlights sweeping through his cab as well. "Damn," he thought. "Where are you Lewis?"

As he twisted around to watch the truck drive out of sight, a voice called out from the darkness beside him.

"So, what do you want?"

The voice startled Jack. He turned his head and found Lewis staring at him through the driver's side window.

"Lewis. Jesus, you scared the shit out of me."

Lewis continued to stare at Jack. Then he said, "So?"

Jack rolled down the window another notch. "Earlier, you said that your brother was out with . . . uh, Sylvie, and you wanted to know if we found her."

"Sylvie?"

"Sorry, That's her name— the woman from the Francis House." Jack pulled on his door handle, pushed the door open, and stepped out of the cab. "You said Richie was out with Sylvie."

"Sylvie?" Lewis repeated her name in a voice not much louder than a whisper.

"Yes. Sylvie. What can you tell me about her and Richie?"

Lewis remained silent.

"Lewis! It's important."

"Like I said earlier, me and Richie weren't real close. but a while back he told me about this sweet deal he had goin'."

"What deal?"

"Sounded like every now and again he'd get a call with some coordinates, you know—latitude and longitude. Then he'd go out, drag a grappling hook around, and haul out whatever he had to retrieve. When he brought it back, he'd get paid a ton of cash for the package."

"Who'd he give the package to?"

"He never said."

"So what makes you think Sylvie killed him?"

"Just before that last trip, he called me. Said it was going to be his last one. Said he was going to make a killing, wouldn't have to fish for a living ever again."

"Did he say anything else?"

"Only that he was taking someone with him on this trip."

"And you think it was Sylvie. Why?"

"A feelin'. Time was, we were close, and I could always tell when he had something going with a girl."

"Did he actually say it was her?"

"No."

Jack was sure he detected the briefest hesitation before Lewis continued. "I asked again who he was taking out, but he wouldn't say."

"Lewis. I don't understand. Why are you so sure it was her?"

"I am. I just am."

Lewis began to turn away, but Jack grabbed his arm and turned him back.

"Tell me! What did he say that makes you so sure it was Sylvie?"

Lewis looked at Jack. Even in the shadows, Jack could tell that he was torn.

"Please."

"He said that you weren't the only one. That she wanted to go with him. I knew it couldn't be Max, and after those rumors, I assumed it was her."

"So he took her?"

"I guess. He said she made him an offer he couldn't refuse."

"And you think she killed him."

"Yeah."

"Why don't you think it wasn't just some freak accident out there?"

"Jack, you know her. You know about all those bodies last time she was in town. Ain't no accident if you ask me. And what I really want to know is if you found her."

"Lewis, no. No, we didn't. First we saw some smoke, then, the smoke disappeared. By the time we got there the boat was gone. Everything was gone. Nothing out there but debris." Jack was glad the darkness was concealing his expression as he lied. He added, "You know a Coast Guard investigator is looking for you."

"I heard. But some other guys have been asking too. Seems best to just not be around."

Jack thought about the guys he had just seen over at the commercial pier.

"Listen, Lewis, thanks for talking with me. Something tells me you're right to be cautious. Here's my number. You need anything, feel free to call."

"What's it to you?"

"Just take care, Lewis."

Jack climbed back into his truck as Lewis walked off into the night. During the brief ride home, he reached a conclusion: With so many questions unanswered, he was going to have to find Sylvie. And Bryan might be the best place to start.

IT WAS MID-AFTERNOON by the time Jack drove back down to Hampton Beach to find Bryan. Max had gone to work.

Since parking at the harbor was sure to be scarce, he parked at Dave's and walked down to the docks. He figured that if *Miss Cookie* were there maybe Bryan would be too.

When he got to the pier, he stopped and surveyed the harbor. Only one party fishing boat remained on its mooring, more than half of the slips in the marina were empty, and the docks were clear. He wasn't sure what he had expected, but that made perfect sense. After all, on a glorious day like this, who wouldn't want to be out on the water. Discouraged at not seeing *Miss Cookie,* he was about to turn and leave, sure that this had been a wasted trip, when a cloud of black smoke belched from the back of that lone remaining party boat. Jack watched as one of the crew on the boat cast off the mooring. Slowly the boat turned toward the dock, smoke billowing from its stern, and behind it he finally noticed *Miss Cookie*, still on her mooring, her skiff trailing off the stern. Maybe he would find Bryan after all.

"Hey, Jack," Dave's voice startled him. He had been alternately staring out at *Miss Cookie* and watching the smoking party boat slowly move toward the dock.

"Dave! What are you doing here?"

"Got out of work early, saw your truck, and guessed you might be down here. What's up?"

"I was hoping to catch up to Bryan. This Sylvie stuff is bugging me and I wanted to talk to him."

Dave pointed to the boat and said, "Skiff's there, so he's on board. *Miss Cookie*'s been gone for a few days. Must have returned last night. I'll go with you."

"How we gonna' get out there?"

Having laid a steady smoke screen all the way to the docks, the party boat had just finished tying up and had shut down the offending engine.

"I know those guys," Dave said, motioning toward the boat. "Come on."

* * *

It wasn't long before Dave and Jack were in a skiff, motoring out toward *Miss Cookie.*

"Nice of them to loan us their skiff," Jack said.

"He thinks they blew a gasket. They'll be there all night trying to fix it. Had to cancel a trip today. Won't be needing it"

"Still, it's nice of them."

"He told me something else that didn't make any sense," said Dave as he guided the borrowed skiff out to the *Miss Cookie.*

"What was that?

"They told me that they saw Bryan picked up a couple of guys this morning here at the dock."

"So, that's what he does."

"I know, but these two guys he picked up with his skiff and took them back to his mooring. Never went out."

Jack gave his friend a puzzled look.

"That's what they said."

* * *

Dave expertly laid the skiff up to *Miss Cookie.* "Bryan!" he called out.

There was no reply. The cockpit had quite a few crushed beer cans strewn about and the door to the deckhouse was open.

"This doesn't look good," said Dave in a low voice.

"Why're you whispering?"

Dave suddenly looked embarrassed. "Don't know!" Then he called out Bryan's name again and knocked on the hull. No answer.

He turned to Jack. "Something just feels wrong."

"Well, you certainly shouted loud enough. He's probably passed out below. Let's go see."

"Bryan! You here?" Dave called out again before climbing aboard. Taking the painter from Jack, he secured the skiff while Jack climbed over the rail.

"Must have been a rough one," said Jack. He picked up several of the crushed beer cans and tossed them into a bucket before moving toward the open deckhouse door and calling Bryan's name.

"Any sign of him?" asked Dave.

"No. Maybe he's up forward."

The companionway door was closed. As Jack stepped into the deckhouse, his foot kicked a bottle, which rattled across the floor and stopped underneath the table.

"Man, no wonder he's not answering us," said Jack. He reached down and picked up the empty rum bottle.

Dave passed him and knocked on the companionway door. "Bryan! You in here?"

As before there was no answer, so he turned the knob, pulled the door open, and peered in.

"He in there?" asked Jack.

Dave was silent for a long moment as he stared into the cabin. Then, quietly, he said, "No."

"Everything all right?"

"No." And with that Dave disappeared down into the cabin.

Jack followed right behind him. The cabin was a mess—torn apart, with broken cups and plates smashed across the floor. The door to the head was open, swinging back and forth as *Miss Cookie* rocked gently. There was a hole in the door, just about fist size, and the bedding was strewn about, but there was no actual sign of Bryan.

"What were you up to, Bryan?" Dave's voice barely rose above a whisper. "What the hell happened?"

"Whatever happened, it certainly doesn't look good."

Dave continued to move through the cabin, picking up objects, starting at them, and then putting them back down again. "I don't think this was all his doing."

"Why not?"

"It's not Bryan. I mean, I've known him a long time. We've gotten drunk together on more than one occasion. He's not a violent drunk. He'd just drink himself to sleep."

"Maybe something happened that set him off?"

"I can't imagine."

"What about Sylvie?"

"What?"

"He'd been having an affair with her. He helped her retrieve that package. Maybe she came back. Maybe something about that went wrong. We've already agreed that she's trouble. What if she did something that set him off?"

"I don't think so," Dave said. "I got the impression that after she hauled her stuff away, he didn't expect to see her again."

"What about those two guys that your friends saw him with? Did they see him take 'em back?"

"Didn't say. They were mostly down in the engine room."

"Well, his skiff's here, so probably a safe bet that he did. I doubt they swam."

"Or, someone came out and got them, leaving him aboard."

"So, where is he?"

"No idea."

"Let's wait a while and see if he comes back."

The tide was coming in so *Miss Cookie* was stern to the west, giving them a great view of the sunset and bathing the nuke plant in shades of pink.

CHAPTER 59

AT FIRST, NEIGHER JACK NOR DAVE paid any attention to the sirens. After all, it was the end of summer, and the hotels and motels of Hampton Beach were still filled to capacity. They both knew that bumper thumpers, beach fires, and disagreements that required official response were common. It wasn't until the first police car crossed the bridge going north with lights flashing and siren screaming that they began to pay attention. As the number of sirens increased, and more emergency vehicles began converging, both from the south and from Hampton Beach proper to the north, they couldn't stop watching.

"What the hell is going on?" asked Jack.

They could see a cluster of red and blue flashing lights out by the entrance to the harbor where the north side breakwater began, and there was a great deal of activity down by the edge of the water.

"Someone probably fell on the rocks," said Dave.

"It's possible, but doesn't that seem to be a bit of an over-the-top response?"

"It does, but you know how they all like to get in on the action, especially when it's not routine."

"Everyone is here. Look, the Marine Patrol has just arrived." Jack pointed to the grey and silver boat that had just appeared with its blue lights flashing.

"We gotta' go check it out."

"What about Bryan?"

"Well, he's not here."

* * *

When they returned the borrowed skiff to Dave's friends, they towed Bryan's skiff in behind them, leaving it tied to the dock. The short walk from the dock to the scene of the commotion took longer than Jack had expected. There was so much traffic it seemed that everyone wanted to see what was going on. By the time they had pushed their way to the front of the crowd, the rescue team was beginning to crest the breakwater with someone—or something—strapped securely into an aluminum-framed rescue stretcher. An EMT walked beside it

Jack's memory flashed back to the Francis House fire, when a body had been found in the ashes. It was the last time he had seen a stretcher like that.

A few minutes later, the last member of the rescue team clambered up over the rocks.

Officers had strung up yellow tape, and as Jack watched he could see that now the police team manning the perimeter appeared to be torn between doing their job of keeping the crowd back and their desire to see what was going on.

Jack turned toward Dave and asked, "So, what do you think?"

Dave was so focused on watching the action, he didn't respond.

"Dave!"

"Yeah, what?"

Jack was about to repeat his question when Dave called out, "Kevin!"

Dave waved at one of the cops inside the yellow barrier. "Kevin!" he called out again.

Jack watched as the cop walked toward them.

"Hey, Dave."

"What's going on?"

"The captain of one of the party boats thought he spotted something in the rocks down by the water as he came in from a trip. He reports it, the tide had just started coming in and this is the result."

"Any ideas what happened?"

"Not really."

"You seen the body yet?"

"Nah. I really don't like looking at bodies. I'll just stay over here. I'm happy just keeping you ghouls away. I'll give you a call if I hear anything. Gotta' go."

"Thanks, Kevin. See you around."

"Damn," said Jack

"That sucks."

They watched as the stretcher was loaded into the waiting ambulance. The doors shut, but it didn't take off immediately.

Jack said, "Sure are taking their time leaving. Maybe he's not dead."

* * *

"Come on, Jack. We've got to go." Dave tugged on Jack's arm and then began pushing his way through the crowd.

The urgency in his voice surprised Jack, but he didn't have time to even respond.

"Dave. Wait up."

He couldn't tell if Dave even heard him, and Jack had to sprint to catch up to his friend. They were nearly at the Wok by the time Jack caught up. "Dave! Slow down."

Dave's pace actually increased, and he said nothing while Jack stayed a step behind.

"Dave! What the hell is up with you?" said Jack. He was finally able to reach out and touch Dave's shoulder as they reached the marina entrance.

Dave stopped and turned suddenly, nearly causing Jack to run into him.

"Did you see that Coast Guard Investigator?"

"No I didn't."

"I did, and I have a bad feeling. I want to get back out to Bryan's boat."

With that, Dave turned and hurried off again. Jack had no choice but to follow.

"I've got to do something. Wait by the skiff, I'll be right back," Dave said to his friend; then he walked off before Jack could reply. All he could do was watch as Dave walked down the dock to the crippled party boat and climbed aboard.

In less than five minutes, Dave joined Jack in the skiff and all he said was "Let's go."

A soon as they reached *Miss Cookie* Dave climbed on board while Jack secured the skiff.

"Are you going to tell me what this is all about?" said Jack as he joined Dave in the deckhouse.

"I think that the body they found was Bryan."

"What! Whatever gives you that idea?"

"Remember the guys on the party boat told us that they saw Bryan pick up two guys and take them out to his boat?"

"So."

"Before, I saw that Coast Guard investigator over where the body was recovered, it just struck me that it might be Bryan. Just now when I stopped at the party boat, I asked them again about those two guys. Before, Stevie, the mate, wasn't there when I borrowed their skiff. He was now, and he told me he saw them getting picked up from *Miss Cookie* by someone in one of those testosterone boats and they headed out of the harbor really fast."

"So from this you've deduced that they somehow killed Bryan and left his body down on the rocks in broad daylight."

"It's possible. Hey, did you notice what's missing?"

"No, what?"

"Sylvie's panties."

"What?"

"They're not here. Now bear with me. We know she's trouble. We know she and Bryan had been getting it on and she left them here—a souvenir. And we know that he helped her retrieve something. What if those two guys who were here today were really looking for her, and as they questioned him, they found the panties and took them as proof that she was around. When he wouldn't or couldn't tell them where she was, they killed him."

"Dave, are you on drugs or something?"

"Come on. Admit it— it's possible."

"I suppose, but it's a stretch."

"You know, we ought to get out of here."

CHAPTER 60

JACK AND DAVE REMAINED on the pier overlooking the floats until the last State Police Crime Scene truck drove away. By now, the afterglow of the sunset had faded to dark, the nuke plant was fully lit, and the tide was more than halfway in. The steady rhum, rhum, rhum of tires on the bridge as the daily beach crowd departed provided a backdrop for the final words of their conversation.

"Listen, whatever happens next in terms of an investigation, we try to stay out of it as much as possible," said Jack.

"Agreed," said Dave. "But those guys who loaned us the skiff did see us go out to Bryan's boat."

"Well, we went out there looking for him and he wasn't there, right? Nothing but the truth in that."

"Right."

"Listen, I've got to get going." Jack paused and then added, "You really think that it was Bryan?"

"Hope not. But I have a bad feeling."

* * *

Jack remembered little of the ride home. He couldn't wait to tell Max about what they had seen. Ben's was still open and he knew she was closing so he stopped in. The bell on the door clingled as Jack walked in. In spite of the steady wrooshing sound of the lobster tanks, he knew Max would hear the bell. Before he was halfway down the hall, he saw her head peeking around the corner from the bar.

When she saw it was him, she rounded the corner and gave him a welcoming hug and kiss. "What're you doing here?'

"You wouldn't believe the night Dave and I just had. How're things here?"

"Not bad. Busy early and now there are only a couple of parties finishing up. Won't be long."

"Good."

They walked into the bar arm in arm. "Beer?" asked Max.

"Sure."

She pulled away from him and went to draw his beer while he took a seat at the bar.

"Hey, Jack." Patti walked in.

"Patti."

"What've you been up to?"

"Not much. I was down to Hampton Harbor and saw Dave. A body was found on the rocks by the entrance to the harbor." He tried to keep his tone as matter-of-fact as possible.

Before Patti could reply, Max returned with his beer.

"You went down to see Dave," she said. "I didn't know that. What's this about a body?" she said as she put his beer in front of him.

"They found a body on the rocks by the entrance to the harbor." He repeated his original statement.

"God, another one?" Max asked. "Didn't they just pull some guy out of a dumpster? Do they know who it was on the rocks? What happened?"

"Don't know. Actually, I went down to try to find Bryan. He wasn't around, but Dave showed up."

Max interrupted. "Bryan?"

"Yeah, between the questions from the Coast Guard and Richie's brother, Lewis, I just felt like I needed to talk to Bryan."

Patti, who had been quietly standing there as Max interrogated Jack, now spoke up. "So you really went down to see Bryan. But I thought you told me you went down to see Dave."

"Not exactly. I went down to see Bryan and then Dave saw my truck parked at your place and walked down to the harbor. He borrowed a skiff and we went out to *Miss Cookie* together. We didn't find Bryan, but his boat was a mess. Looked like someone had been on quite a bender."

"Then what?"

"We saw a lot of emergency vehicles heading toward rocks at the entrance of the harbor, on the Hampton side, so we went to see what was going on." He stopped to sip his beer.

"And?" prompted Max.

"And, we walked over there and they brought a body up over the rocks. I guess they had to work fast because the tide was coming in." Anticipating their next questions, he said, "And no, we didn't get a look at whoever it was. Best guess is that it was someone fishing, probably slipped, hit his head, and, well, that was it."

"Gotta' go finish up my tables," said Patti.

Max had been looking at Jack closely. As soon as Patti was gone she said, "There's more. Isn't there?"

"Why do you say that?"

"Because I know you. So give."

"Fine. Bryan's boat was a mess, I told you. And he wasn't there. When they brought up the body, that's when Dave saw the Coast Guard guy and got all weird. Dave insisted we leave and then we went back out to Bryan's boat."

"And?"

Jack didn't respond right away. He just sat silently with a strange look on his face and sipped his beer.

"Jack— And?"

"And, Dave's pretty sure that Bryan was the one killed because the panties were gone."

"Panties? What panties? What the hell are you talking about?"

Jack blushed, realizing too late that only he, Dave, and Bryan knew this secret. But the way Max stared at him now left him no choice but to tell her.

"Bryan had some black lace panties, a souvenir of—shall we say—a memorable evening. He kept them and said they were 'lucky'."

"*Whose* panties?"

Jack had been afraid this question was coming.

"Sylvie's."

The brief moment of silence that followed his statement only added emphasis to her reaction. "Sylvie's! We have to talk."

Patti walked in at that moment. "What do we have to talk about?"

"Nothing." Max turned away to begin closing the bar and Jack sipped his beer.

"Fine! Don't tell me!" Patti began to march out in a huff, but at the door she turned back and added, "You know you will eventually."

* * *

Max had walked to work so she rode home with Jack. Neither made any move to get out after he parked, switched off the engine, and turned off the lights.

"So, Jack, what's this about Sylvie and Bryan?" asked Max in a soft voice.

Jack didn't answer right away, but Max didn't have to ask again. The silence and the close, confined dark space of the truck cab felt like a confessional, and her question demanded the answer.

"All I know is what I heard from Dave. After we took Sylvie home, she hooked up with Bryan on his boat in Newburyport. The next morning, while he slept, she left, sans panties. A day or so later, she got him to take her out to retrieve that package we hooked on our trip."

"Stop right there. What package?"

"I thought I told you."

"No. You didn't"

Jack told her about the large object and the grappling hook and then continued. "According to Dave, they pulled up three waterproof cases. She wouldn't tell Bryan what was in them, but he looked when he had the chance. Dave said he was pretty shaken up. He never told Dave what was in them. If that really was his body out on the rocks, maybe we'll never know."

CHAPTER 61

"I UNDERSTAND. I'll meet you at one, over at the harbor," was all Jack could say before his phone went dead. Rather than putting his cell phone back into his pocket, he placed a call.

"Dave, you won't believe who just called me."

"You're right, I won't."

"It was that Coast Guard investigator. He wants to meet me. Said he has some questions about Bryan."

"Bryan?"

"That's what he said."

"What do you think he's looking for?"

"No idea."

* * *

Jack went down to the harbor early. As he was talking to Eleanor, Special Investigator Alistaire Peeves drove up.

"Ellie, have you met Investigator Peeves?"

"Yes, we've met," she said, extending her hand.

"It's nice to see you again, ma'am." From his body language and his clipped greeting, it was obvious that this was not a social call.

Ellie got the message and excused herself as he turned his attention toward Jack.

"Shall we?" He gestured for Jack to follow him.

They walked past the launching ramp toward the far end of the parking lot.

"So, what can I help you with?" asked Jack.

"I'm still looking for Lewis. You haven't seen him, have you?"

Jack hesitated for a split second before answering. "No. I haven't."

Special Agent Peeves glanced over at him. Then he continued.

"And your friend Bryan?"

Something about the way he asked that set off an alarm in Jack's head. "No."

"When did you last see him?"

"Few days ago. I actually went down to Hampton yesterday looking for him, didn't find him, wasn't on his boat."

"You went looking for him? Why?"

The alarm got louder. "Had a fishing question. Thought he could answer it."

"What time was that?"

"Don't know exactly. Late afternoon? His boat was there, but like I said, he wasn't on it."

Before the officer could ask another question, Jack said, "Wasn't there something about a body they found down there last night?" Jack watched the agent's face closely.

"Yes, they did find someone."

"You heard anything about it? There hasn't been much in the news."

The agent hesitated. "I'm sure you haven't heard anything because they haven't been able to notify the family yet."

"I suppose."

"What can you tell me about Bryan?"

"Not much. I think I've told you all I know."

"Jack, let me be frank with you. We think Richie was involved with some kind of smuggling operation, and we also think that Bryan may have been involved. If you know anything, it would be a good idea to tell us."

"I'm sorry, but I don't."

"Okay. But I do expect to hear from you if you remember anything else."

Having reached the end of the parking lot, they turned and walked back in silence. When they reached the officer's car, he turned toward

Jack and said, "Jack, I'm going to tell you something that maybe I shouldn't, but you need to understand what's at stake and just how important it is that you trust me."

Jack waited for him to continue.

"It was your friend Bryan whose body was recovered last night."

Suddenly Jack's legs felt weak. Suspecting it and hearing it were really two separate things.

"Nothing has been released to the press yet. We really are still looking for some family to notify. But this isn't a game. I'm afraid that whoever Richie was involved with is now taking steps to make sure that he—or she—can't be identified. It's not unreasonable to expect that anyone who knew Richie or Bryan or was involved with either of them could be at risk also."

The first name that flashed through Jack's head was Sylvie. Was he right to keep her secret? Was she in danger—or was he?

"Jack." The officer broke into his thoughts. "You take care now. And if you see Lewis, let him know I'd like to talk with him."

He got into his car and drove off, leaving Jack dazed and confused.

CHAPTER 62

"COME ON DAVE, LET'S GET THIS DONE," his surveying partner, Smitty, shouted to him.

Today they were down in the Lanesville area of Gloucester. It was an area where it was easier to quarry the granite just under the surface of the land than it was to farm the thin layer of soil on top. The street they were working on had many homes that had been built by the Finnish quarrymen. The houses were long and narrow from front to back, with beautifully crafted stone foundations.

While Smitty drove up and down the street setting up signs to caution drivers that they were working there, Dave began to set up the equipment. In addition to their modern laser and GPS-enhanced equipment, he also set up an antique transit that he owned. Just as some sailors liked to shoot the stars with a sextant and calculate their position manually using the *Nautical Almanac*, he wanted to test his transit's accuracy and exercise his skills in plotting the old-fashioned way.

With his equipment in place, Dave looked through the eyepiece of the antique transit and slowly turned the adjustment knob in an effort to get a feel for its range and clarity. One of the targets he chose was a mailbox next to a wall of arborvitae that screened a house from the street. He could clearly see the number 27 on it. Impressed at how sharp the resolution was, he began to slowly rotate the transit away from the mailbox toward a new target further down the road, where his partner was. As he did, an approaching car filled the eyepiece.

Blurred at first, the driver's face came into perfect focus for a split second before it began to blur again.

"It can't be," he thought to himself as he frantically worked the adjustment knob, trying to bring the driver's face back into focus. He succeeded a split second before the car turned into the drive at number

27. "Sylvie?" he thought to himself.

A voice crackled in his ear. "Dave, you ready?"

He said nothing and continued to stare through his transit at where the car had disappeared up the driveway at number 27.

"Dave?"

"Yeah."

"Stop watching the hot chick in that car."

"What?"

"You heard me. I saw her too. But c'mon, Dave. You've seen hot women before. Let's get this done."

For the next hour they worked together as Dave recorded the readings in a small spiral bound notebook. Later they could compare this raw data to the current data on file and make any needed corrections. Between sights, while his partner changed locations, Dave looked back through his antique transit toward the drive by the arborvitae. As the amount of time that passed without another sighting increased, the more he began to question what he had been so sure of earlier.

* * *

Just as Dave was closing his notebook to call it a day, a new car pulled up and stopped in front of number 27. He still had his antique transit set up, so he walked over and turned the focus knob. As the car came into focus, he saw two men, backs to him, just disappearing from sight up the drive.

When they didn't return, he shrugged and began to pack his equipment. Moments later he heard Smitty shout his name, but before he had time to look up, the sounds of squealing tires and an engine accelerating filled his ears. He barely had enough time to jump back out of the way. Then he watched in disbelief as the car disappeared down the road, certain that again he had just seen Sylvie.

CHAPTER 63

"DAVE, WHAT TIME DO YOU GET HOME TODAY?"

"Should be home about three."

"See you then." The phone clicked dead.

Jack's call had come through not five minutes after the speeding car had nearly hit him. He looked at the phone in his hand, debating whether to call Jack back and explain what had just happened. No, he'd see Jack soon enough.

* * *

Jack was sitting on the tailgate of his truck when Dave pulled in a little after three.

"Hey, Jack. What's up?"

"I had another conversation this morning with that Coast Guard Investigator. Special Agent Peeves."

"So?"

"So, he told me that the body they found out on the jetty was Bryan. I didn't want you to have to find out on the phone."

"What?" Dave stopped dead in his tracks and stared at Jack.

"It was Bryan. I know you guys were friends. I'm really sorry. And listen, there's more. The agent's questions also left me thinking that he may know something about Sylvie."

"Holy shit," Dave murmured under his breath. Then, looking up at Jack, he said, "I saw her this afternoon."

"What! You saw her?"

"Yeah. We were working down in Gloucester—Washington Street, off 127, up by Lanes Cove. It's an old neighborhood; there used to be a quarry around there."

"Sylvie was staying in that area. You're sure?"

"Yeah. She nearly hit me with her car when she peeled out of there."

Jack said, "Tell me exactly what happened."

"Okay, so me and my partner, Smitty, were doing a survey job up on Washington Street. I set up this old antique transit I sometimes use, just to keep in practice. I saw someone pull into number 27. It was a quick look, but I thought it was her."

"Go on."

"Not much else to say. She turned in. A bit later another car stopped in front. Two men got out and went up what the same drive. Then she came flying out and nearly ran me over. That's when I got a good look and knew for sure it was her."

"What about the men?"

"The men?"

"Yes. The guys who parked in front."

"What about them? Their car was still there when we left. Look, Jack, enough about Sylvie. What did the Coast Guard say about Bryan?"

CHAPTER 64

JACK RECAPPED THE DETAILS of his conversation with Special Agent Peeves, concluding, "And that's about all."

"I can't believe it. I know we had guessed as much, but to find out it's really true . . ."

After a moment Dave added, "Why do you think he might know something about Sylvie?"

"Nothing concrete, just a feeling."

"What if she was involved?"

"Then I'd say things are going to get real interesting."

Several moments passed, and then Jack said, "Tell me again about those guys at her place."

Dave described for a second time what he had seen.

Jack listened carefully. Then he said, "There's something I never told you."

"What?"

Jack proceeded to tell Dave about their trip to Sylvie's house, and how she had thought it had been broken into.

"Jesus! Jack."

"I know. But at the time, I think that I just wanted to be done with her."

"And how's that working out for you?"

Again, silence and tension filled the space between the two friends.

This time, Dave was the first to break the silence. "Remember that night I went down to Bryan's boat and he told me about those cases?"

"Yeah, you told me that."

"Did I tell you Bryan said that Sylvie had been spooked by some guys down on the dock? That's why he came to get food. She was hiding in the cabin."

"I don't think so."

"They were gone by the time I got there. What if those guys down on the dock were the men you saw today?"

"That's a stretch."

"I know, but when she came back, she was like a ninja. Creeped me out. What if those guys have been after her all along?"

"That's still a stretch."

"I know. But so is Bryan ending up dead, and now that's actually true. So again, what if?"

"I don't know."

After a pause, Jack added, "You know, if we really want to stretch things and get into conspiracy theories, when I was down at the harbor looking for Lewis, there were some guys there that looked out of place, and Lewis was real nervous. Maybe they're the same guys."

"You're right, that's really pushing it. But who knows?"

Jack said, "I think we should go check it out. Max and Patti are both scheduled to work late at Ben's. Are you up for a road trip back down to her place? We could get a bite at the Agawam on the way back home."

"Yeah. I think we owe it to Bryan to figure out what's going on."

* * *

The closer they got to Sylvie's place the quieter they became. As they turned onto her street, they could see flashing lights from an assortment of police and emergency vehicles.

"This can't be good," said Jack.

"No shit. Pull over so we can see what's going on. And Jack?"

"Yeah?"

"Try to keep a low profile here."

They walked up the street and joined the back of a crowd of curious onlookers who were straining to see what was going on.

"What happened?" said Jack to no one in particular.

A man in a blue pin-striped shirt turned to answer him. "Not really sure, but it looks like there was a break in, found a body inside."

"Dead?" Jack blurted out.

The man looked at the scene for a moment and then turned back to Jack. "Yeah. Brought it out a while ago. Carted him off, but since then there hasn't been much to see."

"Who?" asked Jack.

"No idea. Only saw a body bag."

Jack turned to share that nugget of information with Dave, but realized they'd been separated by the growing crowd.

"Just one?" Jack said as he craned his neck to look for Dave.

"You seem surprised."

"What?" He was still searching for Dave.

"You seemed surprised when I said that there was just one body."

That caught Jack off guard, and for a second his embarrassment rendered him silent. Later, when Jack would recount the story to Dave, he wouldn't be able to recall what the man looked like, aside from the pin-striped shirt. His face was one of those faces that were memorable only for being nondescript.

Finally, after what felt like forever, Jack regained his voice and stammered, "I'm sorry. I didn't expect that."

The man gave no response. Then, after a withering look at Jack, turned away.

Jack, too embarrassed to remain there, retreated through the crowd to find Dave. By the time they met again, Jack had regained his composure.

"Dave, where'd you go? I thought you were with me and then you weren't."

"Sorry. Have you noticed anything missing?"

"No. What are you talking about?"

"The car! The car that those two men came in. I asked around and nobody remembers even seeing it."

"Well, I have something for you. They took a body out a bit ago."

"What! I didn't hear that."

"A guy I was standing by told me. A man, he said. You don't suppose . . . ?"

"Shhh. Look over there." Dave pulled Jack around and back.

"What?"

"Over there, with the cops. Isn't that our friend Special Agent Peeves?"

"You're right. Wonder what he's doing here?"

"Don't know, don't want to find out." He tugged on Jack's arm, pulling him back to the truck.

"Agawam, here we come."

CHAPTER 65

"THIS POT ROAST IS REALLY GOOD," said Jack as he swallowed his first bite.

"Meatloaf's pretty good, too."

Driving away from Sylvie's house, their talk had centered on what they had just seen. But about halfway to the diner, their conversation had turned to food as a stomach-rumbling hunger overcame them. Now, after a few silent mouthfuls, their conversation about the recent events began again.

Jack broke the silence first. "What do you suppose Special Agent Peeves was doing there?"

"No idea. But what if . . ."

Dave paused as he took another bite of meatloaf. "Mmmm, this is good." He swallowed and then added, without looking up from his plate, "What if they're all related?"

"What're all related?"

"All of it. Bryan, whatever was in those cases, the body tonight. Maybe even the body in the dumpster. Did they ever find out who that was?"

Jack shook his head.

"Well, look. I just thought of something. Didn't they find the dumpster after the night that Bryan and Sylvie picked up those cases? What about those guys that spooked Sylvie at the dock? Maybe he was one of them."

Before Jack could respond, Dave continued. "Other than that day, we haven't really heard much about it. And just after they found that body, we got the first visit from that Coast Guard investigator."

"And you think this is all connected in some way?"

The expression on Dave's face said, "Are you dense?" What he said was, "Don't you think it's kind of strange the way she shows up, then disappears, and somehow just after, a dead body turns up? First Richie, then the guy down by the dock, then Bryan, and now this guy at her place."

"When you put it that way."

"I know. And didn't you tell me that Lewis was all spooked up in Rye Harbor and there were some guys there who looked out of place there? And that Coast Guard investigator keeps showing up."

"I suppose."

"You suppose. Come on Jack. Sylvie's involved in something really big here. You've got to see it."

"I'll admit that everything you've said is true. Whether or not it's a grand conspiracy remains to be seen."

CHAPTER 66

MAX WAS STILL AT WORK when Jack got home. Cat greeted him at the door with great displeasure at having been left inside, alone.

"I know, I know. Max left you all alone. How 'bout I get you some supper?"

Her "Mrowh's" turned to loud purrs, which turned to soft num, num, nums as she continued to try to talk while eating. Jack chuckled and took a beer from the fridge. Then he stretched out on the couch with Cat on his chest and promptly fell asleep.

In his dreams, Jack heard a woman calling his name. Sylvie? He couldn't be sure. Max? He heard it again. Then he saw an arm, raised out of the water. The voice seemed to be coming from the arm. As hard as he stroked, the boat remained the same distance from the arm, and the voice kept calling out to him. "Jack! Jack!" He leaned out over the side of the boat, stretching until he felt as if his arm would come out of its socket, but the waving hand remained just out of reach and the voice continued to call out to him. He could feel a hand, or something, touching him, but he couldn't tell where that touch was coming from.

"Hunh!" He sat up quickly, all senses alert, and yet not at all sure what he was seeing or feeling. He heard laughter and looked around, trying to understand what he was seeing.

"Max? What is she doing there?" he thought to himself. "Where is the arm, the boat, and why am I no longer in a boat leaning out over the water?"

He looked at Max again. She was kneeling next to the couch. The laughter he heard was hers. His sleep-addled mind began to sort out what was real and what he had thought was real. Her curly red hair, those green eyes, her smile, those were all real.

"Max! You scared the shit out of me."

"Oh, my God. You should have seen yourself jump. I was whispering your name in your ear. I don't know if you heard me or not, but suddenly you sat up. You nearly hit me in the face." She leaned into him and wrapped her arms around him. "I'm so glad you're here."

Between the way she said that and the way she hugged him, he got the feeling that something wasn't right.

"I'm glad I'm here, too. How were things at Ben's?"

She relaxed her arms, letting go of him, and rocked back on her heels. She continued to kneel on the floor next to him with her hands resting on his knees. "It was okay."

Her answer confirmed what he had sensed. Something had happened at Ben's. He knew it would probably be futile to attempt to pry it out of her before she was ready, but he couldn't help but try.

"Just okay?"

"Unh huh." She stood and walked toward the kitchen.

"Max."

She stopped and glanced back at him but then continued on.

"Come on, Max. Something happened at work today. I can tell. Why don't you tell me what it was?"

She remained silent.

He watched as she poured a glass of wine. Then, after slowly and deliberately re-corking the bottle, she turned to face him and took a sip.

Jack got up from the couch and took a step toward her. As soon as he moved in her direction, he could see a subtle shift in her stance. He stopped, wondering what was going on.

"Jack . . ." She seemed unsure of exactly what to say. She took another sip of wine. "Today, at Ben's, I saw someone." She stopped.

Jack's concern continued to grow. "Who?"

"Sylvie."

He stared at her silently as her words sunk in. "Sylvie? What? How?" He realized he was stammering.

Max took another sip of her wine. Then, in a calm and measured voice, she repeated her news, never taking her eyes off him.

Jack, still stunned by what she had said, stared blankly at her as dozens of questions and thoughts whirled in his head. "You're sure?"

"Yes. It was busy. I was behind the bar and I saw her walk in. She looked around so quickly, I'm not even sure she saw me. I watched her walk out onto the deck, and by the time I was able to leave the bar to see if it really was her, she was gone. I just got a feeling that she was looking for you."

"Me? Why would you think that?"

"Look, you don't have to believe me, but I know what I saw, and I'm sure it was her and that she was looking for you."

"I didn't say I don't believe you."

She gave him a look that told him that this was not an argument he was going to win, so he stopped. After an awkward moment of silence, he started again. "Look, Max, you telling me that she showed up, well, I wasn't expecting that. I'm sorry."

Now it was her turn to ask some questions. "What's going on, Jack?"

"Let me get a glass of wine first."

They sat down on the couch and he told her all about what he and Dave had witnessed earlier. "Then, when you woke me up. I was pretty groggy, and when you told me that you had seen her—"

She cut him off. "I know what I saw, and I'm sure it was her. What are we going to do?"

"We?"

"Okay, you? What are you going to do?"

"I don't know."

"Maybe you should call that Coast Guard investigator."

"Probably should, but I have a feeling that I won't have to. Like it or not, I expect that she'll turn up again."

CHAPTER 67

THE LIGHTS WERE OUT and Max was getting ready for bed. Jack stood by the window and looked out to sea as a thin ribbon of moonlight sliced the harbor in half. On either side, nearest that cut, he could see the shadowed shapes of boats sitting peacefully on their moorings. As his eyes moved away from that ribbon, and toward the spot where *Irrepressible* had been moored for all those years, those shapes gradually faded until they were no longer visible, just as his beloved boat had vanished when she slipped below the waves. Cat must have sensed his melancholy because she jumped from her spot on the couch and began to rub against his legs.

"Mrowh." Her voice was soft and soothing, not scolding or insistent as earlier. When Jack picked her up, he felt her relax. She began purring softly, and then her two front paws began alternately stretching open then closing. "Cat, you are such a good girl. Thank you."

She looked at him and purred louder. Then he turned his back to the window, returned her to the couch, and said, "It's late. Good night, Cat."

The bedroom, which had seemed so totally black when he first walked in, gradually became less so as he crossed the room to the bed. The soft, silvery light from a million stars above streamed through the skylight, illuminating Max as her soft curves blended into the folds and swirls of the single sheet that covered her. He paused, looked down, and listened to her breathing, trying to discern if she were still awake or asleep. As he did so, memories of long-ago nights spent sailing under the canopy of those same stars flashed through his head. When a hint of a breeze ruffled the curtains, bringing with it that light, salty scent of the ocean, he sighed. Then, slowly and carefully, he slid onto the bed, trying not to disturb her.

As Jack settled on the bed, looking up through the skylight at the stars, Max uncurled, stretched, and rolled over toward him. Still not sure whether she was awake or asleep, Jack remained still as she came to rest against him, her head on his chest and one leg draped over his. He had his answer when her arm slid beneath the sheet. With his heart pounding, he sucked in his breath, his body reacting to her touch as her fingers began to explore and caress him.

He began to say her name, but she silenced him with a kiss.

"Shhh," she whispered, and he obeyed.

* * *

Eventually sleep came. Jack awoke with the sun in his eyes, alone in bed, wondering if it had all been a dream. He found Max, sitting on the couch, sipping coffee, with Cat curled up next to her.

"I didn't hear you get up," he said as he made himself a cup of coffee.

Max smiled. "You were sleeping so soundly, I didn't have the heart to wake you." Then, with a teasing lilt to her voice she added, "You must have been exhausted."

He blushed and grinned. "I was."

"Do you understand what happened last night?" That question surprised him and he looked at her. She was smiling and he couldn't be 100% sure, but he thought this time her voice seemed a bit colder.

CHAPTER 68

DAVE WAS AT WORK when C.G.I.S. Agent Peeves found him. He was in Gloucester again, on a different job from the day before, but still near the area where he and Jack had seen the body taken from Sylvie's house. Between the traffic passing by and his concentration on getting the right reading, Dave hadn't heard the footsteps behind.

"Good morning."

Startled, Dave turned and found himself face to face with the Coast Guard investigator.

"Jesus. You startled me."

"I'm sorry. Mr. Wheeler, I have a few more questions for you. Your boss told me I'd find you here."

"Uh, sure. But please call me Dave." He waved to Smitty to take a break. "How can I help you?"

"As you know I'm investigating the death of your friend Bryan."

"We weren't really close friends, more fishing buddies, but yes, I know."

"I need to go over that trip you took with him several weeks back, when you reported the boat that sank."

Dave wasn't expecting that. "Uh, sure. I don't know what else I can tell you, but go ahead."

"When you first described seeing the smoke, you indicated that Bryan was reluctant to turn back and it took some convincing to do so."

"That's right. We said we'd pay for the time and the fuel."

"Why he was so reluctant?"

"I don't know. It's just the way he was. He didn't really like dealing with authorities. He must have assumed that if we went back and something had happened, then he'd have to."

"Tell me again what you found when you got there."

"Just some wreckage and some oil on the water."

"Nothing else to indicate what boat may have sunk? No survivors? Nothing?"

Dave felt more uneasy by the minute. "No. Like I said, we only found some wreckage, not much, nothing identifiable, and no, we found no survivors." They had kept Sylvie's secret this long; there was no way to go back now.

"Mr. Wheeler." The sudden shift from *Dave* to *Mr. Wheeler* matched the sharp look in the agent's eyes. "I'll ask this one more time. You are absolutely certain that you didn't see any sign of survivors."

Dave stood there silently while Special Agent Peeves continued to stare. Finally he said, "No, uh, yes, that's correct, we didn't see any signs of survivors."

"Thank you. I'll let you get back to work."

Before striding away, Agent Peeves turned back and said, "One more thing. When I spoke to your boss, he told me that you were working near here yesterday."

"Yeah. We were."

"Did you notice anything peculiar?"

"Like what? We see strange things all the time. We're invisible to most of the neighbors wherever we go."

Inspector Peeves pulled out a small notebook and thumbed through some pages. Then he looked up and said, "Yesterday, on the street where you were working, a body was found in one of the houses. You didn't notice anything, did you?"

"Sorry."

"Well, thanks anyway, Dave. You take care."

Dave didn't respond. He watched as the agent walked to his car, climbed in, and drove off. As soon as he was out of sight, Dave let out a huge breath. He felt as if his entire body was shaking.

"He knows something and he knows we do too." He said this under his breath as he reached for his cell phone to call Jack.

CHAPTER 69

THE WOODS WERE COOL and Jack found the soft crunching of each foot-fall almost musical. Loose gravel, wet leaves, dry leaves, wood bark, hard-packed dirt—each had its own distinct sound and the rhythm was more complex, unlike on the roads.

After Dave's call about his visit from Special Agent Peeves, Jack had decided that he needed some alone time to think, and as was his habit that meant a run. Hoping to avoid Peeves on the roads in Rye, he had chosen Maudslay again.

He was several miles into his run when he first heard footsteps behind. Anticipating that he was about to be passed on the left, he moved over to the right, but no one caught up to him. In fact, the footsteps faded as he approached a steep descent. For a moment, he forget about the footsteps as his pace increased and he had to focus on his footing. Once the trail leveled out he glanced back but he saw no one.

"Probably turned off," he thought.

He ran on, so lost in his thoughts and focused on the trail that by the time he noticed the footsteps a second time, he was facing much more difficult terrain. Opportunities to glance back to identify the other runner were few and far between, and whenever he did look, no one was in sight.

As the trail became limited to single track with many short hills and quick turns, Jack placed his focus entirely on his footing. On the down sides of each hill he let himself go, seeming to fly down the paths while maintaining just enough control so as to not trip and fall. Conversely, whenever the trail rose, he shortened his stride and quickened the pace, pushing hard until he crested each hill with his heart pounding in his ears and his lungs burning from the effort.

As he was about to crest the top of the last single track section on the longest and steepest hill, he thought he heard someone call his name.

"Jack!"

It was a woman's voice and he knew that voice. Even though he hadn't quite reached the top of the hill, he stopped and turned. Struggling to catch his breath, he looked down the hill. With sweat running into and burning his eyes, he couldn't see clearly, so he lifted his shirt to wipe the sweat from his eyes. As he did so, he swayed and had to catch himself.

"Jack! Watch out."

His ears hadn't deceived him.

"Sylvie?" he managed to choke out as he fought to catch his breath.

Wearing a black sports bra and fashionable skin-tight shorts that left little to the imagination, she too was drenched in sweat and breathing hard as she slowed and then stopped just below him.

"Jack," her words came between breaths, "You're— a— hard— man— to catch."

He stared down the hill at her, blinked, and wiped his eyes again. Memories flashed through his head from the first time they met at the Rockdog. Now, as then, she was stunning, only this time she was stunning in a lot less clothing. All he could see was her, and all he could hear was his labored breathing and the sound of his heart pounding in his ears as he watched her climb those last few steps up the hill toward him.

"What—" He took a deep breath, trying to regain some composure and his voice.

Before he could finish his question, he found her standing right in front of him. She looked up into his eyes, reached up, and touched his lips with her fingers. "Shhh. We've got to talk."

His breathing was nearly back to normal, but his heart continued to race. "Are you all right? How did you find me? What? Why now?"

"Jack, stop and listen to me. Ever since that day out at Jeffreys when you and your friends saved me, things have become very complicated."

"Ya' think?"

"Don't be a jerk. You guys saved my life. Now I have to know . . . have you told anyone about finding me?"

"Besides Max? I haven't, Dave may have told Patti, I'm not sure, and I guess we'll never know about Bryan, will we?" He couldn't quite keep the venom out of his voice.

"Jack, I'm so sorry about that. I had nothing to do with his death. I genuinely liked him, and I tried to keep him safe."

"Okay, let's say that you had nothing to do with that. What about all these other dead guys who keep showing up?"

"What are you talking about?"

"Come on, Sylvie, don't play stupid with me. The guy they found in the dumpster by the dock, the day you went back out with Bryan. I know you went after that package. Bryan told Dave."

He was on a roll and cut her off before she could say anything else. "And what about down in Gloucester? You got home, two guys showed up, you left shortly after, and one was found dead."

She blanched. "How did you know about that?"

"For someone who seems to be so good at sneaking around, you didn't notice that there was a survey crew by your house. Dave was on that crew. You nearly ran him over as you sped out of there."

"I don't live there. I use that house on occasion. I keep some stuff there. I stopped by that day to pick something up that I needed."

Finished, Sylvie now stood in silence, bathed in sweat from the hard run to catch him. She made no attempt to push away the strands of loose hair that were sticking to her forehead and shoulders as she stared up at him with those intense blue eyes and a vulnerability in her expression that he found nearly impossible to resist. Part of him wanted to reach out and push those strands of hair away, take her in his arms, and comfort her, while another part of him wanted to get as far away from her as possible.

"Jack, I don't know what to say. It's not what it looks like, and it's complicated. Please trust me."

"You keep saying that. So how about you trust me and tell me what's going on? No, wait—don't tell me—if you did, you'd probably have to kill me." He could see that his sarcasm wasn't lost on her.

"Jack, that's not fair." She took a half step back away from him. "Okay. I'll tell you what you want to know." As she paused, her face grew serious. "But you're right. I may have to kill you."

As Jack watched her closely, a twitch in the corner of her mouth gave her away. The tension broke and they both began to laugh. Seconds later, she moved into his arms, and they held each other tightly. Their hot, sweaty bodies pressed even closer as their laughter turned to silence.

That moment seemed to last forever. Then she released him and took an awkward step back.

"I'm sorry," Sylvie said softly.

"No, I'm the one who should be sorry."

As Jack found himself caught between anger and arousal, Max's voice echoed in his mind: "She's been nothing but trouble from the day you met."

CHAPTER 70

THEY DID NOT RESUME RUNNING right away. Instead, they walked up the rest of the hill in silence. When they reached the last remaining formal garden of the former estate, Sylvie said, "You're lucky to have Max, Jack."

"So she keeps telling me. But listen, Sylvie. Seriously. What really happened to Bryan?"

"I told you. I had nothing to do with that."

"So you said, but you know, don't you?"

Her silence answered his question.

"Look, Sylvie," he pressed. "You said you'd tell me what's going on."

"I'm parked in the pay lot," she said.

When they reached her car, she turned and faced him. "Jack, I didn't mean for anything to happen to Bryan, but I needed his help." She touched Jack's arm, paused, and then added, "I won't let anything happen to you or your friends."

He had no response and began to turn away.

"Wait."

She opened her car door, and despite his mixed feelings, Jack couldn't help but watch as she stretched and leaned in. She reemerged with a scrap of paper and pressed it into his hand.

"Just in case," she said. "Take care."

* * *

When Jack reached his truck about ten minutes later, he finally looked at the crumpled scrap of paper in hand. It had started its life as a receipt from Dunkin' Donuts, and even though the sweat from his palm had made the ink run, he could still make out a phone number with the letter *S* underneath. He set it on his truck seat, hoping it would dry by the time he reached home.

CHAPTER 71

ON THE RIDE HOME JACK STRUGGLED to put the events of the last few weeks together. He pulled into his drive behind a nondescript car that nevertheless managed to look official. "Shit."

"You're back!" Max's voice rang out as he climbed the last few stairs. "I got your note. How was your run?"

"It was good. Went down to Maudslay."

In a low voice, she confirmed what he had already figured out. "That Coast Guard investigator is here. He's in the bathroom." Then she added, "I was just getting us something to drink. You want some lemonade?"

He would have preferred a beer, but he nodded. "Sure. When did he get here?"

"Only a few minutes ago."

The toilet flushed and Jack whispered to Max, "What has he said?"

"Nothing." Her answer coincided with the sound of the door opening.

"Hello, Jack," Special Agent Peeves stepped into the room.

"Agent Peeves. It's nice to see you again. How can I help you?"

"I'm pretty sure you know."

"No. How?"

Before the agent could reply, Max walked over and handed the men two glasses of lemonade.

"Thanks." Special Agent Peeves took a sip, nodded a thank you to Max, and then refocused his attention on Jack.

"Fine, Jack. Have it your way. I talked with your friend Dave earlier, as I'm sure you already know. We're still investigating that sinking you witnessed—"

Jack interrupted. "We didn't witness anything. What we found was evidence that there had been a sinking."

"I'm sorry. You're right. In any event, we had been keeping an eye on Richie Lowe for quite some time."

"So it was his boat that sank."

"Yes. We found the boat."

"And Richie?"

The officer shook his head. "Presumed lost at sea. But we do have enough evidence to be confident that it was him."

"And that's what you came to tell me?"

"Not exactly. I need your help."

"My help?"

"Yes. I think you know more than you are telling me. And I think that when you hear what else I have to say, you may reconsider your silence."

Jack took a quick breath and reminded himself to keep his expression neutral.

"As I was saying, this was an ongoing investigation. We had an undercover agent working the case, and that agent has disappeared."

Jack didn't see that coming. "An undercover agent?" He could feel his eyebrows rise with the question. So much for appearing neutral.

"Yes." From the intense look he received, Jack knew that Special Agent Peeves hadn't missed the change in his expression either. "We had been watching Richie. Our agent had made contact, and we believe the agent may have been with him on his boat when it sank."

"But you don't know for sure?"

"No, we don't. It's all speculation. We haven't been able to track down our agent, but that isn't very unusual in cases like this."

"I see. So what was Richie involved in?"

"Smuggling."

"Smuggling?"

"Among other activities, and before you ask exactly what he was smuggling, don't."

So many thoughts ran through Jack's mind it was hard to sort them out quickly. Sylvie had never really said what it was she did. Was she actually an agent?

Special Agent Peeves continued. "Like I said, we want your help."

"I don't see how."

"First, let me say that what I'm going to tell you is in the strictest confidence." He paused and looked over at Max, who had been watching and listening to their entire exchange. "This applies to you also."

She nodded her agreement.

Turning back to Jack, he said, "Remember that body that was found in the dumpster down at Hampton Marina?"

"Sure."

"We believe that that individual may have had ties with Richie."

"So?"

"So, that individual was a known bottom feeder named Tommy Fontaine. The question is: what was he doing there, in Hampton? Richie was already dead." He paused for effect then said, "I think he was waiting for Bryan."

"Bryan? Why?"

"Well, we think Bryan had retrieved something, probably whatever it was that Richie had been going to get when he was killed and his boat sunk."

"What makes you think that?"

"Fisheries had a spotter plane out that day—routine monitoring of fishing boats. They saw two people hauling up something onto *Miss Cookie* and they let us know."-

"So why weren't you waiting for them?"

"We're pretty sure that Bryan was mostly a victim. We wanted to know who was with him, what he was going to do and so the decision was made not to pick him up."

"And now he's dead."

"And we're sorry about that. He was just at the wrong place, at the wrong time, doing the wrong thing and . . . well, got caught."

Jack was about to say something when Agent Peeves cut him off. "Now, here's where it gets interesting. Let's assume that Bryan returned with Richie's stash and Tommy was there waiting for him. Who killed Tommy? Remember he was found dead in the dumpster, down by the dock, neck broken."

"You aren't saying that Bryan did that, are you?"

"No, I don't think he did." What he didn't say was more telling than what he did say.

Jack became silent as what Agent Peeves had just told him began to sink in.

"No way Bryan did that," he agreed.

"You sound pretty sure of that. Is there something else you're not telling me?"

"No. Just doesn't sound like something Bryan would have done."

"Maybe, but it is kind of a coincidence, don't you think?

Jack shrugged.

"Look, Jack, I think you know more than you are letting on I don't think that you fully understand the danger you might be in. As this investigation goes on, and we begin to fill in the gaps, I don't want to see you and your buddy Dave getting caught up in something that you could have easily avoided. Remember, Richie is dead, his boat sunk, our agent is missing, and your friend Bryan is dead."

Jack took a breath and composed himself. "I appreciate your concern, but I don't think you have anything to worry about."

Agent Peeves shrugged. "I hope not. I'm going to leave you two now."

As he turned toward the stairs to leave, he paused. "Oh, there's one more thing that I didn't mention. The other day, another body was found, and we think that may also be connected to this investigation."

Jack said, "What body?"

Agent Peeves looked directly at Jack and said in a carefully measured tone, "Down in Gloucester, happened right near where your buddy Dave was working. Dave says he didn't see anything, though I'm not convinced. Turns out, this guy was known to hang around with Tommy Fontaine. His neck was broken too."

As Jack's heart pounded in his chest, he fought to keep his voice calm. "In Gloucester?"

"Yeah. Like I said, the victim was an associate of Tommy Fontaine's. Looks like he broke into a house and then someone broke his neck."

"And because they knew each other, you think they're related?"

"Anything's possible."

As soon as Special Agent Peeves had driven off, Max looked at Jack. "What the hell is going on?"

"You know as much as I do."

"I'm not so sure. Why didn't you tell him about finding Sylvie?"

"I couldn't."

"That house in Gloucester. It was the house where we took her, wasn't it?"

Jack said nothing.

"So. It was."

"Your words, not mine."

"You didn't have to say anything. I saw your reaction—and so did he. He knows."

"You can't be sure."

"Oh, yes I can. I know you Jack Beale, and you had better think about what he said. I believe him when he said that you and Dave could be in trouble."

"Look Max, he's just fishing. He doesn't know that it was her out on Richie's boat or that she had anything to do with those deaths."

"I think he does."

Jack could see that things were going down hill fast. He was worried, and he needed to talk to Dave.

"Look Max, I don't want to fight. I didn't tell him about Sylvie because we promised her that we would not tell anyone that she was alive."

"But, according to him, it sounds like she was his agent. The Coast Guard needs to know."

"If she is, and she wanted him to know, I'm sure she would have contacted him. The way he keeps turning up, he's not exactly hard to track down."

"I think you're wrong to keep this a secret."

Jack's heart skipped a beat as he realized how angry she'd be if she found out that he had just seen Sylvie on his run.

"I don't. I need to talk to Dave. Everything will be all right."

CHAPTER 72

MAX WAS GONE BY THE TIME Jack finished showering. As soon as he was dressed, he made the call. "Dave. You home yet?"

"Just pulling in. Hit the market on the way home. What's up?"

"That Coast Guard inspector just left my house."

"What did he want?"

"That's what I have to talk to you about."

"So, tell me."

"Better we talk in person."

"You had supper yet?"

"No."

"Patti's at work. Wok?"

"Sounds good. I'm on my way."

* * *

The drive to Dave's took longer than Jack had hoped. There was a concert in the center of Hampton Beach, and the traffic was all backed up. When he finally arrived, Dave was waiting outside to direct him where to park.

"So what's up?" asked Dave as Jack got out of his truck.

"I'm not exactly sure."

"Well, I'm hungry. Let's head over to the Wok."

As soon as they were seated, Dave repeated his original question, "So, what's up?"

"That Coast Guard inspector came to see me."

"So you said."

"He told me some things that I wasn't expecting."

"Like what?"

"Like, they know that Bryan went out for those cases. And that maybe Sylvie is a special agent who was working for them."

"What? "

While they talked, drinks and dinner were ordered and served.

As Dave reached for the hot mustard he asked, "What specifically did Agent Peeves say?"

"He said that they had had an undercover agent working with Richie for quite some time. Something about a smuggling operation. Now, he says, the agent's disappeared. Didn't say more than that, but I can't help but think that he was talking about Sylvie."

"Sylvie? An agent? You're shitting me."

"No, I'm not. It gets better. He told me that guy they found dead in the dumpster—the day after Bryan came back with Sylvie and those cases—was some kind of a low-life for hire, name was Tommy Fontaine. Do you remember much coverage about that discovery?"

"No."

"Right. Papers never said much about it. Did you know his neck was broken?"

"No."

"Peeves said they kept it hushed up on purpose. There hasn't been much coverage since Bryan was killed, either, even though it seemed like every first responder was down there."

"Now that you mention it," said Dave.

"Peeves also told me that he asked you about that guy down in Gloucester."

"He did, but I didn't say anything. Do you think he saw us down there?"

"I don't think so, but he does think you know more than you told him. That body they took out? The guy worked with Tommy Fontaine. His neck was broken, too."

"Sylvie?" asked Dave.

"I find it hard to believe. Maybe Tommy and that other guy, but Bryan? I can't see it."

"The panties were missing, though. Think about it. I know she's hot, and I know she has this thing for you, but what do you really know about her? God, Jack. She said she killed Richie."

Jack looked at Dave in silence. At Maudslay, Sylvie had insisted that she hadn't killed Bryan, and he believed her. Finally, he said, "Not Bryan, Dave."

"But the other two?"

"I don't know. I suppose anything's possible, but wouldn't that cross a big line if she was working undercover?"

"It would. But from what you are telling me, sounds like Peeves already thinks so."

Jack pushed away his empty plate. "Listen Dave. I've got to get going. I'm not sure we solved anything tonight, but I do think we need to be careful."

"Agreed."

CHAPTER 73

ON THE DRIVE BACK TO RYE HARBOR, Jack wrestled with his guilt about keeping his meeting with Sylvie from Dave. Still, it was for the best. Dave would have told Patti, she would have told Max, and it all would have gone downhill from there.

Since the concert in the Casino had started, the traffic through the beach wasn't quite as congested, so his ride home was a bit faster. As he crossed over the bridge and was able to see Ben's parking lot for the first time, he was surprised at how many cars were still there. That meant it would be a while before Max would get home. He decided to stop in and make sure she was okay.

The bar was nearly empty, but outside the deck was still crowded. Max was busy behind the bar beginning her closing routine when he walked in. Her back was to the door, and as she turned to face the bar, she said, "Jack! You startled me."

He smiled as she regained her composure. Then she said, "I didn't expect to see you. Didn't you go down to Dave's?"

"I did. We grabbed a bite at the Wok."

"And you didn't bring me anything?"

"Sorry. Next time I will."

"Beer?"

He shook his head, "I'm good."

"Well, I would have loved the Chinese food, but I'm glad you're here. It's been a strange night."

"How so?"

"Not sure if it's just me or because it's the end of the summer or what, but we seemed to have even more odd ducks than usual."

"Probably the full moon."

"Is tonight the full moon? I was so busy, I never even noticed."

"If it's not full, it's close. Really pretty."

"That would explain a lot. Two guys came in, sat at the bar, ordered drinks, and then just sat there, staring at me the whole time."

Patti walked in and added, "Those two guys? They were creepy. And when they left, I overheard them talking in some language I've never heard before."

Jack looked back and forth between Max and Patti. "Let me get this straight. Two guys, not from around here, probably—I don't know, let's just say *on vacation*—come in, sit at the bar, order, watch the attractive bartender, don't say anything else, then leave." He rolled his eyes toward the ceiling. "You're right! That's just so strange!"

Max swatted his shoulder. "You are such a jerk."

CHAPTER 74

EVEN THOUGH JACK HAD BRUSHED OFF their fears, deep inside he was worried. Between all that had happened, the inspector's warning, and his latest talk with Sylvie, anything unusual seemed noteworthy. He stayed and helped Max close Ben's. Then he took her hand.

"Come," he said. Instead of walking directly to his truck, he led her to the edge of the parking lot overlooking the harbor. Jack slipped behind her, wrapped his arms around her, and pulled her close. Max leaned back into him. Holding on to his arms, she pulled his embrace tighter, closed her eyes, and sighed.

Time seemed to stand still as they stood there locked in each other's arms, bathed in the silvery blue light of the full moon. Then Jack felt Max shiver. "You cold?" he whispered.

"I am," she whispered back.

She released his arms and turned to face him. Max leaned up at the same time he leaned down and their lips met. It was a soft, delicate kiss, not held for long, but its effect was far stronger than its force. Every cell in Jack's body tingled as if an electric charge had just passed through his body. As their lips parted, Max exhaled softly and whispered, "Take me home."

* * *

That same silvery moonlight that had bathed the harbor and turned the water's surface into a million sparkling diamonds also lit their bedroom. Only now, it was a softer, more deeply sensuous light, dominated by shadows that accented and redefined each fold and ripple of the blankets on their bed in the same way it illuminated each curve and crease of their bodies. Their fingers and lips alternately traced the patterns of light and shadow up and down legs and arms, over breasts and shoulders, all the while following the path to more private and intimate places. Their coupling was long and slow, and in the end sleep came, their bodies entwined and bathed in the soft glow of moonlight.

CHAPTER 75

CAT INSISTED ON BREAKFAST long before Jack had any intention of getting up, but he did so anyway. "Here you go, Cat."

Clearly ecstatic at how well-trained he was, she purred loudly and chattered while she ate. Jack knew he would not return to bed. As tempting as it was, or more accurately as Max was, thoughts of the previous day's events surfaced in his head and took control.

Looking out his window, he could see dark clouds forming to the northeast, over the ocean. The American flags that were present on most of the boats in the harbor indicated that the wind was coming from that direction too. The forecasters had predicted a nor'easter, and there was little reason now to doubt them.

Jack left the window and made himself a cup of coffee. The jolt of caffeine and sugar was just what he needed. He was still thinking about all that had happened and wondering how it would unfold when he sensed Max behind him.

"Good morning." Her sexy, still half-asleep voice broke the silence and he turned. She stood facing him in her robe, her hair still tousled from sleep.

"Morning."

"Penny for your thoughts?"

"I was just thinking . . ." he paused.

"About what?"

"About you, about all that has been going on, about what that Coast Guard investigator said, about Sylvie—"

He caught himself, but it was too late. In an instant, the look on her face hardened. He felt his face flush and his heart rate increase as she glowered at him. "I . . . I didn't mean what you're thinking."

"And what am I thinking?"

He couldn't speak. Time seemed to slow as he tried to find the words to explain what he meant, but they would not come. He watched helplessly as she turned and walked away. Cat jumped, then ran and hid when the bedroom door slammed.

"What is wrong with you? Sometimes you are so stupid," Jack mumbled to himself. He turned to look out the window again. The darkening clouds over the ocean only added emphasis to the darkness that now enveloped him.

Damn! She had asked what I was thinking. Doesn't she realize that she's the only one for me? Of course I'm thinking about Sylvie—she's a big part of this mess. What am I supposed to do now?

"Mrowh, Mrowh." Cat's voice broke the silence as if to say, "Get over it. Everything will be all right. Now, let me out of here."

Cat dashed out as soon as Jack opened the door. He also stepped out, looking up to survey the darkening sky. He was about to turn and go back in when he saw a white van turn onto the end of the drive down by the road. Normally he would have ignored it—extra tourist traffic was one of the pitfalls of living on a dead end road by the ocean in New England. Curious day trippers tended to ignore the street signs, no matter how clear the cautions were. After recent events, however, he decided to keep an eye on the van.

When it reached Courtney's place, it stopped for a moment, but instead of using the area in front of her cottage to turn around and head back to the road, it began creeping forward until it finally stopped close behind Jack's truck. The windows were tinted and dark enough that he couldn't see in, but the dirt, dents, and rust made it was obvious that the van had had a hard life.

At first, no one climbed out or even rolled down a window. Then both front doors opened and two men got out. The passenger crossed between the van and Jack's truck to join the driver. The passenger was short and stocky, with piercing eyes, and the driver was much taller and powerfully built. Dressed in rumpled suits, with ties loosened, they looked like low-level overworked bureaucrats doing a job they would rather not. The driver had a piece of paper in his hand and alternately looked at the paper and Courtney's house. Finally he focused on Jack.

"Morning," said Jack, stepping toward them, "You look lost. Can I help you?"

The driver looked at the paper again and then back at Jack. "No, I don't think so. I think we found what we're looking for."

As Jack paused to try to identify the driver's distinct accent, he spotted the gun in the passenger's hand. Suddenly, Jack remembered the story that Patti and Max had told him about the two men in the bar last night, and his heart went cold.

"Please come with us."

Jack froze. Images in his mind flashed between the package they'd hooked on the boat and the sight of Bryan's body being hauled up to shore. Somehow, he just knew that these men were behind it.

"Mr. Beale. You will come with us now, or my partner will go find that pretty little friend of yours and . . . well, I think you understand, yes?"

"Fine." He began walking toward the van.

* * *

High above Jack, Max had been looking out the window to see if she would need to bring an umbrella to work. The clouds were now so dark she glanced down at the drive to see if the ground was wet. She watched as the van stopped and two men get out. "Probably lost tourists," she thought to herself as she began to turn away. But something about the men looked familiar. She turned back and watched as Jack stepped toward them.

"What are they doing here?" she said under her breath.

As she watched, the three men briefly exchanged words, and then together they walked toward the van. "What the—"

Before she could finish her question, Jack had disappeared around the back of the van, followed by the two men. Moments later, the van shot backwards, cutting sharply in front of Courtney's. Gravel splayed as it accelerated down the drive. In that moment, her jealousy and anger were replaced by panic and fear.

Max ran from the window and grabbed the phone.

"Patti! Let me talk to Dave."

"He left for work a while ago. Why?"

"They just took Jack!"

"Who?"

"Those men! The guys from the bar last night! They were just here. I was looking out the window and they pulled up in a van. Jack was already outside, and they took him away."

"Oh, my god. Max. You have to call Tom."

CHAPTER 76

MAX HAD JUST DIALED THE STATION and was waiting for Tom to pick up when the call waiting tone beeped and Patti's number came up on the screen.

"Oh, my god, Max," Patti said for the second time in just minutes. "I just went outside and Dave's car is still here. His keys and his cell phone are on the ground near the mailbox. The cell phone is smashed like he dropped it. They must have taken him, too! What are we going to do?"

"Patti, I'm waiting for Tom to pick up. Melanie said he's there, but she put me on hold. Get in your car and come over. I'll call you back on your cell."

"Tom Scott."

"Tom! Two guys just took Jack away in a van. We think they also have Dave. You've got to get after them."

"Max?"

"Yes."

"What do you mean two guys just took Jack away?" His voice sounded calm and steady, in direct contrast to the way Max felt.

"Tom! There isn't time."

"Max. Slow down. Did you call 911?"

The phone went silent for a moment. Then, in a quieter voice, she said, "No. I called you."

"Okay. Now, Max, tell me exactly what happened."

She took a deep breath and began recounting what had occurred.

"Max. You said Patti is on the way over?"

"Yes. She should be here soon."

"Here's what I want you to do. Stay there and don't do anything. I'll be right over."

"Thanks."

* * *

Tom hung up the phone and looked across his desk at Coast Guard Investigator Peeves. He was about to say something when Inspector Peeves said, "She was shouting so much I heard. I've got a huge favor to ask. I need you to step aside. Let me handle this."

"What? She called me."

"Tom. Listen to me. These people are dangerous. They have no regard for anything except what they want."

"Terrorists?"

"I can't answer that."

"You can't or you won't? I thought we were on the same team."

"We are. But I need you to give me this. I need to go talk to Max and her friend— alone."

"Why?"

"It's complicated."

"Bullshit. Try me," said Tom.

Peeves stood and stared at him.

Tom took a breath and softened his tone. "Look, before I can agree, you've got to give me some idea of what's going on. Jack and Dave are friends."

Special Agent Peeves looked at Tom long and hard as if weighing his options. "Okay, but this can't leave this room. It's just between us."

"Understood."

For the next five minutes Tom listened in near disbelief. Finally Inspector Peeves stopped and stood. "Tom. This is important."

"You'd better get going. Max and Patti will getting anxious."

"Thank you. I'll be in touch."

CHAPTER 77

MAX WATCHED FROM THE WINDOW as Patti came up the drive and parked in front of Courtney's. She was about to go down to meet her when she saw another car approach. It parked behind Jack's truck and Agent Peeves climbed out. That's all she needed to see.

Max burst out the door just as he was about to say hello to Patti. She put her hands on her hips and yelled, "What are you doing here? Where's Tom? What the hell is going on?"

Ignoring her outburst, he said, "Hello, Max, Patti. Can we go inside?" His voice was calm and firm.

"You didn't answer my question."

"Please, let's go inside."

Patti moved toward the door and went in, but Max was giving no quarter and stood her ground.

"We have a situation—"

Max cut him off, "A situation! Damn straight we have a situation. Jack was forced into a van and we think they took Dave too and all you can say is, 'We have a situation'?"

Agent Peeves stepped toward Max. "Please, I understand that you're upset. Can we go inside? I'll explain everything."

Max continued to hold her ground. He stepped closer and said again, "Please," while motioning with his arm.

With a final glare, Max turned and led the way inside.

Clearing the top step, Max saw that Patti was standing by the window, staring out, her shoulders shaking slightly. "You okay?" Max asked.

Patti turned. Her eyes were red. With a soft sniffle, she managed a feeble, "Yes."

Before Max could say anything else, Special Agent Peeves, who had followed her up, cleared his throat.

The two women looked over and faced him. With an edge still in her voice, Max said, "Okay, we're here. What's going on?"

"I need your help."

"Our help?" Now Max was nearly shouting. "What about Dave and Jack? What about them? Who's going to help them?"

"Let me start again. Believe me when I say that I had hoped that nothing like this would happen. I warned Jack and Dave."

"But—"

He held up his hand and continued. "As I'm sure you both know, I've been investigating the sinking of Richie Lowe's boat and his subsequent disappearance. Since then, there have been at least three other deaths that I think are all related, including the death of Dave's friend Bryan, and the last thing I want is for there to be two more."

He paused to let that sink in. "Richie was involved in a smuggling operation that we have been investigating for several years now. We've had an undercover agent working on the inside, but she disappeared at the same time that his boat sank out at Jeffreys. I believe that the agent is alive and that Dave and Jack know where she is."

Max stared at him, sucked in her breath, and then blurted out, "She? Are you telling us that she's an agent who works for you?"

"So she is alive," he said softly, as if to himself.

"She who? And what does any of this have to do with Dave and Jack?" Patti asked.

The agent looked at the women and said, "Okay, Max. I think it's time we stop playing games."

She nodded in agreement and turned to Patti. "It's Sylvie."

"Sylvie! That woman who was after Jack? What does she have to do with this?"

Officer Peeves broke in. "I can tell you that the woman you know as Sylvie has worked for me for quite some time. At this point, I am concerned for her. Something, I don't know what, happened to her a while back, and it seems that she has, shall we say, strayed off the reservation."

Max interrupted. "So now you're telling us Sylvie's an agent and you're saying you've lost her?"

His silence confirmed that she had heard the story correctly. Patti sniffled and blew her nose on a tissue from her purse.

After a few minutes of awkward silence, Max asked, "So what does Jack have to do with any of this?"

"And what about Dave?" Patti chimed in.

"We . . . uh, I think that they found her during their first fishing trip with Bryan and somehow she convinced them to keep her existence a secret. I also think that later she somehow coerced Bryan to help her retrieve whatever it was that Richie had been after when his boat sunk."

"And you know this how?" asked Max

"I don't. This is all speculation, but circumstantially, it all fits."

CHAPTER 78

JACK'S HEAD WAS POUNDING. His arms had been twisted behind his back and something was cutting into his wrists. He tried to sit up, but couldn't. Even if he were not tied up, the motion of the van as it sped along was such that it would have been difficult. It took a few moments before it all began to come back to him. He remembered the van coming up the drive, the two men getting out, and the gun. The gun. He especially remembered the gun. The passenger had used it to direct him to the back of the van. He remembered his own surprise at seeing Dave on the floor, and then it all went black. Now, as it came back to him, he twisted around to check his surroundings. The back of the van was empty save for him and Dave. A loud pounding techno beat filled the van, and even if his head hadn't hurt from getting knocked unconscious, that music would have done the job.

"Dave."

At first there was no answer, but when he managed to turn enough to nudge Dave with his feet, his friend responded.

"Jack?"

"You all right?"

"I'll live."

"Who are these guys?"

"Don't know. But I know what they want."

"What?"

"Whatever Bryan and Sylvie pulled up. They think we know where it is."

"Do you?"

"No. You?"

"No. But we better find a way to convince them we do or we'll end up joining Bryan."

"And how do you propose we do that? We really don't know."

"Yeah."

"Any idea where we're going?"

"None. This feel like the *Fugowee Run* to you?"

"Yeah, it does, but I'll take blindfolds over a knock on the head any day."

"Me too."

* * *

Agent Peeves watched as Max walked over to take Patti's hand. Both women stared at him.

"So what are you going to do?" asked Max.

"I . . . we need to find Sylvie. It's obvious she has some kind of connection with Jack." From the look that Max gave him, he knew instantly that this was a touchy subject. "Look Max, as difficult as this may be, it's our only hope."

"I know. But I don't have to like it."

Patti had been silent through this exchange, but now her voice broke the icy silence. "So how do we find her?"

"Unless either of you know how to reach her, I'm afraid there's not a lot more that either of you can do right now but stay put and see if she contacts you. Tom's put out a general alert on the van, and I'm going to return to my office to see if I can dig up anything else."

As he walked down the stairs, he remained convinced that they knew more than either was letting on, Max in particular. There was something, he couldn't say exactly what, but there was something about the way she reacted to even the mere mention of Sylvie that convinced him that she knew more than she was willing to admit. *If I read her right, she's going to do something,* he thought to himself.

CHAPTER 79

JACK HAD NO IDEA HOW LONG they had been in the van, but it seemed as if they had been riding for hours. He had finally managed to get into a sitting position and was leaning against the side of the van. The pounding in his head wasn't helped by the techno beat that still filled the van. Making matters worse, the throbbing in his head seemed to be keeping the same rhythm.

Dave, lying on his side across from Jack, croaked in a loud whisper, "Jack, can you see anything?"

Jack's first reaction was to shake his head to indicate no. That was a huge mistake. His head felt like it was going to explode. He winced and wished that his hands were free so he could hold his head, rub his temples, or do something to lessen the pain. Instead, all he could do was close his eyes and take long, deep breaths until the throbbing settled back into that incessant techno beat coming from the front of the van.

As bad as his neck and shoulders ached from his arms being twisted behind, and the fact that his hands were beginning to go numb, when Jack looked down at Dave, with his split lip and swelling cheek, he told himself to suck it up, after all. After all, they had only hit him once. He twisted to his right and strained to see out the front windshield.

"Can't really see anything. Sky out of the front window. Our friends seem to be having a discussion."

"Probably about where to dump us."

Jack looked over at his best friend. Dave tried to smile, but it was more a grimace and his chuckle more a groan.

Jack started to grin. As grim as their situation was, there was a certain dark humor to it. *Yep, just like the "Fugowee,"* he thought to himself. He returned his gaze toward the front of the van as the beat went on and Dave closed his eyes.

Jack continued to stare toward the front windshield, looking for any clue that might give a hint as to where they were going: a sign, an overpass, anything. Whenever their direction changed so that the sun streamed in through the windshield, he had to close his eyes tight against the pain, which felt like red-hot pokers were being stuck into his eyes. With that loud techno music serving as a metronome, the throbbing in his head never missed a beat.

The music also made it hard to hear any outside sounds that might provide clues to their location. He tried to visualize their route from the swaying of the van whenever they changed direction, but that proved impossible. In short, he had no real idea where they were going. Still, that didn't stop him from saying, "I think we're heading south, maybe southeast."

When there was no immediate response from Dave, Jack looked down at his friend again. Dave appeared to be either asleep or unconscious, so he nudged him with his foot.

Dave lifted his eyes. "You see something?"

"Nothing specific. Just a feeling that we're going in that direction."

"Ohhhh." Dave made a sound that seemed to be part groan and part acknowledgement of what Jack had just said and closed his eyes again.

Shortly after that the van stopped abruptly, causing Jack to tip over onto his side. Craning his neck around he was able to catch a glimpse out the front again. This time instead of blue sky he saw mostly tree limbs and leaves. Then Jack felt as much as heard the van being shifted into reverse. It turned sharply, accelerated back, and then jerked to a stop. The engine continued to run and there was no relief from the music. Looking forward, Jack could see that the two men were having an animated discussion, and even though he couldn't hear what they were saying, their gestures indicated that it was about him and Dave.

He nudged Dave and whispered, "I think we've arrived." Before he could say anything else, the engine stopped. The smaller man in the passenger seat glanced back and reached for something that was behind the driver's seat. As soon as he turned back and opened the door, the music stopped. It was strange. At first the music continued to reverberate in Jack's ears, but by the time both men had climbed out and closed their doors, the silence finally won out.

Jack looked over at Dave and saw him looking up.

"Where are we?" Dave said.

"Don't know." They were whispering, unlike the two men, whom they could hear talking just outside the back of the van. Their voices were muffled and the language was foreign.

Suddenly one of the back doors to the van was yanked open and Jack found himself staring at the same gun that he had been introduced to earlier.

"Quiet. Don't move."

Jack froze and stared at the man who filled the doorway. He tried to see beyond him for clues as to where they might be, but that proved to be impossible.

The man leaned in. With his free hand he deftly dropped a black cloth bag over Jack's head. That's when Jack heard the other door open.

"Get him out."

Jack couldn't be sure which of the men spoke, but instantly a pair of strong hands grabbed him by one of his arms and yanked him toward the door. His shoulder exploded in pain. He cried out, but it made no difference. He was being dragged out and it was all he could do to get his feet out first to keep from falling on the ground. Outside, he was pushed up against the van. The gun barrel pressed into his ribs and a voice told him not to move.

He could hear Dave receiving the same treatment, only it sounded like Dave was led away immediately.

"Now, move!"

Jack moved, guided by the barrel pressing hard into his back. He nearly fell as the ground suddenly sloped away. The surface felt grassy under his shoes, and when it flattened out, a hand grabbed his shoulder, sending more waves of pain through his body and signaling him to a stop.

A door opened and he was shoved through the opening. "You will be quiet," said his captor. Then the door was shut and he could hear a lock click.

"Dave? You in here?"

"Over here."

Jack tried to follow the voice, but with the bag over his head it was nearly impossible. He steadied himself and took several tentative steps. He nearly tripped as his foot hit something.

"Hey, take it easy."

It was Dave. He was on the floor.

"You okay?" Jack asked.

"Yeah. As okay as I can be, considering."

"Any ideas?"

"No. And I have a bag over my head."

"Me too. You sitting or lying down?"

"Sitting."

"Okay then. My hands are still tied behind me, so I'm going to turn around and try to grab your hood with my hands and pull it off."

"Go for it."

It took several tries, but finally the bag was pulled off. Jack could hear Dave taking several deep breaths. "Thanks man, I was dying in there."

"I can imagine. So what's it look like?"

"Empty."

"What do you mean, empty?"

"There is nothing in here."

"Nothing?"

"Nothing— just us."

"So how about you help me get this bag off my head."

"I don't know. Kind of looks good on you."

"Thanks, wiseass."

Ten minutes later the bag was off Jack's head and the two friends were sitting next to each other in the middle of the one-room building.

"You're right. It is nice. Wonder why it's empty? There's nothing in here," said Jack. "My hands are going numb, how're yours?"

"I hate zip ties. That's all I'm going to say."

CHAPTER 80

AS SOON AS SPECIAL AGENT PEEVES drove away, Max turned to Patti. "I have an idea."

"What can we do?" Patti said. "He told us to stay here."

"I know, but . . ." Max paused. "Patti, I never told you this, but the day after that fishing trip, Sylvie called Jack for his help. Her car had been stolen, and we gave her a ride to her place in Gloucester."

"You and Jack drove her home? You're kidding."

"No, I'm not."

"Why would you even do that?"

"I don't know. Somehow Jack made it seem like the right thing to do. I sure as hell wasn't letting him take her alone."

Patti just shook her head.

"It was a cute house."

"Max!"

"Sorry! When we got there, she got all funny and said that someone had been in the house. She insisted that we leave right then. "

"How come you never told me this?"

"I guess I just wanted to forget that it happened."

"You should have told me."

"I know. I'm sorry. Anyway, what do you say to a road trip to Gloucester?"

"What?"

"Look, we need to find Sylvie. I think I remember where her house is. Hopefully she's there."

"Max, No. Agent Peeves will be back soon."

Ignoring her friend, Max began gathering her things. "You coming with me or not?"

"No. I'm staying."

"Fine, suit yourself. Dammit, where are they?"

"What?"

"The keys to Jack's truck."

"Why don't you take your car?"

"No gas. The keys must be in it. At least come down and help me look."

Max told Patti to check under the passenger's side while she checked the usual places: in the ignition, on top of the sun visor, or under the driver's seat. Frustrated, Max hit the wheel with her hand.

"Damn it, Jack," she muttered under her breath. As she said those words, she pulled the ashtray compartment open. Inside, amongst spare change and bits of paper, were the keys.

Max started to pull the keys out of the ashtray but a scrap of paper was stuck to the ring. It looked like a stained Dunkin Donuts receipt.

"God, Patti, I don't think Jack ever cleans out this truck," she said as she peeled it off the ring. Some writing caught her eye.

"It's a phone number," she said, "with the letter *S.*"

"Try it!" Patti said.

CHAPTER 81

AS MAX COUNTED THE RINGS, she held her breath. On the fifth ring a voice answered.

"Hello?"

The voice was so soft, Max couldn't tell if it was Sylvie or not. Just as much as Max wanted to find her, she didn't want to confirm the fact that Jack had been hiding her number.

For a moment, a wave of relief washed over Max as she convinced herself that it wasn't Sylvie. Then the voice said "hello" again, and this time she wasn't so sure.

"Sylvie?"

There was a long pause before the voice said, "Max?"

A chill ran through her as some of her worst fears were realized. "Yes."

"How did you get this number?"

"I found it."

"Is Jack all right?"

"No . . . Yes . . . I don't know." Max was beginning to become unglued.

"Max! Tell me about Jack."

"I'm sorry. He and Dave have been taken. We don't know where they are, or what their captors want."

"Who took them?"

"Two men. One is tall and muscular and the other is shorter, built like a tank. I saw them in the bar the other day. They spoke with some kind of an accent. Apparently they grabbed Dave first and then they came for Jack. I saw him walk to the back of the van with them and then they sped off."

"And then?"

"I called Tom but he didn't come. Special Agent Peeves showed up instead."

"Special Agent Peeves?"

"Yeah. He's a Coast Guard Investigator who keeps turning up to ask Jack questions about finding the debris from Richie's boat. He's looking for you, too. Look, Sylvie, do you work for him?"

"It's complicated, Max. Meet me in the second parking area on 1-A as you head into Hampton Beach from the north in twenty minutes."

* * *

Twenty minutes passed, then another twenty. Max was getting progressively more agitated as her wait neared forty-five minutes. With each passing minute and every car that drove by looking for a place to park, her emotional roller coaster fluctuated from a sense of relief at the reprieve, no matter how short, to an increasingly greater dread of having to face Sylvie in person.

Sitting on the tailgate of the truck waiting for Sylvie's arrival, Max could feel the temperature rise. She rubbed her sweaty palms on her jeans and wished that she had worn shorts like the dozens of beachgoers streaming past her. As she pulled her sweatshirt over her head, she heard a deep rumble that was steadily growing louder.

Sweatshirt off, she looked and saw a motorcycle approaching. The rider was dressed in black: boots, chaps over jeans, leather jacket, and a helmet with a dark tinted visor, which remained pulled down. "It must be hot wearing all that black leather," she thought.

The bike stopped in front of Max. Without a word, the rider unstrapped the helmet and pulled it off. "Hello, Max."

It was Sylvie.

"Sylvie," she replied. She hopped off the tailgate and stepped toward the bike. "What the hell is going on?"

Sylvie stared at her, but before she could respond, Max repeated the question. "I asked you—what is going on? Where's Jack? And Dave?

What have you done?"

"Max, I haven't done anything."

"Bullshit. You're involved in something and because of whatever it is, Jack and Dave are in trouble."

"Poor choice of words on my part. I'm sorry."

Sylvie climbed off the bike. In bare feet she would be about the same height as Max, but in her boots, with their heels, she seemed to tower over her.

"Max, we can sit here and bitch at each other, or you can sit and listen to what I have to say. I don't want anything to happen to Jack or Dave any more than you do."

"Fine." Max crossed her arms over her chest. "I'm listening."

"Simply, the people who have Jack want something that I have, and I know they will do anything to get it."

"What do you have?"

"That doesn't matter."

"Yes, it does. According to Agent Peeves, it's the reason that Richie was killed, the reason you were left in the middle of the ocean, and the reason Bryan was killed. Now Jack and Dave have been kidnapped. So, yes, I think it matters."

"Come." Sylvie climbed back onto the bike.

Max didn't move. "I want some answers."

Sylvie put on her helmet and pressed the starter button. The cycle roared to life. She looked at Max, lifted the visor, and said, "Not here. You coming?"

Max looked at the bike and shook her head. "Not on that thing. I'll follow you in Jack's truck."

Sylvie closed the visor on her helmet. Max heard the bike click into gear and watched it begin to roll.

"That bitch," she said aloud as she jumped into the truck. Her hands were shaking, which made it hard to get the key into the ignition. As soon as the engine started, she slammed the shift into reverse and, without even looking, hit the gas. As she pulled away, she looked into her mirror and saw a runner in a Winner's Circle Singlet standing near where she had been parked. He was waving his arms and flipping her the bird.

"Shit," she mumbled. At least she hadn't hit him.

CHAPTER 82

SYLVIE WASN'T WASTING ANY TIME, and Max had to work to keep her in sight. Fortunately, the beach traffic was heavy enough that it slowed Sylvie down, and Max was able to keep her in sight as they rode past Salisbury Beach, over to Route 1, and south across the Merrimack River. By the time they drove through Ipswich, Max guessed that they were going to Sylvie's place. She was certain when they rounded the traffic circle at the end of Route 128 and headed north on 127.

However, Max was caught off guard when Sylvie slowed, turned, and then drove around to the back side of an unassuming red building. There were gas pumps in front, cars parked helter-skelter, and a steady stream of people going in and out. The name above the door was *Willow Rest*.

By the time Max finally found a place to park the truck, Sylvie was already standing in front of the door, waiting. As Max approached, she noticed that the bike was nowhere to be seen. But before she could say anything, Sylvie said, "I'm hungry. This place has great sandwiches. Come on. My treat."

Max followed her in. The building served as a general store, produce market, deli, and local gathering place. Crowded and cluttered, it had the same kind of feel that Paula's did in Rye Harbor. A large bulletin board near the entrance was filled with notices of future events as well as some that had already passed. Business cards for local services were tacked up everywhere, and there was a definite buzz to the place. Max couldn't help but notice how at home Sylvie was and how many people acknowledged her. Dead indeed.

"You like pastrami? This place has a great pastrami sandwich."

"Uh, sure," said Max, still wondering exactly what Sylvie was up to.

"They're big. I'll get one and we can split it. There's a table over there. Go grab it before she does." Sylvie nodded toward a couple who had just walked in and were clearly eyeing the table. She handed Max her helmet and added, "Drinks are in the cooler."

She said it in a way that left no room for discussion. Then she turned to place their order, leaving Max no choice but to claim the table and get some drinks.

As Max placed the helmet on the table, she noticed that along with everything else in the place, there were also some local crafts on display. A rack of beaded necklaces caught her attention, and since Sylvie was still at the counter, Max went over to check them out. Above the rack was a handwritten card with the name of the artist: Jeanette Johnson, JJ for short.

"She really has a good sense of design and color. I have several."

Max turned. It was the woman who had just walked in.

"This one would be stunning on you," the woman said, pointing at one that was black with some small gold accent beads.

"It is beautiful. Do you know her?" said Max, fingering the necklace.

The woman looked at Max, obviously surprised. "You don't know her?"

"No, I'm sorry."

The woman started to chuckle. "That's just like her. You're sitting with her."

Max tried to cover her surprise. "We just met. She never mentioned that she was an artisan."

"She's quite amazing, isn't she? Looks like your lunch is ready. It was nice talking to you."

Max looked over toward their table as her new friend walked away. Sylvie had just put the sandwich down and was looking around the store. Max went to the cooler and got an iced tea and a lemonade.

"I didn't know which you would prefer . . . JJ." Max kind of spat out the *JJ*.

"Lemonade. Look Max, I don't expect you to understand, or even to like me. But the fact is, we—yes, we—have a problem, and I'm going to try to fix it."

"You're going to try! Trying isn't good enough. You've got to fix it."

"You're not eating your sandwich. It's good." Sylvie took another bite of her half, ignoring Max's reaction.

Max took a bite. It was good, and she was hungry, but that was not enough to fully temper her anger. "So what's with this JJ stuff?"

"Oh, nothing."

"What do you mean 'nothing'?"

Sylvie looked at her. "I use it . . . uh . . . think of it as a pen name. Authors do it all the time."

"And you make jewelry." Max was having a hard time buying what she was hearing.

"Yes. It relaxes me. Do you have a hobby?"

"It relaxes you?"

"Yes."

"And you live here?"

Sylvie nodded.

"In the house where Jack and I took you?"

"Some of the time."

Max looked at Sylvie, still trying to wrap her head around all this new information.

"Okay, you live here some of the time. You make jewelry under the name JJ, and people around here know you by that name. What else is missing from this story?"

Sylvie said nothing and took another bite of her sandwich.

"Okay, never mind your story. Right now I really want to know what you are going to do about Jack and Dave."

"Fair enough. You finished?"

Max nodded.

"Then let's go. And by the way, we're taking Jack's truck from here on out."

CHAPTER 83

"WHERE'S MAX?" Agent Peeves asked Patti. He hadn't been gone long, but he had hoped that during his absence the women might have agreed to tell him more.

"Gloucester, maybe. I'm not sure."

"What do you mean you're not sure?"

"She took off to look for Sylvie. That's where she thinks Sylvie lives."

"And why does she think that?"

"Apparently after that fishing trip, Sylvie called Jack. Her car had been stolen. They gave her a ride to Gloucester, and I think that's where Max is going now."

"They knew!" he thought, It was all he could do to contain his anger. He took a deep breath and forced himself to remain calm. "I wish she had waited for me to get back."

"I don't think she trusts you."

"So I gathered."

"What are you going to do?"

"Here's my number. You stay here, I'm going to head to Gloucester to see if I can catch up with her before she does something really stupid."

"Do you know where she's going?"

"I have a hunch."

* * *

C.G.I.S. Agent Peeves was furious. She had withheld information from him. She and Jack had been in contact with Sylvie. "What's wrong with these people?" he asked himself as he backed down Jack's drive. He knew that the quickest way to Gloucester would be via the highway. He also knew that from Rye Harbor there was no quick way to the highway, and as hard as he pushed it, the tight roads, slow-driving tourists, and red lights conspired to make the ride painful, which only increased his anger and anxiety.

Different scenarios began forming in his head. He would get to the house and find no one, which would mean this was a wasted trip. He would get to the house and find evidence that Dave and Jack had been held there, but they were gone. He would get to the house and find only Max there, nothing else. He would get there and find evidence that Sylvie had been there, but no sign of Max, Dave, Jack, the kidnappers, or the stuff that Richie had been after. Or, he could find a complete cluster-fuck—the place a complete mess, possibly dead bodies, no Sylvie, no stuff, Jack, Dave, and Max maybe dead, maybe wounded, maybe . . . he didn't even want to think of that possibility.

He was mulling over that last scenario as he finally got onto the highway, and it just added to the sense of urgency he was feeling. Sixty, seventy, eighty. He watched his speedometer climb, and when he hit eighty-five he quit accelerating and focused on the road. He had just crossed the Massachusetts border when he began to see red taillights ahead.

CHAPTER 84

AN ICY SILENCE FILLED THE CAB OF JACK'S TRUCK. "Are we going to the place where we took you before?" asked Max. They had been driving for fifteen minutes, and other than a few cryptic instructions from Sylvie, little had been said.

"Pull in here," she instructed as they reached a church that was just down the street from her house.

Max pulled in, and only when she was as far from the road as possible, did Sylvie tell her to stop.

"Okay, Max. Here's the deal. What those guys want is in my house."

"So why don't we just go and get it?"

"Because I don't think that would be a good idea. When I was ordering lunch, the cook told me that a guy had come in looking for directions to my place. Based on his description, I'm pretty sure he was one of the guys who grabbed Jack and Dave. He bought four meals to go. You do the math."

"So they're here."

"Seems probable, but there's too much we don't know to just go barging in."

"So let's assume they're here. Who are these guys?"

"I don't know, but I'm guessing that they work for the same people who killed Bryan, and want me dead. From your description and what I was told by John back at the Nest . . ."

"John?"

"The cook. Friend of mine."

Sylvie took a deep breath. "Max, do you trust me?"

"No, I don't. But what choice do I have? Give me some answers and maybe I'll change my mind."

"Fair enough. I'll try. Go ahead."

"What is it you do?"

"I can't tell you. Next?"

"What about your real name. Is it really Sylvie or Jeanette or is it something else entirely?"

"Jeanette Johnson is the name I use for my jewelry making, otherwise Sylvie will work."

"Sylvie what?"

"That's not important."

"For the record, 'Sylvie,' we're not building a whole lot of trust here. What about Jack?"

"Jack?"

"I know you're attracted to him . . ."

"Max, stop right there. I will admit that I find Jack attractive. I find many men attractive. But Jack belongs to you . . ." Sylvie turned her head and looked out the passenger window, as if the discussion was closed.

By this point, Max had had enough. "Just forget it!" she said. "I'm going to look for Jack."

Max had just put her hand on the handle when Sylvie turned back and said sharply, "Don't open that door."

"And what if I do? What will happen?"

This time, when Sylvie stared at Max, her eyes were as cold as black steel. She said again, much more slowly, "Don't open that door."

Max looked back at her and then, slowly and deliberately, took her hand off the handle.

"Thank you. Now here's what's going to happen. You're going to stay here in the truck while I go and check out the house. Believe me when I tell you that these are not nice people, and if they do have Jack and Dave, they won't hesitate to kill them at the first sign of trouble. So please, don't be stupid."

Before Max a chance to say anything else, Sylvie opened her door, slid out, and without looking back moved briskly to the woods behind the church.

CHAPTER 85

JACK HAD TO TURN HIS HEAD and close his eyes when the door opened. The blast of sunlight blinded him for a moment, and it wasn't until a large shadow passed over him that he was able to open his eyes. Standing in the doorway was one of their captors. "Okay, you two. Time to go."

Jack still couldn't place the accent, but as he looked at the large silhouette framed in an aura of sunlight, he realized that the doorway faced west.

Jack was yanked to his feet first and then Dave was pulled up. As the hoods were dropped over their heads again, Jack said, "Hey, you got a bathroom? If I don't go, things will get really ugly, really fast."

His captor stopped. Jack could hear him catch his breath as if taken aback. "Wait here. Don't move," he said. It sounded like he turned away and stepped toward the door.

Jack could hear that a conversation was taking place, but because of the hood covering his head, the words were muffled.

"Let's go." His arm was grabbed and he was dragged out of the building, nearly losing his balance as he was pushed forward.

* * *

Sylvie watched as the two men walked out the back of her house and down to the building that she had been turning into a studio. As one went inside the other stood outside. His attention seemed to be divided between watching what was going on inside and then turning away and scanning the grounds. Sylvie knew he couldn't see her, but there was a moment when he looked right at her. She didn't recognize him, but she knew that in the future she'd never forget his face.

Her house was situated on the edge of the abandoned quarry that, a hundred years ago, had provided the economic life-blood of the area. Ever since that time, Mother Nature had quietly been reclaiming what was once hers. Now it was a tangled mess of low-lying scrub brush and trees that had anchored themselves into the tiniest of cracks and crevasses in the rocks, hiding the quarry from view.

After leaving Max, she had followed the trail that ran along the rim of the quarry. Originally a shortcut that the local kids had made with their bikes to get from one neighborhood to another, it was now a trail that everyone used, but travelers still had to be careful. Anyone who was not aware of the local history might never know that just off the trail, hidden by that overgrowth, were some steep drop-offs that could be deadly.

The spot on the trail that led to her house was near one of those drop-offs, and she had almost missed it because it had become so overgrown. Twice she had needed to catch herself to keep from losing her footing. Moving slowly and carefully so as to make as little noise as possible, she had made her way down until she had come to the place where she knew she could watch the house without being seen. Several large blocks of granite lay there, having been cut but never removed, and they created a natural blind from which she could watch the house. From here she would be able to remain hidden and still have a clear view of the back of her house.

She watched as one of the men pushed and prodded Jack up toward the house. Jack's arms appeared to be bound and he had a bag over his head. Then the second man, whose face she had first seen, went inside and brought out Dave, who was also pushed and prodded up to the house. Then they all disappeared inside.

As she waited, she became increasingly impatient and concerned. As she was working out in her mind how she was going to approach the house without being seen, she heard the sound of car doors slamming and an engine starting. "Could they be leaving?" she thought.

Without any further consideration of sight lines or stealth, she left her spot in the rocks and hopped and skipped down the last vestiges of the old quarry until she reached the back yard. From there it was a fifty-yard sprint up a gentle slope, past the shack where Jack and Dave had been held, to the back of the house. Because the property had been defined by the long-gone quarry, the front of the house was at street level, but in the back its foundation was fully exposed, and there, a door led into the cellar. Above that door and jutting out from the house was a deck on which she had spent many pleasant evenings watching the sun set.

As soon as she was under the deck, she knew that she couldn't be seen from inside the house if anyone remained. She took several deep recovery breaths and listened for any sign that someone was around and she had been seen. The only sound she heard was that of her pounding heart. Satisfied that they were indeed gone and she was alone and undetected, she turned her attention to the door. The top half of the door had six glass panes that were so dirty that seeing inside was virtually impossible. It was locked, but locked doors were never an obstacle for her. Seconds later she had pulled it open and slipped inside.

CHAPTER 86

IT HAD BEEN FIFTEEN MINUTES or so since Sylvie had walked off. Max was sitting in the truck growing increasingly impatient. She got out and began pacing. At first she stayed near the truck, but as she paced, she began to consider following Sylvie down the path. Several times she turned toward the path, and each time as she neared it, she would stop, consider what she was about to do, then turn back and return to the truck. On the third cycle, as she neared the beginning of the trail she heard the sound of people running. Fearing the worst, she turned and sprinted back to the truck. Breathing heavy and with her heart pounding, she got to where it was parked just as two runners came out of the woods. She laughed at her overactive imagination as she watched them run past the truck, across the parking lot, on to the street, and out of sight.

As Max watched them head down the road, a car turned onto the street and began driving toward her. Without thinking, she stepped back behind a large bush that was in front of the church and watched it approach. She began to feel embarrassed for a second time until she realized that driving the car was Special Agent Peeves. Holding her breath, and with heart pounding, she watched as he drove slowly by, his gaze focused on the road ahead. As soon as he was past, she returned to the truck and climbed in. As she sat there, hands shaking, she realized that she was worried for Sylvie.

* * *

It was dark and cool. As her eyes adjusted to what little light came in through the grimy panes of glass in the door, she listened again for any sounds that might indicate that she wasn't alone. Looking up she saw that the single light bulb for the cellar had been broken. Hearing nothing, she began to feel more confident as she felt her way across the cellar. It was filled with years of accumulated stuff—boxes, old bicycles, furniture and all the other reminders of past lives. It was a minefield of things that could easily be tripped over, so she took slow and deliberate steps as she made her way deeper into the shadows.

When she reached the far wall, she knew that she was under the front entrance of the house, so she stopped and listened again. Not having heard a single sound to the contrary, she was now confident that the slamming car doors that she had heard were from the van, and that the house was empty. With cobwebs tickling her neck and a strong urge to sneeze, she began moving boxes until she found the cases she had hidden.

"If they only knew," she thought to herself as she moved the last box under which she had stashed the three cases she and Bryan had recovered from the ocean. A wave of relief washed over her. She opened the first case. The cash was all there as were the flash drives in the second. Removing the long flat case, she then replaced everything she had moved, hiding again the two smaller cases.

As she worked, she was a little surprised that the cases hadn't been found. They had to have known that the house was hers, so the questions became, "Why hadn't they searched down in the cellar, and why had they brought Jack and Dave here?" As she pondered these questions, she began to see several possibilities. First, there were those two guys who had visited before. Probably had been sent to search for the cases, but she had surprised them. One ended up dead, with a broken neck and the other avoided the same fate by running. When the local police arrived, there would have been no reason for them to search the cellar since everything had taken place upstairs and it had looked like a break-in gone bad.

But then there was Peeves. He wanted her as much as Endroit did, and if Peeves did know about the cases, it made sense that he'd search more thoroughly if he showed up. The more she thought about it, the more she was convinced that the two men who had Jack and Dave were low-level thugs, hired by someone—probably Endroit in an effort to get to her. And if that failed, they, along with Jack and Dave, were probably expendable. That's how Endroit worked.

CHAPTER 87

SYLVIE DECIDED TO TAKE A LOOK around upstairs, but first she opened the case and removed a handgun that had a silencer attached. Then she closed the case, left it in the shadows, and went up. The house was empty. The only sign that anyone had been there was a really nasty smell lingering in the bathroom. She was about to head back to the cellar when some movement out a front window caught her eye. Curious, she stood to one side of the curtains and took a quick look out. Peeves.

She knew why he was here. She also knew that he was a by-the-book kind of guy, so without proper authorization it was unlikely he'd come into the house. Slipping back down into the cellar, she made sure that the door to the cellar was locked, grabbed the case, and moved back into the shadows.

Her eyes had adjusted to what little light there was that came through the grimy windows in the cellar door and from her vantage point she could watch it. The first indication that he was there occurred when the cellar became darker and she could see him trying to peer in through the windows. She heard the knob rattle, and then the door clicked before slowly opening.

Didn't I leave it locked? she thought. *Yes. I know I did. Oh, Alistaire, you must really be desperate. It's not like you to behave like this.*

She watched as he slipped in and pushed the door closed until it made the telltale snick of the latch catching. He turned from the door, paused, looked around, and then walked to the stairs and went up. As much as she wanted to run, she knew she couldn't. She could hear his footsteps on the floor above as he slowly and deliberately walked about the house. It seemed like a very long time before she heard the door at the top of the stairs open again, followed by his footsteps on the stairs.

Sylvie held her breath as he reached the bottom of the stairs and stopped and looked around. *Please leave*, she repeated over and over in her head. *Yes!* she thought as he stepped toward the door, followed by, *Oh, shit*, as he turned and began walking in her direction. She was confident that he could not see her, but he began moving things about. A tiny flashlight appeared in his hand and she watched as the beam passed back and forth around the cellar.

All of a sudden, the beam clicked off. He strode to the door, opened it, and was gone. Sylvie took a deep breath to calm herself. Moving toward the corner of the cellar that was nearest the driveway, she listened to see if she could hear him leaving. She thought she heard a car door shut and an engine start, but she wasn't sure. The only way to know for sure would be to leave the cellar and go look.

Luck was on her side. When she peeked around the corner, there was no sign of his car. Grabbing the case she ran quickly across the yard, retracing her steps back to that natural blind where she knew she could watch the house without being seen. She opened the case, put the pistol into its nest, and then took out the rifle for a quick inspection. Satisfied, she replaced the rifle, closed the case, and pressed it into a hollow on the ground beside her that was covered in weeds.

CHAPTER 88

AFTER MAX SAW AGENT PEEVES drive by, she began checking her watch. Each passing minute increased her anxiety. Five minutes. Ten minutes. Fifteen minutes passed. "Come on Sylvie," Max said under her breath. After another ten minutes had gone by, she couldn't wait any longer. Sylvie's instructions be damned. She had to do something.

As soon as her feet hit the pavement, however, the resolve that had brought her to the point where she had to do something began to fade. She looked toward the trail one more time, hoping that Sylvie would suddenly appear. Nothing. The only movements she saw were leaves rustling in the breeze.

"Okay then," Max said to herself as she turned to head for the road. But before she could take a step a voice in her head made her stop. If Peeves was still around, her red hair would make her too easy to spot. She looked in one of the side mirrors and began to fuss with her hair until she had gathered it onto the top of her head and decided that it would suffice. Only thing was, she needed some way to hold it there, out of sight. Heaven only knew what was in Jack's truck. She let her hair drop and began rummaging through the truck's cab.

Behind the seat, under some old rags, a length of chain, and several coiled ropes, she found it. "Sweet!" she said softly as she pulled out a shapeless mess that was once an old ball cap. As she pressed it back into shape, she realized that it was Jack's old boat-work hat from when he had *Irrepressible*. Faded, sweat-stained, and stiff from dried paint, it was pretty nasty, and she began to reconsider her idea. But, as she looked at it, memories flooded back.

"Jack! Why do you need to keep this nasty old thing?"

"It's loyalty, Max. That cap is like an old friend."

It was springtime, and she was helping him get Irrepressible *ready to go back in the water.*

"Jack, how can you enjoy such a tedious, back breaking, knee-bruising, muscle-aching job?"

"It's the delightful promise of your post-work massages, Max. That's what always keeps me going!"

Now Max thought, "I wonder if he even knows that it's back here?" In the end memories trumped nastiness, and she put it on, carefully tucking her hair into it. Another glance in the mirror and she was ready.

As she walked out to the road, it struck her how quiet it was. There were no cars driving by, no kids playing, and other than the cries of a few seagulls, there was no other signs of life. Was the road closed?

Standing in front of the church, she looked in the direction she and Sylvie had come from and saw no indication that that was the case. Besides, Peeves had come by earlier. In fact, as she turned and began walking up the street toward Sylvie's house, she saw his car backing out of the driveway. Immediately Max knelt down with her back to the road and pretended to be tying her shoelace. She cocked her head just enough to see him drive off away from her. She was about to stand again when she saw a white van coming toward her up the street.

Even though she was still kneeling, now she stared at the approaching van. She watched it as it drove past and then slowed, finally turning into the same drive that Special Agent Peeves had just left. "That was close," she thought to herself.

Heart pounding, Max stood as soon as the van was no longer in sight. Her first reaction was to run over to see if Jack was there, but then she recalled that Sylvie had said that the men were likely armed and dangerous.

She looked back toward the church. There was no sign of Sylvie, and Max realized that her questions had multiplied. Had Sylvie met up with Peeves? Did he leave to get help, or was he gone for good? Did the guys in the van have guns? Whose side was Sylvie really on, anyway?

Max's fear turned to panic as she remembered Sylvie's last words, warning her to stay with the truck. She ran back to the church, feeling both relief and dismay that Sylvie wasn't there.

CHAPTER 89

AFTER TUCKING THE CASE into the hollow, Sylvie sat down and looked back at the house, thinking about her options. First, she needed to get those other two cases out of the house. Without them, she would not be able to finish what she had started. Second, Jack and Dave needed to be rescued, but she had no idea when or if they would return. And finally, she had to disappear.

A flash of sunlight off a side-view mirror caught her eye as the van returned. "What the hell?" she said in a hushed whisper. "Did they forget something?"

Sylvie reacted by quickly pulling the case from its hiding place beside her. Glancing up she saw the two guys pulling Jack and Dave out of the back of the van. By the time they were out of the van, she had opened the case, assembled the rifle, and attached a powerful scope and the silencer. With the rifle propped on the rock in front of her, she began watching them.

Jack and Dave had hoods over their heads, hands secured behind their backs, and each was being escorted down to the shed in the back by one of the men. Because of the down slope and the blindfolds, their escorts were having some difficulty in keeping them upright. Jack seemed to be having an easier time of it, and as he was led down first, a gap developed between the two pairs.

Sylvie took a deep breath and, without thinking, sighted in on the man who was escorting Jack. For the next few moments her entire universe existed inside that small round circle, which she kept centered on the man's head. As if trapped in the vacuum of space, she heard nothing and felt nothing. All she saw clearly was a tiny spot of pink flesh in the circle's very center. Then, in less than a blink, that tiny spot became a larger black dot and he fell from sight.

Without hesitation she refocused on the second man. It had happened so quickly that he hadn't had time to react to the shooting, and the expression on his face was one of complete incomprehension. She focused and pulled again, and he too dropped to the ground.

In just seconds, she had solved two problems and created a whole set of new ones. With practiced precision she disassembled the rifle and returned the pieces to the case. From a quick glance toward Jack and Dave, she could tell that they were not sure exactly what had happened. The calm and singular focus she had experienced during the past few seconds were now replaced with an urgency—and the need to act.

She sprinted from her vantage point in the rocks toward the house, giving little attention to stealth. Sure that Special Agent Peeves would return, probably sooner than later, she had to get those cases and disappear.

As she neared, she could hear Jack and Dave calling back and forth to each other, trying to figure out what had happened. Ignoring them, she ran to the cellar door, yanked it open, and moved straight to the front wall where the cases were hidden. As she had done only a short while before, she carefully moved all that hid the cases, pulled them out, and put everything back. It wasn't perfect, but it'd do for the moment. Exiting the cellar, cases in hand, she glanced over at where Jack and Dave were attempting to pull the hoods off their heads, and she ran.

* * *

"Dave. You all right?"

"Fine. What the hell just happened?"

"I hate to think. Help me get this hood off, like we did in the shed."

"Holy shit," said Dave as his hood was pulled off. Then he said, "You're not gonna' believe this. Your turn."

Jack knelt and Dave moved in front of him, back to, so he could grab Jack's hood

"Got it," said Dave.

Jack sank down and rolled to his right, leaving Dave standing there, holding the hood.

"Oh, my god," said Jack when he saw the two bodies each with a neat dark hole in the center of the forehead and blood pooling below.

"We gotta get out of here. This was an execution. Did you hear someone run by just after the two shots were fired?"

Dave shook his head.

"Well I did. Whoever it was ran past me and into the house, and then just as fast ran out. Never even offered to help or anything."

"Maybe it was the killer."

"I suppose."

"So how 'bout we get up into the house, maybe find a knife and get our hands free, and then call the cops."

"Sounds like a plan."

For the second time in as many hours, the two friends climbed the stairs to the deck. The door was closed, but not locked. Inside Sylvie's kitchen, they found a knife and managed to cut their hands free.

CHAPTER 90

WHEN SYLVIE EMERGED from the end of the trail into the parking lot, Max saw that she was carrying three cases. They must have been heavy because she dropped one at just that moment.

"Sylvie. What happened?" Max said. She left the truck, ran over, and helped her with the case. "Are you all right? Did you see Jack and Dave? Agent Peeves was there—did you see him?"

Sylvie didn't answer but kept moving toward the truck.

"Throw that in the back. We've got to get out of here."

Max stopped. "What do you mean we've got to get out of here? What about the guys?"

"We've got to get out of here," she repeated. Her voice was hard and commanding. She threw her cases in the back of the truck, grabbed the one Max was holding, and did the same. "Get in," she said while turning toward the passenger side door.

"No. Not until you tell me what is going on. Are Jack and Dave all right?"

Sylvie stopped and walked over to Max. "I'm not going to say this again. They are all right and we have to get out of here—now!"

Her tone left no room for debate, and even as anxious and wound up as Max was, she knew that she was no match for Sylvie. She turned and walked around the truck and climbed in.

"Drive. Back to my bike."

Nothing else was said until the Willow Rest was in sight."

"Are you going to tell me what's going on?" Max asked finally.

"It's best you don't know."

"But I saw Inspector Peeves show up and then leave. I saw the white van. It was them, wasn't it?"

"I thought I had told you to stay in the truck."

Max said, "Tell me what happened."

"Drive around. My bike's back there."

Max was getting pissed off. She hit the gas, swerved around a parked car, reached the back of the building, and then slammed on the brakes, stopping inches from the motorcycle.

"There. Now tell me."

Sylvie gave Max a look that would cause hell to freeze, opened her door, slid out, and went to the back of the truck, where she opened the tailgate.

As Max jumped out her door, a police car flew by, lights flashing and siren screaming. By the time Max had reached the back of the truck, Sylvie had pulled the long flat case to the tailgate and opened it.

Ready for a fight, Max stopped when she saw the open case, gasped, and stared first at what was in the case, then at Sylvie.

Sylvie, ignoring Max, took the handgun out of the case and put it in one of the saddlebags on her bike.

"What did you do? You've got to tell me what happened," said Max. This time her tone was more pleading than demanding.

Sylvie continued to ignore her. Instead of answering, she began removing the parts of the rifle, adding them to the same saddlebag.

She then took the case and tossed it into the dumpster. As she walked back to the bike, she stopped and looked at Max.

"The less you know the better, and I'd suggest you forget everything you've seen today. Just like when we first met, I don't exist." She paused then added in a softer tone, "What I will tell you is that our problem is solved. Jack and Dave are alive and safe. They're back at the house. You should go to them."

"What are you going to do?"

"Disappear for a while. Take care of some unfinished business. Maybe visit Jack now and again."

As Max began to bristle Sylvie's face suddenly softened and Max could see the hint of a smile. With a conciliatory tone to her voice she said, "Relax, Max. I was just kidding. Jack is yours. You have nothing to worry about. Now go. Go to him."

Sylvie grabbed the other two cases from the truck and motioned for Max to get going.

CHAPTER 91

THE FIFTEEN MINUTES IT TOOK MAX to drive to the house were the longest fifteen minutes of her life. As Max turned onto the street, she could see the blue flashing lights from a police car. She drove as close as possible and pulled over. The cruiser was parked across the front of the drive, creating a barrier to help keep curious neighbors away. A crowd was already beginning to form, and she could see an officer trying to string up some yellow tape in an effort to keep them back.

Max didn't get out right away. Sylvie had never really told her what had happened, but after seeing the guns, deep inside, Max knew. She was almost sick thinking about it. Her hands were shaking, and she squeezed the wheel tightly to force those dark thought away. Finally, remembering that Sylvie had said that Jack and Dave were okay, Max left the truck and headed for the drive, where she pushed through the crowd to the yellow tape. There wasn't much to see, but there was enough to confirm her fears. The white van was parked as far up the drive as possible. Next to it, on the ground, was a sheet-covered form. She didn't see Jack or Dave.

Behind, she heard a few short whoots as an ambulance arrived. Two men climbed out, grabbed something that resembled toolboxes from the back, pushed their way through the crowd, and ducked under the tape, where they were met by one of the officers. Too far away to hear what was being said, Max could only watch. Their conversation involved lots of gesturing, pointing, and head nodding until suddenly one of the men abruptly walked away and disappeared behind the white van.

"Excuse me." The voice sounded familiar, and when Max turned to see why, she found herself face to face with Special Investigator Peeves.

"Well, look who's here," he said in a mocking tone.

Max froze. Even though she had known he was around, she was still surprised by his sudden appearance. "In– – Inspector Peeves," she managed to stammer.

"What are you doing here? You were supposed to stay at your place with Patti. I don't suppose you'd like to tell me why you're here instead?"

Max struggled to think of a quick reply.

Seeing her panic, he softened his tone, "We'll talk later. From what I understand, Jack and Dave are here and they're all right. Why don't you come with me and let's go find them. Maybe they'll shed some light on things." He lifted the tape for her to pass under.

A soft murmur went through the crowd as Max ducked under the tape. Peeves put his hand on her elbow and guided her toward the officers, where badges were shown and handshakes exchanged.

After the formalities were completed, he said, "Come," and guided her toward the front door of Sylvie's house. "They're inside."

* * *

She didn't see him at first, but she did hear his voice.

"Jack?"

Peeves gave her a soft nudge forward and said, "I think they're out back in the kitchen."

She moved forward. When she reached the doorway to the kitchen, she stopped. Each man had his back to her, and it looked like an EMT was working on Dave.

"Jack."

Three faces turned toward her voice. About to rush to Jack, she froze when she saw Dave. His face was bruised and swollen, and a butterfly bandage was covering the corner of his right eye.

"Max?" said Jack. That was all it took.

She rushed to him and they came together. She could feel herself trembling as she buried her face against his chest as they held on to each other. When she finally relaxed her embrace, she looked up at him with tears in her eyes and said, "Oh, my god, Jack."

Cradling her face in his hands, he wiped the tears from her eyes with his thumbs. Then he leaned down and gently kissed her, a move she then returned with more vigor.

"Ahem." The voice of Investigator Peeves interrupted their moment.

As they pulled apart, Max whispered in Jack's ear, "We have to talk." Then she gave him another small kiss.

The EMT turned to Peeves. "I'm finished here. It definitely looks worse than it is. I'd say Dave has been very lucky."

One of the local cops came in to take statements from Dave and Jack, and Inspector Peeves guided Max outside onto the deck overlooking the backyard. "So, are you finally going to tell me why you were really here?"

"What do you mean?"

"Max, let's skip the games. I left you in Rye Harbor with strict instructions to stay there. You do remember the part about staying put?"

She nodded.

"So why are you here?"

"You said we needed to find Sylvie. Well, I didn't tell you, because I wasn't sure she'd even be here, but Jack and I took her home once. I thought I'd come down and see if I could find her for you."

"And did you find her?"

"No. I didn't see her car in the drive, so I just kept going. On the way home I stopped in town for some lunch. I heard sirens go by, and then someone came in and told the cook there'd been a shooting or something. I panicked, in case it was Jack and Dave, so I rushed out. Another cruiser went by and I followed it. That's how I ended up here."

Seeing the disbelief on his face, she knew it was time to change the subject. "When can Jack and Dave come home?"

"I'm sure that when they've finished giving their statements, they'll be free to go."

"And me."

"You too. I will be checking out your story, so please remain available."

"I will. Promise."

"Stay here. And this time I mean it. Stay Here!"

As he walked away, she had no doubt that Agent Peeves realized that he had just been fed a complete crock, but, hey, there was a bit of truth in it. She just hoped he wouldn't figure out which was which.

CHAPTER 92

IT WASN'T UNTIL NEARLY SUNSET that Dave, Jack, and Max were allowed to leave. By that time the bodies had been hauled off, the canine units had thoroughly sniffed over every square inch of the area, and the crowd had mostly dispersed.

"So Max, what did he say just before we left?" asked Jack.

Jack was behind the wheel, with Max in the center. Dave, with eyes shut, was leaning against the passenger door.

"Nothing really. I don't think he completely believed me."

"What did you tell him?"

"I told him that I was looking for Sylvie but I couldn't find her."

"But that's not what happened, is it?"

Max didn't say anything. Jack glanced over at her several times before she finally answered. "No." Then in carefully measured tones she asked, "Jack, have you been seeing Sylvie?"

He hadn't expected that. "No."

"Then why did I find her number in your truck?" The tone in her voice was deadly.

Dave opened his eyes again and looked at his two friends.

"It's not like that," said Jack.

"Then tell me what it's not like." Her voice was cold and measured.

"Look Max, A few days ago when I was running in Maudslay, she came up behind me. Scared the shit out of me. We talked. She said that she was going to take care of some loose ends and then she'd be gone."

"What about the phone number?"

"Just as she left, she gave it to me. She wanted me to have it just in case. I was never going to call it."

"Jack, that's stupid. You expect me to believe that?"

"Believe what you want, but it's the truth."

"Hey, guys. Can you give it a rest?" said Dave suddenly.

They both looked at him.

"You're making my head explode." Then, as the truck began to drift, he added, "Eyes on the road, Jack."

They rode in awkward silence. By the time they were on Route 95 going north, Dave had started to snore.

Jack finally broke the silence. "Look Max," he said in a hushed tone as he glanced over at Dave, "I'm sorry I didn't tell you about seeing Sylvie, but I'm guessing that if our roles were reversed, you wouldn't have told me either."

"That's not the point."

"Hey, remember when you first came into the house, you whispered in my ear that we had to talk. What was that all about?"

She didn't answer right away. Then, in a low voice she said, "I know who shot those men."

"What?" Jack spoke so loudly now that Dave jolted awake.

"Yes." She paused and then repeated what she had said.

Stunned, Jack asked, "And you know this how?"

"I kind of helped."

"You 'kind of helped'? What do you mean 'you kind of helped'?"

Max didn't answer right away. Then she said, "It was Sylvie."

The truck jerked to the right as Jack and Dave both turned to stare at her.

"Jack, watch the road!" said Max.

"I am watching the road," he snapped. His knuckles began to turn white as he squeezed the wheel.

Dave was wide awake now. "Max, please explain what you meant."

For the next ten minutes or so, hers was the only voice in the truck. When she finished they rode in silence for another five before Dave said, "Holy shit, Max."

"Yeah, I know."

Jack remained silent, staring straight ahead as he drove.

CHAPTER 93

WHEN THEY GOT TO DAVE'S, Patti was waiting for them in the driveway. It took a few minutes for her to calm down after her initial shock at seeing Dave's bruised and bandaged face. "Does it hurt?" she asked.

"They gave me something for the pain, but what I could really use is a beer."

"Not with painkillers," Patti said, "but I'm sure we have some tea somewhere." She took his arm and guided him toward the door. "You guys coming in?" she said to Jack and Max.

"In a minute," Max said.

After Dave and Patti went in, she turned to Jack. "Look, I'm sorry. It's over. You're safe. And as far as I'm concerned, she doesn't exist. Now, you going to come in?"

He stared at her, then stepped toward the door. Before she could open it, he took her hand and looked at her. "Thanks."

That one word was all that was needed. She leaned into him, wrapping her arms tightly around him, and he pulled her close. They stood there holding onto each other, neither willing to be the first to let go.

"I was so scared," she said, her voice muffled by his chest.

"I was too," he whispered over the top of her head.

Then Patti opened the door again. "Oh, jeez. Get a room. Listen, I'm going over to the Wok to pick up some food. Join us for dinner?"

"I'll come with you," said Max. She relinquished her hold on Jack and wiped a tear off her cheek.

* * *

Dave lifted the mug of tea that Patti had given him and raised it to Jack. Jack returned the gesture with his bottle of beer and then they clinked the vessels together and drank. He never saw that the mug was emblazoned with the slogan "Girls Rule!"

"Jesus, this tastes like dishwater. Jack. Can you believe that story?"

"It's hard, but, yeah, I do."

"Think we'll ever see her again?"

"I kind of hope not."

"Kind of?"

Dave was not surprised when Jack flipped him the bird.

"Right." Dave grinned and then took another sip of tea, holding his pinky finger up for emphasis.

"Just think, if we hadn't pulled her out of the water how much simpler life would be."

"True. But we did. And in the end, she saved our asses."

Jack nodded in agreement. "You know, we can't ever tell anyone about this."

"I know."

Dave just couldn't resist needling his friend a bit further. "So, now that she and Max are BFFs—"

Jack cut him off. "I don't think so."

"Oh yeah, face it, you are so fucked."

CHAPTER 94

AS SOON AS MAX turned the truck engine off, Jack jerked himself awake. For a moment, he thought he was still in Sylvie's shed.

"We're home, sleepyhead."

He looked around. "Oh."

When he pulled on the door handle and slid out of the cab. Cat came running up, talking a blue streak as she head-butted his leg. He bent down and picked her up. She nuzzled his face and he said, "Yes, I missed you too."

Max had already opened the door, and Cat wriggled out of his arms, jumped to the ground, and ran inside.

"Come on," said Max. "You really need a shower."

Jack crinkled his nose and agreed.

* * *

The water was as hot as he could stand. He leaned forward into the wall and closed his eyes, letting the shower run over his bowed head and beat on his shoulders. He closed his eyes and let his mind go blank. It felt so good it was almost painful, as his tired muscles began to relax. He was so into the moment that he didn't hear the shower door snick open. He barely noticed the small breath of cool air when it hit him, but when the shower door clicked shut and he felt two warm arms wrap themselves around him, followed by the soft warmth of Max's body pressed against his, he sucked in his breath and a new kind of tension took over.

It wasn't until after they had been fully satisfied that they realized that the water was beginning to cool. She was first out, as he stayed, enjoying the last few moments of warm water.

Max had already dried off and was brushing her wet hair when Jack stepped out of the shower.

"I hate cold showers," he said as he grabbed a towel to dry off.

"Me too," said Max.

He looked at her and smiled. Her skin was pink and he wasn't sure if she was blushing or pink from the hot water or flushed from their lovemaking, but it didn't matter.

* * *

"You know Jack, she's not so bad."

Those were words he had never expected to hear. He turned his head to look at Max. Then he felt it coming: one of those moments a guy faces when, regardless of what he says or whether he agrees or disagrees, he will pick the wrong reply. He chose a noncommittal "Mmm" and closed his eyes.

But apparently, Max was just getting started. She rolled onto her side, head propped on her elbow, and looked at him.

"I mean, she did save your life, I don't know how she could do what she did. It was like what they do in some sort of a spy movie. Do you have any idea how bullshit I was when I found her number in your truck? I almost didn't call it. Think what would have happened then. Did you know she was like that, or were you just flattered that a hot young woman was interested in you?"

Jack moaned.

"Are you falling asleep?"

He chose long, deep breaths to announce his reply. Max continued to watch him until her eyes too became heavy. "I love you Jack Beale," she whispered. Then she rolled on her back and closed her eyes.

* * *

Bacon. He smelled bacon, and coffee. He was still asleep, but gradually real sensations began to mingle with his dreams. Something was prodding him gently in the face, and a weight was pressing down on his chest. Then, there was a whirring sound. A helicopter? It was far off in the distance. He looked but couldn't see anything. Another poke in the face was followed by a soft "Mrowh," and the helicopter sound changed into purring. Cat wanted him awake. He opened one eye to see her staring at him. She was sitting on his chest and was about to gingerly prod his cheek with her paw again.

"Cat. Go away." He pushed her off his chest and rolled over.

"Good morning, sleepyhead."

"Ohhh," he moaned. "What time is it?"

"Time to get up if you want to see me before I have to go to work. Courtney had to cover my shift yesterday. Coffee's ready, and I cooked bacon."

He couldn't resist, and besides, Cat wouldn't let him. She was walking back and forth over him and Mrowhing loudly, making it impossible to go back to sleep even if he wanted to.

* * *

Max was standing by the window looking out over the harbor, a cup of coffee cradled in her hands, when he came up behind her. "Did I ever thank you for saving my life?" he whispered in her ear.

She leaned back into him. "It was Sylvie who saved your life."

"Technically, yes, but if you hadn't called her . . ." His voice drifted off.

"When you put it that way, you're right. I did save your life — again. And speaking of saving your life, I found your work hat from *Irrepressible* in your truck. Maybe you'll need it again someday."

Jack turned her to face him. "Max, without you . . ." He paused.

She touched her fingertips to his lips. "I know. You don't have to say anything."

CHAPTER 95

AFTER MAX SET OFF FOR BEN'S, Jack decided to take a ride down to Dave's. Cars lined both sides of the street, so he parked his truck by Dave's mailbox, and Dave called down from the kitchen window to come on up.

As he cleared the top step he heard, "Mornin' Jack. How're you feeling?" It was Special Investigator Peeves. "I was just going over a few things with Dave."

"Agent Peeves." Forget the early hour. He walked over to the fridge and grabbed a beer.

* * *

Nearly two hours passed before Peeves finally left.

"I don't think he believes us," said Dave.

"He doesn't. But as long as we leave Sylvie out of it, I don't see that we can have any problems."

"What about Max?"

Jack got quiet. Then he said, "She's okay. We talked, and I think she understands that Sylvie is not a threat to her . . . uh, us. I also think she's scared of her, or at least what she's capable of."

"I can see that. She scares me. Do you actually know what her story is now?"

"Not really, but from what I can gather, Peeves is or was her boss. She was working undercover . . ."

"Undercover?"

"Apparently. And somewhere along the line something changed for her and he lost her. When he heard about the sinking of Richie's boat, and as more bodies began to accumulate, I think he began to put the pieces together and decided that she was alive—and well, behind those events. At first, I think he was just trying to reel her back in. Now—I don't know."

"That's messed up."

"Do you remember that guy who was involved in that stuff in Rye with the development by the harbor?"

"Yeah. En— Endre—"

"Endroit."

"That's right. What about him?"

"I think he's the key. I think Sylvie's after him, although I'm not sure why. Most likely he was behind the smuggling operation that Richie was involved with."

"Okay."

"From what Lewis told me and what has happened, here's what I think—Richie was hired by Endroit to recover the cases and kill her. Richie's mistake was not recovering the cases first and when he tried to take her out, she killed him instead. Burning the boat was a spur of the moment decision and seemed to be a good way to disappear. Almost. Had we not found her, she probably would have drowned and that would have been the end of it. Instead she ended up on Peeves' radar."

"What a mess."

"So after we saved her she had to change her plans and recover the cases."

"And that's where Bryan came in."

"Exactly. I'm guessing they'd been fuck buddies for a while. Who knew? Anyway, he helped her get the cases, but Endroit must have gotten wind of it and sent his guys to recover the cases. First time, one of them ended up in the dumpster. Then they killed Bryan, and she took out another down at her place in Gloucester. By this time, our friend Agent Peeves began to have suspicions that Sylvie wasn't really dead and was hot after her as well."

"Okay. So Peeves was chasing her, Endroit was after her and the cases and in turn she was hunting him. Then lucky us, we became pawns in this chess game. And—who knew that she and Max would partner up and save our asses."

"Yep."

"So, Jack, how was it that you *really* came to have her number?"

"That story I told Max in the truck yesterday was true. She caught up to me at Maudslay. We talked, and that's when she gave me the number."

Dave looked at him. "You talked."

"We talked."

"Well, I suspect that you're leaving out significant details, but in the end she did her good deed by saving our butts."

Jack lifted his beer and said, "Amen."

EPILOGUE

SYLVIE DID DISAPPEAR. Special Agent Peeves continued to check in with Jack and Dave from time to time, clearly to remind them that he was still looking for her. However, there was no sign of her, and as the cool autumn weather approached, gradually life returned to normal.

Late one afternoon after Max left for work, Jack decided to go for a run. The air was cool against his bare skin, and as he ran by Ben's, he noticed how few cars were in the parking lot. Only a month earlier it would have been full by now. Another summer had definitely come to an end.

When he reached the boulevard, he didn't even have to slow down; there was no traffic anymore. Running past the Francis Place his thoughts began to drift, and he remembered all that had happened there: June and her involvement in that whole fiasco and how much the harbor would have changed had her plan succeeded. A few weeks ago, they had received word that she had died of heart failure. She had never come out of her coma. Now she was gone.

Settling into a comfortable rhythm, he had just turned left in the center of town and was heading west on Washington Road when he caught a glimpse of a car in the distance driving toward him. It was late enough in the day that the sun was shining directly in his eyes, making him squint to see the car.

When he reached one of the few patches of shade on the road, he could see that the car approaching was a classic cherry red convertible. He slowed to check it out, and as the car passed by, its radio blaring, something caught his eye about the driver—a woman. He stopped to get a better look, but the car was already too far away. The car disappeared around a bend, leaving only the final strains of Roy Orbison's great hit "Pretty Woman" in his mind.

As he turned left at West Road, he remembered his final moments with Sylvie at Maudslay. Now she had disappeared, which could only be a good thing, yet he couldn't help but feel that she was still nearby. She had said that she had some loose ends to tie up. What did that even mean? Part of him hoped that he wouldn't find out, but another part wanted to know.

The shaded parts of the road got darker as the sun sank lower in the sky. He turned onto Garland Road and began heading back home. As he ran, his thoughts alternated between the cherry red convertible and the moments at Maudslay with Sylvie until part of him was convinced that she had been the one behind the wheel.

It was nearly dark by the time he got home. There were no lights on and Max's car was still gone. He decided that after a quick shower he'd go over to Ben's for a bite to eat.

Thirty minutes later, he was ready to go. Cat raced in as he walked out the door. When he opened the door of his truck, a piece of paper fluttered from the seat to the floor. He picked it up and unfolded it, fully expecting that it was a note from Max. It was a Dunkin Donuts receipt instead.

His hands shook as he turned it sideways to get a better view of the words.

You looked good out there running tonight.
I've taken care of the last loose end.
Take care, S

OTHER BOOKS BY K.D. MASON

HARBOR ICE (2009)

The winter has been brutally cold, leaving Rye Harbor frozen solid. Finally, the weather warms and the ice begins to breakup and drift out to sea. That's when a woman's body is found under a slab of ice left by the outgoing tide. Max, the bartender at Ben's Place recognizes that it is her Aunt's partner and that begins a series of events that will eventually threaten Max's life as well. It is up to her best friend, Jack Beale, to unravel the mystery.

CHANGING TIDES (2010)

Fate, Chance, Destiny . . . Call it what you will, but sometimes life changing events begin in the most innocent and unexpected ways. For Jack Beale that moment came on a perfect summer morning as he stood overlooking Rye Harbor when something caught his eye. In that small space between the bow of his boat and the float to which it was tied, a lifeless body had become wedged as the tide tried to sweep it out to sea. That discovery, and the arrival of Daniel would begin a series of events that would eventually take Max from him. Who was the victim? Why was Daniel there and what was his interest in Max? Was there a connection? And, so began a journey that would take Jack from Rye Harbor to Newport, RI and, eventually Belize, as he searched for answers.

DANGEROUS SHOALS (2011)

Spring has arrived in the small New Hampshire coastal town of Rye Harbor and all seemed right in the world. Jack Beale and Max, the feisty red haired bartender at Ben's Place, are back together after their split up the previous year and are looking forward to enjoying a carefree summer together. Then, someone who they thought was just a memory reappears, pursued by a psychotic killer. When he ends up dead, Jack and Max become the killer's new targets. What should have been an easy, relaxing summer for Jack, Max and his cat, Cat, becomes a battle of wits and a fight for survival.

KILLER RUN (2012)

Malcom and Polly were living their dream, running a North Country Bed
& Breakfast they named the Quilt House Inn. The Inn was known for two
things, the collection of antique quilts on display and miles of running and
hiking trails for their guests use. Jack, training for his first trail marathon,
The Rockdog Run, heard about the Inn and hatched a plan whereby he and
Max could enjoy a romantic get-a-way and he could get in some quality
trail training. For his plan to work, Dave and Patti joined them at the Inn.
Meanwhile, in the weeks leading up to the marathon, a delusional antique
dealer developed a fascination with one of the quilts on display in the Inn
and It wasn't long before Malcom and Polly's dream and the four friends
became forever entwined in a deadly mystery spanning two hundred years
and 26.2 miles. Running a marathon is challenging enough by itself. Doing
so on trails and starting before sunrise, in the dark, on a cold November
day is even more daunting. When Jack trips and falls, landing on the lifeless
body of an unknown runner, the race becomes a true "killer run".

EVIL INTENTIONS (2013)

Unseen forces at play may dramatically change the quiet seaside town of
Rye Harbor forever. It's early spring, and one of the town's oldest homes, the
Francis House, has just gone up in flames, revealing a badly burned body in
the ashes. With help from an unexpected source, Jack and his friend Tom,
the Police Chief, unravel the mystery fueled by a broken heart, a secret real
estate deal, and a deadly double-cross.